ORBIT 21

ORBIT 21

Edited by Damon Knight

HARPER & ROW, PUBLISHERS, NEW YORK
Cambridge, Hagerstown, Philadelphia, San Francisco,
London, Mexico City, São Paulo, Sydney

1817

Grateful acknowledgment is made for permission to reprint three lines by W. H. Auden in "Love, Death, Time, and Katie" by Richard Kearns. Reprinted by permission of Random House, Inc.

ORBIT 21. Copyright © 1980 by Damon Knight. All rights reserved. Printed in the United States of America. No part of this book may be used or reproduced in any manner whatsoever without written permission except in the case of brief quotations embodied in critical articles and reviews. For information address Harper & Row, Publishers, Inc., 10 East 53rd Street, New York, N.Y. 10022. Published simultaneously in Canada by Fitzhenry & Whiteside Limited, Toronto.

FIRST EDITION

ISBN: 0-06-012426-1

LIBRARY OF CONGRESS CATALOG CARD NUMBER: 78-20207

80 81 82 83 84 10 9 8 7 6 5 4 3 2 1

CONTENTS

	Introduction: About Fifteen Years of *Orbit* Damon Knight	vii
	LOVE, DEATH, TIME, AND KATIE Richard Kearns	1
	THE GREENING Eileen Roy	10
	ABOMINABLE Carol Emshwiller	23
	UNDERWOOD AND THE SLAUGHTERHOUSE Raymond G. Embrak	33
	HOPE Lelia Rose Foreman	44
	THE MOTHER OF THE BEAST Gordon Eklund	62
	ROBERT FRASER: THE XENOLOGIST AS HERO Sydelle Shamah	81
	PERSEPHONE Rhondi Vilott	101

THE SMELL OF THE NOOSE, THE ROAR OF THE BLOOD 109
John Barfoot

AND THE TV CHANGED COLORS WHEN SHE SPOKE 131
Lyn Schumaker

THE ONLY TUNE THAT HE COULD PLAY 137
R. A. Lafferty

SURVIVORS 151
Rita-Elizabeth Harper

ON THE NORTH POLE OF PLUTO 164
Kim Stanley Robinson

INTRODUCTION:
ABOUT FIFTEEN YEARS OF *ORBIT*

In the sixties, when glossy special-interest magazines such as *Popular Psychology* were beginning to appear on the newsstands, it occurred to me that I, for one, would be willing to pay as much as a dollar for a good science fiction magazine in that format. I was on the road to inventing *Omni,* but I gave it up and began to think instead about the Science Fiction Book Club, which had a ready-made subscription list for books at a dollar each. They could not publish the collections I had in mind—their advances were too small to pay for the material—but they could reprint them. A series of original anthologies, like Fred Pohl's *Star Science Fiction,* if it had hardcover, paperback, and book-club editions, could easily pay its way. I made up a proposal, called it *Orbit* more or less at random, and my agent sent it around.

Thomas A. Dardis, then editor-in-chief of Berkley, bought it, and we worked out the details. For a while Doubleday was interested in doing a hardcover edition, but that fell through; then Berkley was acquired by Putnam, and there was our hardcover edition. It was a funny arrangement in some ways, because Putnam had no science fiction editor and nobody knew quite what to do with *Orbit.* They handed the first volume over to an editor in the juvenile department and put a "Young Adult" label on it. It was an ugly book, too tall for its width, with a jacket the color of dog-do.

While this was in the works, I found out that the juvenile editor had changed two words in the text which he thought might offend librarians: they were "breasts" and "heterosexuality." The second change made hash of the ending of Jim Blish's story, "How

Beautiful with Banners." I made an amazing stink, and the text was restored. Subsequent volumes were published as adult books.

What I wanted to do in *Orbit* was to bring about a revolution in science fiction, like Campbell's in the early forties, Gold's and Boucher/McComas's in the fifties. My thesis was that there was no inherent reason why science fiction could not meet ordinary literary standards, but that the pulp tradition of forty years had encouraged ideas at the expense of writing skill. It seemed to me that the only way to cure this was to set high standards at the beginning, even if it meant publishing a lot of fantasy and marginal material because most hard-core s.f. could not make the grade. Later, cocky with success, I followed this trail too far.

In its first few years *Orbit* got submissions from many of the best-known writers in the field, and I rejected nearly all of them. I would have loved to have those authors in the book, but they were sending me the same kind of mechanical-repetitive science fiction that was appearing in the magazines.

I was a little shocked once, in the early fifties, when Tony Boucher mentioned casually that in a recent issue of *F&SF* there was only one story that he had bought solely because of the author's name. I thought that was one too many. Famous names may help sell a magazine; they don't always, but if they do, it's because those writers have written good stories in the past. Every time you publish a poor story by a famous writer, you diminish the value of that name and defeat your own purpose.

One thing that was wrong with the field in the sixties was that there were only three editors buying short fiction—Campbell, Pohl, and Robert P. Mills, then the editor of *The Magazine of Fantasy & Science Fiction*. Their combined tastes covered a large part of the spectrum, but not enough; there were good stories that none of them would buy. I bought some, and two of them won Nebulas—"Mother to the World," by Richard Wilson, and "The Secret Place," by Richard McKenna.

Introduction

Today there are so many editors that it is hard to believe that any story of the slightest merit is going unpublished. I have mixed feelings about this. It's great for writers, and more new ones are coming into the field now than at any time since the fifties. At the same time, the level of quality of the anthology series has fallen (while that of the magazines has risen a little) until there is not much to choose between anthologies and magazines.

Four or five times I have written rejection letters about stories from unknown writers, then torn the letters up and written contracts instead. These invariably turned out to be the first stories of writers who would become *Orbit* regulars. One of them was Gardner R. Dozois.

Gardner had been discharged from the Army in Germany, and was sharing an apartment with other ex-GIs in Nuremburg on next to no money. When he came back to the U.S. in 1969 or thereabouts, he had about thirty dollars. Late one evening he called me from a tavern in Milford where the bus had let him off, and I went down to fetch him. I had pictured him as a small Boy Scout soldier, pink-cheeked and fragile. What I saw was a giant in a scruffy black coat, with Alice-in-Wonderland hair down his back and the beard of a yak down his front. He saw my start of horror, and said later, with a chuckle, "I freaked Damon out." He stayed at our house for two or three weeks, until we had to kick him out of the nest, and later he came back many times. After the first shock, we discovered he was gentle and shy, endearingly awkward, but with an instinct for survival; somehow he never poked his eye out with the spoon in his perpetual coffee cup. He went on long walks up the hill with my small son Jonathan, carrying him on his shoulders part of the time. There was a rusty abandoned tractor up there; they called it the Golden Tractor and played on it a lot.

One year I had sent Milford invitations to a lot of unfamiliar names I found in the magazines: one of them was Dobbin Thorp, and he accepted. I met him on the highway between my place and the White House Inn, where he was staying—a tall, pale, kind of skinheaded young man with a distracted look in his eye. I said, "Dobbin?" and with a grin he admitted that Dobbin Thorp was a pseudonym—he thought it would be funny to name himself after a horse—and that he was Tom Disch; and I felt like a fool.

Jim Sallis and Gene Wolfe, who had been corresponding, came to the Milford Conference together a year or two after that. Neither one was what I had expected. Sallis was slender, dark-haired and intense, with an almost inaudible voice; Wolfe looked like a large Sergeant Bilko. Later I met Jim's wife Jane, who looked like a large cuddly doll, and their son Dylan. They stayed in our house, with Tom Disch, when we went to Florida in 1968; Tom wrote a story about that and sold it to *TriQuarterly* or the *Paris Review*, I forget which.

I didn't meet R. A. Lafferty until the 1974 World Science Fiction Convention in Washington: he was a white-haired man with an enormous waistline, something like a giant leprechaun. He was always wandering through the lobby, and so were we, and when we met, three or four times a day, he would waggle his hands despairingly and croak, *"Same pee-pul."*

Some things I am proud of: four Nebula Awards; first or early stories by Gene Wolfe, James Sallis, Carol Carr, Gardner Dozois, George Alec Effinger, Vonda N. McIntyre, Gary K. Wolf, Dave Skal, Steve Chapman, Kathleen M. Sidney, Doris Piserchia, Joan D. Vinge, Kim Stanley Robinson . . .

I could claim to have discovered some of these writers, but I don't think that's how it appears to them. When you write a story the best way you know how, and send it to editors, and one finally buys it, you don't feel discovered, you feel lucky.

But it isn't luck. Any half-decent editor has his senses fine-tuned all the time in the hope of detecting a good new writer on the way up. If you show any sign at all that you know what you're doing, an editor will write you letters, encourage you, and maybe buy a story that is just barely good enough because he has a hunch the next one will be better.

Sometimes there wasn't a next one, and that was disappoint-

Introduction

ing. But I kept trying. I asked myself what would have happened in 1939 if John Campbell had bought all his stories from Arthur J. Burks, Eando Binder, John Russell Fearn, and Nat Schachner, the big names then, instead of from the unknown Isaac Asimov, L. Sprague de Camp, Lester del Rey, Theodore Sturgeon, and Robert A. Heinlein.

Mea culpa: Every editor bounces stories that later win awards, and I found out I was no exception. I rejected, among others, "Time Considered as a Helix of Semi-precious Stones," by Samuel R. Delany, "Eurema's Dam," by R. A. Lafferty, "When It Happened," by Joanna Russ, " 'Repent, Harlequin!' Said the Ticktockman," by Harlan Ellison, and "The Death of Doctor Island," by Gene Wolfe, for reasons that seemed good at the time. About some of these I later thought I had been wrong.

Would I have bought stories I thought were bad if I had known they were going to win awards? I hope not. Would those stories have won the awards if I had published them? I don't even know that. Well, then, should I have bought stories I didn't like because I *thought* they were going to win awards? No again, because I would have had to buy ten bad stories to get one winner, and because everything an editor buys is a signal to writers that that's what he wants. Then he gets more of the same, and has to buy it, because that's all he gets, and he's in a positive-feedback cycle. This happens to nearly every magazine, and there's no way to break out of it except by heroic measures or by changing editors.

One thing I remember with pleasure is an exchange at a convention: Somebody asked me, "What do you really want for *Orbit?*" I answered, "I'm trying to keep you confused about that," and he said, "You're succeeding."

When George Ernsberger took over as editor-in-chief at Berkley in 1973, he reviewed the royalty statements and found out something that nobody else had noticed, that sales had been falling off gently ever since *Orbit 6*. We discussed this a little; his impulse was to blame the contents, and mine to blame the package. Finally he said that he wanted to hold off on a new contract until new sales figures came in. I refused, and left Berkley/Putnam. It was a gamble that paid off: Victoria Schochet, then the science fiction editor at Harper & Row, bought the series. Meanwhile *Orbit 13* appeared, the last from Putnam: it was a grab-bag of everything that was left in inventory.

Even though I had landed on my feet at Harper, a much better house than Putnam, I was alarmed enough to make some changes in *Orbit*. I began trying to cut back on marginal items and fantasy; I invented some departments; I tried to find stories that both the conventional reader and I could enjoy.

I was going to say earlier that *Orbit* had published very few stories about spaceships and alien planets, but when I counted those in the first twenty volumes, there were forty-seven. Four of them are by Gene Wolfe—his first story, "Trip, Trap," "The Fifth Head of Cerberus," "Alien Stones," and "Many Mansions." In "Cerberus" he used a colonial planet as a given of the story, and the spaceships were just assumed as part of the background, but in "Alien Stones" he remade the spaceship story as thoroughly as Heinlein did in "Universe."

My acceptance is that when any category of science fiction writing has become dull and repetitive, there is always a brilliant story waiting to be written by *giving up the assumptions that made the story easy to write.* This is what Heinlein did in "Universe": he said, What if energy considerations make the convenient, quick interstellar flights of pulp s.f. impossible—what then?

The interstellar exploration story is waiting to be rediscovered in the same way. Suppose we assume that pulp s.f.'s quick and easy adaptation of human beings to alien worlds is impossible—what then? Solve the problems of economic return, allergic reaction, systemic poisoning, irradiation, etc., instead of sweeping them under the rug "for the sake of the story." Then we'll have a new wave of interstellar stories which will be exciting once more because they will be honest and therefore believable.

My relationship with the editors at Harper & Row's trade department was harmonious; we never had a single quarrel. After Harper took over, however, there was no paperback edition of

Introduction

Orbit, and the series could not make a profit on hardcover sales alone. Harper bravely held out for six years, hoping for better times, but the end had to come, and *Orbit 21* is the last.

The aim of this series has always been to demonstrate that science fiction is a flourishing branch of literature, not a bastard subliterary twig (a view which I have maintained since 1952), and that, as I wrote in *In Search of Wonder,*

science fiction is a field of literature worth taking seriously, and that ordinary critical standards can be meaningfully applied to it: e.g., originality, sincerity, style, construction, logic, coherence, sanity, garden-variety grammar.

It is true, of course, that subliterary s.f. far outweighs the other kind—the twig, in my image, is larger than the branch—but this is true also of every other form of literature, including the "mainstream" novel—take a look at the paperback best-sellers in your local supermarket—and it is merely a restatement of Sturgeon's Rule: "Nine tenths of *everything* is crud." (When has so much wisdom been condensed into six words?)

Coming to the end of this road is a lonesome thing in a way, but I have the satisfaction of knowing that the idea of *Orbit* is alive in other anthology series, in the hands of other editors. What is especially satisfying to me, and quite marvelous, is the emergence year after year of strong new writers, in the Clarion Workshop and elsewhere. As long as science fiction can attract and nurture so much talent, we haven't got much to worry about.

D. K.

LOVE, DEATH, TIME, AND KATIE

Richard Kearns

I saw Death walking, moving toward the rainbow spires and softly-painted eaves of Elsinore.
 I knew he'd come for Katie.
 This really burned me up—he was trying to welch on an old friendship. We'd fought in a couple of campaigns together, one against fire demons who'd been harassing the theocrats in Rutland back around the turn of the century, the other against a contingent of lizard men that had tried to stage a takeover in Rumeria. That was even further back. We were good soldiers, Death and I. And good friends.
 Damn.
 The fink knew I'd be on duty. I grabbed my cloak and started down the stairs.
 The gods had been fickle for as long as I'd known them. Arrogant, too. Those were the main reasons divinity had been banned in Elsinore—Death wasn't any exception.
 I was one of the reasons the ban worked.
 I emerged in the Watchtower gardens, and paused for a moment to fiddle with the small gold clasp on my cloak that had somehow managed to get caught in my beard. Then I headed north, running through the parks that paralleled the entrance

avenue, careful to blend my form with the ashen and sunlit greens that flickered in the breeze. I didn't want Death to spot me until I was ready for him.

The flowers in the trees became molten bursts of color that sped past, red and yellow, glaring as they leaped out at me, vivid as they receded into the dappled shadows. I let my actions become automatic, the smells, the textures, the colors guiding my motions, accelerating my pace.

I left the wooded strip, crossed the avenue and rushed up the steps of Welcome House. This was as good a vantage point as any; I could watch Death's approach without being seen. Additionally, there would be plenty of room for maneuvering—the street and steps were deserted, and no trading caravans were due until late tomorrow. Casting about, I located a dozen clouds well within range to the southeast, hooked into them, and began waiting.

I had been leaning on the pillar without really noticing the bright blue scales, edged in red and gilt, that covered it. I stood back to take a good look. Katie had painted this. The pattern washed across the column, splashing in and out and over the eavebeams, cascading down the wall behind me to the floor of the huge porch. When seen from a distance, Welcome House looked like a big blue dragon, wings folded, head resting on her paws, dozing peacefully in the warm sunlight.

Katie had painted most of the buildings in Elsinore. That was before her fall, when she could still walk, still clamber around in the architecture, wielding a fistful of color.

The time passed slowly.

I waited until he had nearly walked past the House. "Greetings, O Death!" I called. I knew that'd get him. He was a real sucker for formalities.

He stopped and stood with his back to me for almost a full minute. He was bald. His robes were orange, shot through with golds, pinks, purples, and deep reds. The only problem with this was that the colors tended to swirl within his form, shifting continuously. That was disconcerting to anyone who hadn't been trained to withstand the effects of vertigo.

He turned, smiling serenely as usual. "Hello, Jehan." He studied me. "It's been a long time since Rutland. Still no grey hairs, I hope?" His eyes were like his robe, always changing color. That bothered me.

"No. And it's been even longer since Rumeria." I moved down the steps. "What foolishness brings you to Elsinore?"

He arched his eyebrows. "Business. I think you know that. I never go anywhere unless it's on business."

I was in the street now, the sun behind me. "We don't have to go through with this. You can go back. I can ignore the fact you came into the city—for old times' sake. But don't make the mistake of trying to go after Katie. I'll fry you in your own flames before you take a second step."

The smile wavered, just slightly. He sighed. "You understand things very poorly, Jehan. I wish I could go back. I wish I didn't have to come here. I wish I didn't have to fight against my friends. Freedom of choice is something the gods never had." His eyes narrowed. "Humans can choose, though. *You* still can." He licked his lips and stepped forward. "Don't make this difficult for both of us. Let me pass." Another step, his fingers twitching. "I don't mind bargaining with you. It would please me. Do you want divinity? I can give it to you."

I laughed, turning, reaching, pulling down the sky in pieces, casting them at Death. Sunlight, cloud, or shadow, it didn't make any difference. He was caught. A pale, silvery mist, twelve feet across, curled, flared, and twisted around him as I began the sealing spell.

He tried to fight back only once. Cherry-red pellets broke through the outer barrier, spilling flame on the white pavement.

Then nothing.

I walked up to the eighteen-foot-tall marble cube where Death had been imprisoned and ran my hand along the smooth sides. I could sense him inside, waiting.

He'd been my friend, once.

He was also a fool.

Damn.

It was a long climb back up the stairs inside the Watchtower.

The caravan from Lum showed up earlier than expected. I got off duty and picked my way through the merchants' stalls. The smells of spices and perfumes, the glitter of glass jewelry, the haughty prostitutes, the interweaving rhythms of the different hawkers' chants—they all assaulted my senses, inviting me to drown myself in a world of gentle illusions.

The staff at Welcome House had barely enough time to finish off the private rooms for the wealthier guests. The common rooms were a shambles. When the bulk of the entourage finally cornered the manager, demanding service, a heated argument developed, and I had to step in and beat on a few heads. Then I assigned a squad of City Guards to help prepare the common rooms.

No one had asked me about the giant marble cube, which was probably just as well. I decided to wait and remove it after the caravan had left.

Everything was cheap. I couldn't find anything nice enough for a gift, so I left for Katie's empty-handed. I wondered how I would explain the morning's events to her. I figured I had to.

She lived in one of the few unpainted buildings, a small, pagodalike wooden structure in the center of town. We'd built it for her, raising up a hill for its foundation so that it would overlook Reese Park and Pand Lagoon. Serenity House.

She still liked to paint pictures, even though her skills were far from what they used to be. She also resented efforts to offer her special care: carting her around Elsinore, assigning a staff to see to her needs, providing her with nurses or companions.

Katie was stubborn.

Serenity House had been a successful compromise.

I climbed the hill slowly, admiring the gardens as I went. The roses had just begun to open, and dead crab-apple petals littered the ground like snow.

There weren't any doors in Serenity House. Only doorways. I

went in and headed for the western porch. I knew she liked to go there and paint in the afternoons.

"Jehan—is that you?"

"Yeah." I walked out on the porch.

"Stop! Don't move! That's right where I need you to finish this painting!" She was totally obscured by a huge canvas.

I froze. A couple of minutes passed. Then a bright blue eye, framed by a shock of white hair, peered around the edge of the frame. We both giggled.

She came scooting out from behind her work, propelling her wheelchair as fast as she could. I scooped her up when she reached me, swung her around and around, and then settled her carefully back in the chair.

"What a ham! You fall for that same line every time!"

We both laughed again. I grabbed a nearby stool and sat on it. "The caravan's in town. It just arrived."

"I know. Did you bring me anything?"

"No."

"That's all right. There's nothing much from Lum that's worth buying until fall gets here. Come and see what I painted today." She took my hand and led me around to the front of her canvas.

It scared me. She'd painted a sunset churning over Pand Lagoon. It looked like Death, though. His eyes. His robe.

Damn.

She squeezed my hand and smiled at me. "I thought of it when I was reading today. Something Narvi had translated from the past. A little passage, really." She closed her eyes. "Auden wrote it.

> *"There is less grief than*
> *wonder on the whole,*
> *Even at sunset . . ."*

She paused, staring at the painting. "It was a long poem, but that part moved me the most. What do you think?"

I tried to study the thing. "I think I've only seen one other thing like it."

She frowned. "Oh."

"I like this better."

She backed away from the painting and wheeled over to the porch railing. The real sunset was just finishing up, and she watched it slowly fade. "I suppose it's just as well."

I moved over and joined her, sitting on the railing. We were both silent for a couple of minutes. "Katie?"

"Hm?"

"Marry me."

She smiled again. "You're sweet, Jehan."

"No, I mean it."

She studied my face. "I know you do. Tell me why you think I should marry you. You know we wouldn't be able to have any children."

"I know that."

"Then why should I marry you?"

"I love you."

"I love you, too. That's not reason enough."

"We would always be together."

"We're together now."

"I could protect you. Take care of you."

She stared at the palms of her hands, her lips compressed in a thin bitter line. "Jehan, I'm old. I'm older than Elsinore."

"Look, I wasn't born yesterday either, you know."

"No. You weren't." She sighed. "But I'm weary. I can't tell you how weary. I'm so tired of watching the years glide by. I'm sick of all the children. I've had it with learning new names, new faces. Even Elsinore has changed too much for me to be happy here." She stroked the rubber treads on her wheelchair. "I've seen the *land* change, Jehan. The mountains. The oceans. It's not the same planet. And when that happens—" She looked at me again. "You—you can face the prospect of the centuries ahead, the living, the waiting, the changes, the little births and deaths that happen every day. I can't. I'm not going to be around much longer, Jehan. Face up to it. Death is going to come after me, one of these days. Soon, I hope."

Now it was my turn to stare bleakly at Pand Lagoon, watching the dim reflections of the starblaze overhead, counting the million shadows that danced around every tree, every bush, every

flower and blade of grass. "He was here this morning."
"What!"
"He came for you today. I defeated him."
"I don't understand."
I recounted the morning's battle. The silence lasted a long time after I finished.
"I didn't think anybody could do that," she said, heading back into the house. "But I've never had a better gift. Ever."
I started after her. "Then you'll marry me?"
"No." She stopped. Turning, she confronted me. "You really *don't* understand, do you?"
"No! I—"
"Death was right, Jehan. Accept it."
"Accept what? I don't—"
"You defeated him once. Fine. But you can't stop him."
"But—"
"You've given me time, Jehan. Not life. Just time. That's your real gift. I'll be ready when he finally does get here."
I watched her disappear into the house, unsure whether or not I should follow. Better to wait until morning and try talking again.
I retreated to the porch, only to find I was not alone. That bastard.
"Hello, Jehan."
"How did you get out?"
"I didn't."
I studied his swirling robes, considering the possibility. Katie's picture was gone. "You're lying."
"I'm sorry, Jehan. I'm not. I wish I didn't have to be here, but I do. I have no choice. Please don't try to stop me a second time."
I snarled. Moving, striding, I grabbed handfuls of starfire overhead, shaping them with my anger. Whitehot. Sizzling. Driven bars of a cage, through the porch, tying the knot on top with my furious hands. They circled him, calling out his name, cursing, made of pain.
He seated himself on the floor in a full lotus position. Eyes closed and burning.

I kept vigil, watching the night spin by, contemplating love, death, time, and Katie.

He stirred, somewhere near morning, opening his eyes. "Jehan?"

I didn't want to answer. I thought back to the night watches in Rutland, when the demons called out our names in the dark, over and over, burning anyone who answered. We lost three men that way. I remembered their names: Art, the windmaster; Benjamin, his 'prentice; and Karim, the shape-changer.

We buried Art and Karim on the spot. Benjamin came from Rutland, though. We took what was left of his body to his family for burial. I could see their faces, the way they glared at Death, mounted on his black stallion. He wept bitterly at the funeral, however. I had been unable to. Benjamin was eighteen.

I gave in. "What?"

"I'm sorry."

"Me too."

"I wish there was another way."

"Yeah."

Silence for a space. The sky was pinking over from the east, and I wished I could watch the sunrise. It looked spectacular.

"I hope you'll forgive me."

Alarms started going off inside, sucking at my stomach, dumping gallons of adrenaline in my blood. "What do you mean?"

"There really wasn't any other way." He was crying, huge hot tears dripping down his cheeks.

I tore through the house, wailing, destroying everything in my way. Katie's bedroom opened to the east, and she watched the sun rise every morning.

I stopped in her doorway, my hands gripping the frame on either side. The room was filled with violent golds, violet and rusty reds pooling in the shadows. There he was again, free, helping her walk through the window like it was a set of stairs, and it was Katie, and it wasn't, and the house shook to its foundations when I screamed out her name.

She turned.

I'll never forget her face.

Her one eye was the sun, her other fading off into the distance, beyond the horizon where I couldn't see it. Her hair spilled over the sky, electric blue, baby fine, brushing back the horizon like a fluttering wing, driving out the dark, scattering perfume in billows of jasmine. She smiled, all lilyteeth and roselips, and I felt the earth tremble, shape and bud beneath my feet, across the meadows and mountains, under the seas, summerblossoms burning in the lazy yellow heat.

She was gone.

I looked Death in the face and understood, finally.

We buried her poor, broken body in Reese Park. All of Elsinore attended the funeral.

We wept sweet tears of joy, Death and I.

THE GREENING

Eileen Roy

Time slipped through her fingers like ash in the wind. Two weeks ago—three?—she had been aboard one of her father's ships, touring the asteroid belt. Now she lay on a grass cot on a planet light-years from Earth, and her father and everything she had known were two hundred years in the past.

Dea lifted her head from her arm as a banging thundered through the flimsy trade hut. She stood reluctantly, brushing off the clothes that never wrinkled. Aliens waited outside, impatient for her to join them—

She was Andeana Lucita Maria de Carvalho da Fonesca, daughter to one of the wealthiest *granfinos* in Brazil, heir to all his lands and estates. She would do what had to be done to get home again.

One of the aliens towered outside the door, leaning on a two-meter spear. Its tail flicked irritably and its orange eyes narrowed at her. "Will you come, human?"

"I come," she said steadily, tilting her head back to look it in the eye.

Tail twitching, the alien snorted and stalked away. She followed.

Leathery purple skin; teeth and ears like a horse and pouched to round it off—she did not like her first alien species. But then she did not care much for the human beings of this time either.

Dea paused for a moment, ignoring her guide as it ignored her. Worn bones of mountains shimmered in the heat haze. Trees clumped casually into brushland; behind that was a distant line of green. The jungle.

Dea shivered, staring intently toward that shadowy wall. She hated jungles.

Her guide left her without ceremony in the middle of the primitive village, knocking its spear against the entrance pole as it went, as if to shake it free of contamination. Mud and wattle huts, untidy as termite nests, surrounded her in an uneven circle. The smell was worse than any Brazilian *favela*. Small alien forms ran at random, screaming at her or at nothing. The sun beat down on her.

"It is a very old planetary system, one-point-six billion years older than Earth," Kathin had told her. "The natives are, however, technologically unsophisticated. Their most advanced mechanical system is a wind-driven irrigation system."

"How far is it from Earth?"

"Immaterial. Our interstellar flight capacity is adequate to the purpose. We travel through space quite well. You will go there."

"Why?" she had asked. "What can I do that your people cannot? What report from a primitive world about time travel could possibly interest you?"

"For the first point—our investigators have failed. You are closer to them than we are, culturally and emotionally. It may prove to be the only way you can return home. You are strongly motivated, therefore, to find the answer. You will go. It may be our last hope."

The alien spoke just above her left ear. Dea had not heard this new one come; she repressed a start. "What would you have of us, human? What is this foolishness?"

Dea pivoted with deliberate slowness. The alien seemed old. There were lines running from mouth to neck, the pouch was shrunken and skin bagged loosely on its legs. An elder male, speaking for the others? She used the to-equals tense, her voice level. "It has been spoken of before, elder one."

The elder snorted, "Speak of it again, female."

"The Ymon."

"Ymon—they are animals! They know nothing but the beasts and the jungle demons. We took them from the devils of the jungle, so they need not fear the monsters. They could be safe, working for us as our Ymon. Do they work? No! Would you see them, female? See the worthless Ymon?" He gestured with his smallest finger crooked. A shorter, slighter version of the alien scrambled across the compound. Adult in proportion, it was only Dea's height. A string of black beads clinked around its neck.

"Idle and lazy," the elder said, aiming a kick. The Ymon yelped and cowered—somewhat perfunctorily, Dea thought. "They beg, or steal, or cheat our men in games of chance. They are foul and sullen. They will not work. They have no souls, and no warrior would dirty his foot by stepping in their paths—"

"Do you wish for the human trade, elder?" Dea asked. "You have heard of metal, of spearheads that will not shatter, of shafts that will not crack, of knives and snares and throwers that would make a hunter great. Has this talk reached your ears, elder?"

The elder stood like a rock. Dea faced him down. With a sudden whipsaw shout, the elder snatched at the Ymon's necklace. The string broke; black bits fell in the dust and lay, trembling, in the elder's clenched fist. "Beads!" he cried. "What do the humans want with Ymon beads?"

Dea let her silence fill the air until there was quiet. "You will let the Ymon go with me to the jungle," she told him. "You will not hinder them or me. If we trespass on the shrines or sacred places, unknowing, you will not kill us. I go with them, and our safe passage has been fairly paid."

Six of the Ymon gathered with her outside the village wall. "Where are you going, funny-shaped?" one asked her. Its tail waved in gentle sweeps.

"To—the jungle? With you?" Dea said.

"The forest?" They conferred, talking with hands and tails, frequently glancing back at Dea. Finally the first one turned back to her. "Where is the forest?" it asked plainly.

Mute, Dea pointed to the line of green on the horizon. The Ymon stared vaguely in that direction; their eyes did not focus on the distant target. After another brief conference:

"We'll let you show us," the Ymon said graciously. They lined themselves up behind Dea. Feeling suddenly older, she started for the jungle.

It had been good, growing up in her father's house. The mornings sunlit: a breakfast of fruit and hot chocolate in the coolness of the patio, she and her brother teasing each other, their mama keeping a lazy peace. Then Papa would put down his cup of steaming cafézinho *and issue the instructions for the day. Off they would scatter, for lessons or riding or new bits of their world to conquer. It was good to be young in the morning of the world. . . .*

Papa had aged years when Josinho died; his eyes were old overnight. Mama never wailed, never told her anguish, but her tears ran like water at the funeral. Dea resolved then that she would take Josinho's place. She would be everything to her parents and the fazenda *that he had been. She would never leave them. Never.*

They moved among brush and clumps of trees for hours before they came to the rain-forest proper. A stream marked the boundary with mindless, natural precision. Greenery made an imposing wall on the other side. The Ymon stopped to splash in the water. One sat down and poured water over itself, handful after handful. The others shouted and laughed, spraying each other, getting enormously wet. The reserve and quiet she had come to associate with them might never have existed. The water sparkled. Briefly, the heat was gone.

Dea forded the stream and knelt on the other bank to watch the Ymon. One of them splashed to her. She drew back, then waited.

"Bina," it named itself.

"Bina," she repeated. "Dea."

"Dea."

Carefully, it brought a cupped handful of water up to her face and let it drip down.

She had taken her brother's place, trying to live up to everything he had been and could have become. She worked harder in those two years after his death than she had in any of her previous sixteen. She learned accounting, iron-smelting, and how to gather the wild pampas cattle. She supervised crews clearing land for coffee and rubber. She fought against the jungle, as members of her family had fought for eight generations, and learned to hate it with a personal and unrelenting enmity. And her father's pride in her grew.

The jungle hit her like a silent explosion. Her eyes fled from birds to flowers to the dim towering roof of trees to the grand cathedral spaces, clutching at detail after detail and refusing to accept the whole. The roar of insect noise was a wave of sound, deafening before her ears tuned it out. It was immense and terrifying. The Ymon took the lead quickly, seeming to recognize landmarks by smell and instinct. They traveled at a half-lope, chatting, telling jokes, laughing. As if it were a playground—

Soon Dea was panting hard, trying to keep up. Insects whirred in her ears and roots twined around her feet. The dimness could hold anything, snakes, animals— Dea kept her eyes on the line of Ymon, barely more than animate shadows, and doggedly followed.

They were in the Ymon village before she was aware, stupidly, of anything but the jungle. The Ymon kept going to the central stream. Dea collapsed on a rock. The villagers piled out to them like ants; greetings, explanations and critical comments flew at large. From her vantage point, Dea could see the strings of black beads around their necks.

"Pitchblende," Kathin had told her, breathing shallowly and evenly as all future humans seemed to do. Her pale eyes did not quite encompass Dea, as if she contemplated a more absorbing, a more destructive vision. "The Ymon use the mineral for decorative and ornamental purposes. Pitchblende is an ore of uranium and radium. The half-life of—"

"I know about radioactive half-lives, Kathin. Radioactivity *was* known by the twenty-first century."

"Very good. You will know, then, how radioactive isotopes, while diluted to such a degree in natural materials as to be harmless to living organisms, may be used to date artifacts and once-living objects. The Ymon beads come from times ranging from two thousand years in the future to five hundred million years in the past."

Dea gaped. "But how do they do it? What do the Ymon do?"

"We do not know. As far as our investigators have been able to find out, the Ymon—walk through time. You will find out how they accomplish it and tell us."

For the first time Kathin's eyes shifted to focus on Dea. After a moment Dea nodded. "Yes."

The two groups of Ymon rapidly became one, more adults emerging from huts and jungle while children danced in excitement. Dea hung back until Bina came to get her.

"This is Dea, the funny-shaped-ash-skin," Bina announced. "She's come with us to the forest."

There was a rush of comments, both interested and critical. "What for?" "Are you sure it's alive? Does it talk? Maybe we should eat it." "No, it must be a person, it wears clothes, doesn't it?" "But it *smells.*" "How can it walk through the forest on feet shaped like that?"

"She can walk through the forest," Bina insisted. "She walked here. Didn't make much more noise than a wounded *droxil.*"

Half of those assembled thought that hilariously funny, retiring from the discussion to clutch their sides and yelp with laughter. Doubters persisted, nonetheless.

"It doesn't look like a person. I think it's an animal."

"I'm a person," Dea said a little too loudly. "May I stay with you in your village?"

A wizened creature with bright, suspicious eyes inspected Dea thoroughly, tail making lazy waves. "What for?"

"I want to—I want to learn to walk in the forest the way you do. I want to earn a Ymon necklace."

"But how can you walk, with feet like that?"

"Ho, Kie, you should ask. You have to fall on top of a *branz* to kill it."

"I speared it! It's not *my* fault—"

"You can sleep in the end hut with Esst. There'll be a woman festival there soon, sometime. Ambik is fostering her sister's daughter," Bina explained, leading her toward the end of the clearing.

"I don't wish to be a trouble," Dea said stiffly.

Bina's tail flicked. "Nine in the hut, ten in the hut—it'll be warm."

That was one way to put it, Dea thought. She looked involuntarily up. There were nothing but branches, vines, lianas, leaves, for what seemed like miles. She couldn't see the sky at all. She wouldn't see open sky for the next—

"But how can she walk with feet like that!" Kie shouted.

"She'll learn!" Bina shouted back. Dea stood stock-still for a moment before ducking into the low hut. She would have to learn.

Dea wiped her mouth, shivering. She felt light-headed, more than a little sick. Ambik, one of the few Ymon she could recognize by now, set the pot down with a bang.

"If you won't eat, then don't!"

"It has bugs in it! It's dirty and it has maggots in it—"

"*Erl* larvae are good food. It'll work its own way down your throat." Dea covered her face with her hands. Ambik's tail whipped angrily.

"Starve, then." It—she?—stalked away.

Dea hugged her knees and wept quietly. She was so hungry. She wanted to go home, she wanted to go home—

Not looking at it, Dea put her finger in the pot of *erl* honey and, still crying, licked it off.

Moving along the trail, panting, Dea stopped to swab at her forehead. Bina turned impatiently. "Why are you stopping? We have to get vines for the nets."

"It's so hot," she pleaded. "I can't breathe." The air weighed heavily on her. The screeches and sudden screams of birds were slowly becoming familiar—if there were only some sunlight! It was always gloomy, hot, moist and unbearable. She recognized a flower growing on a nearby vine, absently plucked and started to eat it.

"You wear too many clothes," Bina told her. "They make you dirty. You smell all the time."

"I do not!"

He snorted, loping off down the trail. "Get a loincloth!" floated back.

Angry and hot, she pounded after him. Thorns tore at her shirtsleeves, ripped at her trousers. "Oh—" She pulled off her jacket and, enraged, kicked it into the thorns. Let the jungle scratch and sting and cut her to *branz* bait! She didn't care anymore.

"You smell too!" she yelled after Bina. He started to laugh.

Clad in shorts and breastband, Dea waited comfortably beside the buttress roots. The hunters should be almost finished setting up the nets by now, ready for them to drive animals into it. She sniffed, raising her head to catch the trace of musk. *Droxil* scent? As she stepped forward, a stick cracked like a gunshot under her boot. There was a scurrying rush and an immediate, angry hubbub.

"It was an accident," Dea said weakly as Ymon appeared and converged on her.

"They did it." Esst pointed an accusing tail-tip downward. "Those stupid hard-feet of hers." There was another rush. Bina landed on her chest, a half second before Dea landed on the ground. Esst and Ambik tugged at her boots.

"I need them!" Dea said, kicking. "I can't walk without them, they protect my feet!"

"You'll have to do without them now," Bina informed her sweetly, breathing hard, pointing upward with his chin. Kie had scrambled twenty meters up a tree with the offending boots and, as she watched, dropped them into a hole in the trunk. There was no opening at the bottom of the tree. The boots were gone. "*Stupid* human. Do you think we eat air? If we starve, you starve. That was a forty-person *droxil,* and it got away because of your stupid human hard-feet."

"I'm not a *droxil* with hoofs or a *branz* with paws," Dea insisted in a small voice. "I need boots to walk."

"She has little wiggling things at the end of her skin-feet," Esst announced, fascinated. "Do you think we should cut them off?" Dea jerked her feet underneath her.

"The boots are gone," Bina said. "Learn to walk again, human. Learn to walk right this time."

"Ho, Dea," Ambik greeted her as Dea climbed down the slanting tree trunk. Dea placed her feet carefully, but without fear, and she made little more noise than a Ymon. "Get more fungi when you're done with that. There's going to be a woman festival for Esst and Tendati. We're storing up."

"When is the festival?" Dea asked, sitting back. The earth was cushiony with fallen leaves and debris, like a mottled living carpet; she wriggled her toes in it casually. A sapling had fallen here last week during the storm; the forest had already absorbed it, in the ceaseless process of decay and regeneration.

"The festival?" Ambik repeated vaguely. "Soon, soon, any day now."

Dea swallowed. "Esst, Tendati—and me?"

The Ymon watched the forest, tail-tip waving in gentle circles. "Maybe, maybe . . ." She moved off, pausing only to shout over her shoulder, "And bring plenty of vine beer with you!"

On Dea's eighteenth birthday her father had thrown a huge coming-of-age party. That evening he told her that as a present and a sign of trust he was sending her on a luxurious triplanet tour, to inspect family holdings on the other planets and in the Belt. Dea hugged him, laughed, cried, did not believe it. It was her first time offplanet, and her father trusted her to represent him.

The mining base was the third she had visited. It was much like all the others—until the shock-wave hit, a glassy wave, breaking upon human works and crushing them. Domes cracked into webwork; men ran shrieking toward death. Dea saw an invisible line of black racing toward her feet, like a whip cracking. She screamed, and that was the last she remembered.

For a very long time. . . .

"Why did you rescue me from the time crack!" Dea had cried out, railing against Kathin, protesting an incredible and unwanted future. "Why didn't you just let me stay in stasis and rot!"

"We felt—" Kathin tested the word gingerly—"responsible. It was our unsuccessful experiments in time-travel that caused the shock-wave up and down the line of history. Your mining base was not the only instance of destruction. So far we have recovered four hundred seventy-three bodies, and you."

"I don't care. This isn't my time. This isn't my world. You made me come here. I have my own place and time, Kathin. Send me home!"

"Our experiments in time-travel continue, Dea, and will do so until we have achieved success. Please believe us. We will learn to manipulate time. It is not a matter of choice."

The forest surrounded her with its own rhythms. It was a vast, pervasive organism in which the insects and the animals and the people spun out their daily lives, living in the green heartbeat of the forest. "Life here is good," Ambik said once. "We are children of the forest. It is good."

Dea had been accepted. She had learned which grubs and roots were safe to eat, which leaves shed rain, which vines gave water. She had run the woman races with Esst and Tendati through the night-long festivals, sung with them, danced with them. She slept in the hut with the unmarried females and, usually, a few courting males. She was propositioned once or twice. She rarely dreamed of Brazil.

Once she tried for an entire afternoon, sitting lizard-still in the shade of an herb tree, to remember her father's face. She could not.

They were gleaning shellfish on a stream bank when Dea saw something glisten, tumbled among the pebbles. She picked it up, pleased with its smooth black weight.

"A Ymon bead," Tendati identified it, seeming genuinely glad for her. "Good luck coming, Dea."

"Pretty," Dea said. She dropped it in her belt-pocket. Perhaps she would knot a string about it, to tie around her neck. Like them, a child of the forest. . . .

The forest was eternally the same. It had existed for over a billion years without change. Outside, mountains reared themselves up from the plains, seas dried, animals disappeared, wheels or atom bombs were invented. Not in the forest. There a way of life, meshing evenly with the trees, continued without time—as narrowly constricted and as absolutely free as any life that had ever existed.

"No more hunting here," Kie said, a month or so later. His tail was drooping. Everyone knew he was right.

"Time to go walking?" Bina hinted.

"The animals are all gone." "The leaves on the hut are dead and dry." "There are no more nut trees close." "Time to walk." "Woman, pack up the baskets, we're walking!" "Ho, man, you walk, you pack the baskets!" "No more animals." "Time to go."

"My feet are sore!" Tendati wailed.

"Too bad. It's time to walk."

"Yes."

Were they going? Leaving her behind? As she hurried to gather things together, a last, dim flicker of memory assailed Dea. Some ride she and Josinho had taken to a far corner of the *fazenda*. Both of them laughing, at something— Their horses danced, picking their way through the rotting logs. They were pushing the forest back hard that year. And the momentary glimpse of an Indian, silent, staring after them from the felled trees.

Dea snatched up a last bundle and hastened to catch up. She could walk as they did. She was one of the Ymon, a child of the forest. Her breath steadied, her head came up. She walked with the Ymon.

In the gentle dimness of the forest she left herself behind, washed by the rain and recombined by forest soil into something new. Her father's world lost to her now, forever.

The planet altered around them unseen as they walked.

"Better game that way." Kie pointed right. Ambik's nostrils flared, sniffing.

"Ay-yii," she agreed. They turned, time flowing around them like water.

"Further up . . ." "That way—" "Across the stream!" Once Dea, glancing through a wall of brush, saw things like dinosaurs cropping the pampas a kilometer away. Once she heard a screech like no bird she had ever heard before, and she knew them all. Those things were not important and she ignored them. She was one of the Ymon; she felt the time they sought pluck deeply inside her, turning her, tuning her to its own unmistakable song. "Over the rise, now—there."

"Good hunting here," Kie announced with satisfaction.

"Good hunting," Dea agreed.

She left the Ymon a few days later, with a word of farewell and words of thanks. She walked to the edge of the forest, walked to the time they'd left her there. The transmitter was waiting; she activated it. A human ship arrived within days. Kathin was aboard.

"You have been gone only ten days," Kathin began. "What progress do you expect to have made—"

"I have been gone eight months," Dea told her. The other woman's eyes widened, traveling slowly over Dea. Dea smiled faintly. Was the change so obvious? "Take me back, Kathin. Take me to Earth, and I will walk time for you."

They conveyed her to Earth with all reasonable and even unreasonable speed. She stood in the transport that was taking her down to walk Earth's surface for the first time in two hundred years, absently zipping her softsuit up and down. She had asked to disembark at a spot near the old *fazenda*. That was close enough to the forest for a starting point. When the ramp arched out she went down, head bowed. She had a debt to repay, to help these future humans get whatever they seemed to need so desperately—

The wind slammed into her like falling timber. She staggered and half fell. Then the heat blasted the rest of her senses like an open flame and she slipped to her hands and knees. Kathin was at her side, helping her up, explaining. Dea heard only part of it. She was staring at the single colorless blade of grass between her feet.

". . . massive deforestation by the twenty-first century . . . continued in the twenty-second . . . by our time . . . tropical rainforest produced eighty percent of the oxygen on Earth. We needed the land. We didn't realize . . . the greenhouse effect, erosion, climate changes . . . atmosphere rapidly deteriorating . . ."

Dea stood, turning in a full three-hundred-and-sixty-degree circle. The forest of Brazil, the most immense untapped natural resource in the world—the forest was gone. No trees. No green. No life. Just the grey rocky soil, stretching endlessly to the horizon.

"Our world is dying!" Kathin yelled at her. Her face was contorted. "Tell us what to do to put it back. Tell us!"

Watching the untouchable, unreachable woman of times that had come, Dea told her the truth.

"Nothing can be put back, Kathin. Nothing can ever be put back. All you can do is live with what time has left you. . . ." Disbelieving, Kathin raged at her, demanded— Dea held her like a child and wept for the loss that was not hers alone.

ABOMINABLE

Carol Emshwiller

We are advancing into an unknown land with a deliberate air of nonchalance, our elbows out or our hands on hips, or standing one foot on a rock when there's the opportunity for it. Always to the left, the river, as they told us it should be. Always to the right, the hills. At every telephone booth we stop and call. Frequently the lines are down because of high winds or ice. The Commander says we are already in an area of the sightings. We must watch now, he has told us over the phone, for those curious two-part footprints no bigger than a boy's and of a unique delicacy. "Climb a tree," the Commander says, "or a telephone pole, whichever is the most feasible, and call out a few of the names you have memorized." So we climb a pole and cry out: Alice, Betty, Elaine, Jean, Joan, Marilyn, Mary . . . and so on, in alphabetical order. Nothing comes of it.

We are seven manly men in the dress uniform of the Marines, though we are not (except for one) Marines. But this particular uniform has always been thought to attract them. We are seven seemingly blasé (our collars open at the neck in any weather) experts in our fields, we, the research team for the Committee on Unidentified Objects that Whizz by in Pursuit of Their Own Illusive Identities. Our guns shoot sparks and stars and chocolate-covered cherries and make a big bang. It's already the age of frontal nudity, of "Why not?" instead of "Maybe." It's already the age of devices that can sense a warm, pulsing, live body at seventy-five yards and home in on it, and we have one of those devices with us. (I might be able to love like that myself someday.) On the other hand, we carry only a few blurry pictures in our wallets, most of these from random sightings several months ago. One is thought to be of the wife of the Commander. It was taken from a distance and we can't make out her features, she was wearing her fur coat. He thought he recognized it. He has said there was nothing seriously wrong with her.

So far there has been nothing but snow. What we put up with for these creatures!

Imagine their bodies as you hold this little reminder in the palm of your hand . . . this fat, four-inch Venus of their possibilities . . . The serious elements are missing, the eyes simple dots (the characteristic hair-do almost covers the face), the feet, the head inconsequential. Imagine the possibility of triumph but avoid the smirk. Accept the challenge of the breasts, of the outsize hips and then . . . (the biggest challenge of all). If we pit ourselves against it *can we win!* Or come off with honorable mention, or, at the least, finish without their analysis of our wrong moves?

Here are the signs of their presence that we have found so far (we might almost think these things had been dropped in our path on purpose if we didn't know how careless they can be, especially when harassed or in a hurry; and since they are nervous creatures, easily excited, they usually *are* harassed and/or in a hurry) . . . Found in our path, then: one stalk of still-frozen asparagus, a simple recipe for moussaka using onion-soup mix, carelessly torn out of a magazine, a small purse with a few crumpled-up dollar bills and a book of matches. (It is clear that they do have fire. We take comfort in that.)

And now the Commander says to leave the river and to go up into the hills even though they are treacherous with spring thaws and avalanches. The compass points up. We slide on scree and ice all day sometimes, well aware that they may have all gone south by now, whole tribes of them feeling worthless, ugly and unloved. Because the possibilities are endless, any direction may be wrong, but at the first sign of superficialities we'll know we're on the right track.

One of us is a psychoanalyst of long experience, a specialist in hysteria and masochism. (Even without case histories, he is committed to the study of their kind.) He says that if we find them they will probably make some strange strangling sounds, but that these are of no consequence and are often mistaken for laughter, which, he says, is probably the best way to take them. If, on the other hand, they smile, it's a simple reflex and serves the purpose of disarming us. (It has been found that they smile two and a half times as often as we do.) Sometimes, he says, there's a kind of nervous giggle which is essentially sexual in origin and, if it occurs when they see us, is probably a very good sign. In any case, he says, we should give no more than our names and our rank, and if they get angry, we should be careful that their rage doesn't turn against themselves.

Grace is the name of the one in the picture, but she must be all of fifty-five by now. Slipped out of a diner one moonlit night when the Commander forgot to look in her direction. But what was there to do but go on as usual, commanding what needed to be commanded? We agree. He said she had accepted her limitations up to that time, as far as he could see, and the limits of her actions. He blamed it on incomplete acculturation or on not seeing the obvious, and did not wonder about it until several years later.

I'd like to see one like her right now. Dare to ask where I come from and how come they're so unlike? How we evolved affectations the opposite of theirs? And do they live deep underground in vast kitchens, some multichambered sanctuary heated by ovens, the smell of gingerbread, those of childbearing age perpetually pregnant from the frozen semen of some tall, redheaded, long-dead comedian or rock star? Anyway, that's one theory.

But now the sudden silence of our own first sighting. One! ... On the heights above us, huge (or seems so) and in full regalia (as in the Commander's photograph): mink and monstrous hat, the glint of something in the ears, standing (it seems a full five minutes) motionless on one leg. Or maybe just an upright bear (the sun was in our eyes) but gone when we got up to the place a half hour later. The psychoanalyst waited by the footprints all night, ready with his own kind of sweet-talk, but no luck.

The information has been phoned back to the commander ("Tell her I think I love her," he said), and it has been decided that we will put on the paraphernalia ourselves ... the shoes that fit the footprints, the mink, fox, leopard (phony) over several layers of the proper underwear. We have decided to put bananas out along the snow in a circle seventy-five yards beyond our camp and to set up our live warm-body sensor. Then when they come out for the bananas we will follow them back to their lairs, down into their own dark sacred places; our camera crew will be ready to get their first reactions to us for TV. They'll like being followed. They always have.

We hope they are aware, if only on some dim level, of our reputations in our respective fields.

But the live warm-body sensor, while it does sound the alarm, can't seem to find any particular right direction, and in the morning all the bananas are gone.

It's because they won't sit still ... won't take anything seriously. There's nobody to coordinate their actions, so they run around in different directions, always distracted from the task at hand, jumping to conclusions, making unwarranted assumptions, taking everything for granted or, on the other hand, not taking *anything* for granted (love, for instance). The forces of nature are on their side, yes, (chaos?) but we have other forces. This time we will lay the bananas out in one long logical straight line.

When we step into those kitchens finally! The largest mountain completely hollowed out, my God! And the smells! The bustle! The humdrum *everydayness* of their existence! We won't believe what we see. And they will probably tell us things are going better than ever. They will be thinking they no longer need to be close to the sources of power. They may even say they like places of no power to anyone . . . live powerless, as friends, their own soft signals one to the other, the least of them to the least of them. And they will also say we hardly noticed them anyway, or noticed that they weren't there. They will say we were always looking in the other direction, that we never knew who or what they were, or cared. Well, we did sense something . . . have sensed it for a long time, and we feel a lack we can't quite pinpoint. Unpaid creatures, mostly moneyless, but even so, noticed. We will tell them this, and also that the Commander thinks he may love one of them.

But this time they have refused the bananas. (What we offer them is never quite right.) Okay. The final offering (they have one more chance): these glass beads that look like jade; a set of fine, imported cookware; a self-help book, "How to Overcome Shyness with the Opposite Sex"; and (especially) we offer ourselves for their delight as sons, fathers or lovers (their choice).

The psychoanalyst says they're entitled to their own opinions, but we wonder how independent should they be allowed to be?

One of us has said it was just a bear we saw at the top of that hill. He said he remembered that it humped down on all fours after standing on one leg, but they *might* do that.

The psychoanalyst has had a dream. Afterwards he told us never to be afraid of the snapping vagina (figuratively speaking) but to come on down to them (though we are climbing up, actually) and throw fish to the wombs (nothing but the best filet of sole, figuratively speaking).

This is the diagram the psychoanalyst has laid out for further study:

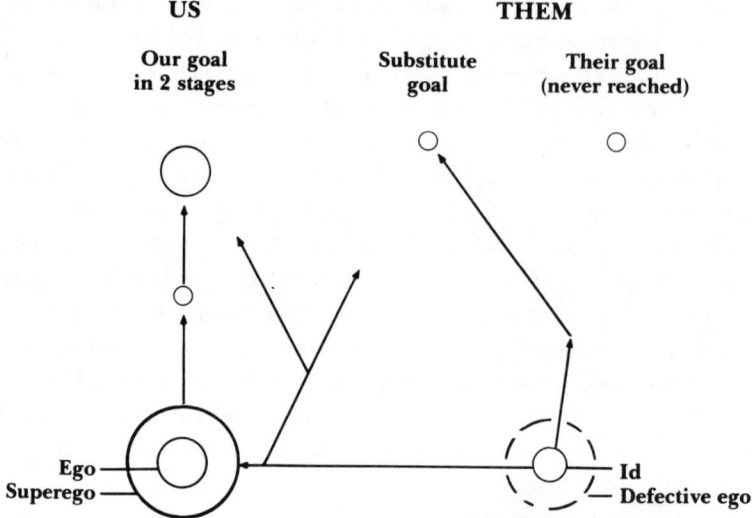

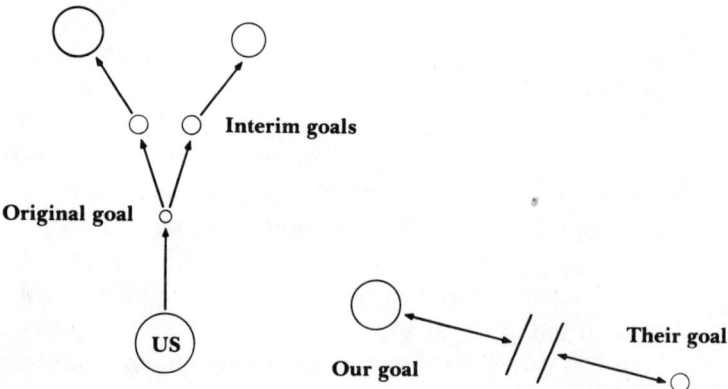

ABOMINABLE

Well, if I had one I'd wash its feet (literally) and the back. Venture the front, too. Let the water flow over both of us. Let their hair hang down. I'd take some time out now and then, even from important work, to do some little things like this of hardly any meaning, and listen, sometimes, to its idle chatter or, at least, seem to. But as to Grace, it must be something else I have in mind, though I'm not sure what.

We are telling all the old tales about them around our campfires in the late evenings, but it's not the same kind of frightening that it used to be when we were young and telling the tales in similar circumstances because now we know they may actually be lurking out there in the shadows, and what's scary is that we have really no idea of their size! We're not sure what to believe. On the one hand, whether they are twice our size or, as the Commander insists, whether almost all of them are quite a bit smaller and definitely weaker. The more mythically oriented among us have said that they are large enough to swallow us up into their stomachs (from below) and to ejaculate us out again months later, weak and helpless. The anthropologically oriented say they may be the missing link we have searched for so long and stand, as they believe, somewhere between the gorilla and us (though probably quite a bit higher on the scale than pithecanthropus erectus) and that they are, therefore, (logically) distinctly smaller and somewhat bent over, but may not necessarily be weaker. The sexually obsessed among us wonder, among other things, if their orgasm is as specific a reaction as ours is. The romantics among us think they will be cute and loveable creatures even when they're angry and regardless of size and strength. Others think the opposite. Opinions also vary as to how to console them for the facts of their lives and whether it is possible to do so at all since 72 percent of them perceive themselves as inferior, 65 percent perceive themselves to be in a fragile mental balance, only 33⅓ percent are without deep feelings of humiliation simply for being what they are. How will it be possible, then, to penetrate their lines of self-defense and their lines of defensiveness? Altercations are inevitable, that's clear. (Eighty-five percent return to rehash old arguments.) We dislike unpleasant emotional confrontations, try to avoid such things at all costs, but we also realize that playing the role of dominant partner in intimate interaction won't always be easy. How nice, even so, to have a group of beings, one of these days (almost invisible, too) whose main job would be to tidy up!

Pedestals have already been set out for them.

Even if (or especially if) they are not quite up to our standards, they will, in any case, remind us of the animal in all of us, of our beastliness . . . our ebb and flow . . . of life-forces we barely know exist . . . maybe some we never suspected.

But now we have had a strange and disturbing message from the Commander telling us that some very important political appointees have said that these stories of sightings are exactly that, stories . . . hoaxes, and it's been proven that the photographs have been doctored, in one case a gorilla superimposed on a snowy mountain, in another case a man in drag. (Only two pictures still unexplained.) Several people have confessed. Some have never even been in the area at all. Whatever we have seen must have been a trick of light and shadow or, more likely, one of the bears in this vicinity and (they're sure of it) we have a hoaxer among us, stealing the bananas himself and making footprints with an old shoe on the end of a long stick. Besides, think if we should discover that they do, in fact, exist. We would only be adding to our present problems. Committees would have to be set up to find alternatives to boredom once their dishwashing years were over. Cures would have to be discovered for cancers in peculiar places, for strange flows, for vaginismus and other spasms. A huge group of dilettantes (Sunday poets and painters) would be added to society, which society can well do without, according to the Commander. And why should we come searching them, as though they were Mount Everest (and as important), simply because they're there? Anyway, the funding for our search has run out. The Commander even doubts if we can afford any more phone calls.

We are all very depressed by this news, though it's hard to pinpoint exactly why. Some of us feel sure, or fairly sure, that there *is* something out there . . . just out of sight . . . just out of earshot. Some of us seem to see, sometimes, a flash of color out of the corners of our eyes, as though the essentially invisible had been made *almost* visible for a few seconds. Makes one think, too (and some of us do), how socks and underwear might someday return, magically, from under beds to be found clean and folded in the drawer, as if cups of coffee could appear out of nowhere just when most needed, as if the refrigerator never ran out of milk or butter . . . But we are at the service of our schedule and our budget. We must return to the seats of power, to the service of civilization . . . politics . . . We turn back.

For a while I think seriously of going on by myself. I think perhaps if I crept back alone, sat quietly, maybe dressed to blend in more. Maybe if I sat still long enough (and stopped telling, out loud, those old, scary stories about them), if I made no proud gestures . . . shoulders not so stiff . . . maybe then they'd get used to me, even eat bananas out of my hand, and come, in time, to recognize an authoritarian figure by the subtle reality of it, and perhaps learn a few simple commands. But I have to stick to my orders. It's too bad, though I do want to pick up my pay, my medals, and get on with the next project. Still, I want to make one more move toward these creatures, if only a symbolic one. I sneak back along the trail and leave a message where it can't be missed, surrounded by bananas. I leave something they'll be sure to understand: the simple drawing of a naked man; a crescent that can't help but stand for moon; a heart shape (anatomically correct) for love; a clock face with the time of the message; the outline of a footprint of my own next to an outline of one of theirs (looks like a question mark next to an exclamation point). "To Grace" at the top. I sit there for a while, then, and listen for sighs and think I hear some . . . think I see something vaguely white on white in the clarity of snow. Invisible *on purpose,* that's for sure (if there at all), so if we can't see them, it's not *our* fault.

Well, if that's how they want it, let them bark at the moon alone (or whatever it is they do) and dance and keep their own home fires burning. Let them live, as was said, "in the shadow of man." It serves them right.

I ask the psychoanalyst, "Who are we, anyway?" He says about 90 percent of us ask that same question in one form or another, while about 10 percent seem to have found some kind of an answer of their own. He says that, anyway, we will remain essentially who we already are whether we bother to ask the question or not.

UNDERWOOD AND THE SLAUGHTERHOUSE

Raymond G. Embrak

The trashmen came upon a nest of maniacs in the cool shelter of what had been a parking garage. They had been sitting around a fire frying a skinned bird, drinking sour water out of gin bottles. When the trashmen ran in, they scrambled to their feet, scuttling off in different directions.

The trashmen split up, Kane going through a black cavity in the cracked green wall, Glaser darting down a corridor, and Underwood flinging open the door labeled STAIRWELL and bounding up the steps.

Dammit, thought Underwood, this'll take a while. It made killing harder when you had to chase maniacs through their own territory. They had spots where they hid, waiting for you to come along so they could bust open your head when your back was turned.

His scuffling echoed hollowly in the shaft, paused as he bounced off the wall of the landing, then charged up the next flight of stairs. He stopped, his back against the wall; he listened for steps above. For a few moments the only sound was his ragged breathing; then the door on the landing above banged against the wall.

Underwood took the steps three at a time, whipped open the door, and a bar slammed into his chest, flinging him back into the stairwell. The edges of steps were jammed against his back as he watched a tall, pimply teenager come at him with a rusty pipe.

Underwood's rifle lay on the floor, a thousand miles away. He jacked his combat boots into the boy's chest, knocking a sharp grunt out of him as he slammed against the wall. Underwood snatched up the rifle. The boy had run out the door.

He was bolting down the sunlit corridor as Underwood took aim at the center of his head. The body was jerked forward, spraying the walls and floor.

Glaser did the driving for their car pool. He liked to drive. Easy-listening music poured through the car. Kane was intent on a crossword puzzle. She always worked on crossword puzzles in her spare time. Underwood sat in the back, idly observing how Kane's brown hair was stirred by the wind blowing in her open window. He could still smell the industrial-strength cleanser on his hands; he had gotten used to it, but he still didn't care for it.

"I'm putting in the swimming pool this week," Glaser said, half turning his craggy, middle-aged face toward them. "I'm going to open it up with a barbecue next weekend after it's filled. I want to see you two there."

"I'd be a fool to pass up an offer like that," Kane said vacantly, concentrating on the magazine in her lap.

"Why don't you bring the old man by, Underwood? It's been about a year since I last seen him."

Small wonder, Underwood thought. The last time, his father had tried to club Glaser with an ivory statuette.

Underwood fished through his pockets for his keys, opened the door of his townhouse. The place he had rushed from in the morning was a beautiful sight in the evening. He took off his brown leather jacket, tossed it on the couch, walked across the plush white carpeting to the kitchen, where he took a can of beer from the refrigerator.

"Just come back from the slaughterhouse, eh, son?"

He turned to face the short, old black man with the white goatee. That was his father.

Every day when he came home from work he heard the same line. It irritated him, but he had to ignore it because it was inevitable.

"We got an invitation to Glaser's: he's putting in a swimming pool next week."

J. P. Underwood stared at his son with a look of astonishment.

"You're shittin' me. What makes you hang around with that idiot?"

"I admit he isn't the world's brightest man, but I like him. And he was good enough to invite *you,* after the way you tried to maul him." Underwood pulled off the tab and took a cold sip.

"The way he sat around talking about the sexual habits of the plague-deranged? During dinner? Come *on,* Max, you can do better than that."

"Look. Why don't you go—get out of the house for a change—see how people live. *Modern* people. It's been—what?—more than a *year* since we got out of the death zone; have a little fun." He handed J. P. a beer from the refrigerator.

"I oughta go, just to see how they reconstruct suburban mediocrity."

Underwood grinned, sipped the beer, and began to relax.

Underwood swam up from under the sheets, blindly reaching out to shut off the blaring alarm clock. He sat up, slid his feet into his slippers, shuffled into the bathroom.

He idly watched Kane's brown hair stir in the wind blowing in her open window. Her head was bent over a crossword puzzle. The radio was on. Glaser was talking about something.

They came down through the huge hole in the roof, landing on the rubble and plaster, firing the submachine guns at the scampering maniacs. They had gotten six, but four others had dashed away into the recesses of the building.

Underwood ducked into a hole in a grey wall, stepping over soft plaster. The dust was thick and dry-smelling. He came out in a large room where the sun filtered down through gaps in the ceiling. He stepped over the rubble, crunching, raising dust.

He went through various rooms, found nothing. He didn't mind that.

He met Kane and Glaser back at the grey van outside. They had a short break and opened their lunch boxes, poured coffee from a vacuum bottle.

Kane said, "It's odd: some of them look almost normal. I mean they don't have the scaly skin or the paws that you normally see."

Underwood looked over at her squinty-eyed gaze, said, "They're still contagious, though. The war really fucked them over, didn't it?"

"Yeah," she answered grimly.

They watched the massive grey trashwagon parked down the street.

The trashwagon ground toward the black cube in the middle of the dusty plain.

Kane backed it to the hatch as Underwood and Glaser, in masks and gloves, walked around the sides. Glaser yanked down the iron lever on the box and the hatch clanked open slowly. Underwood pulled the lever on the trashwagon. The top rose high in the grey sky, the dirty bodies sliding down into the black hatch, landing with a sound like a thousand falling potatoes. The iron machinery whined and shrieked, the noise barely diminished by their earplugs. Underwood could see blue and yellow sparks beyond the hatch as the corpses were fed to the furnace.

Underwood stood in line with the trashmen of other districts to punch out. He read the same posters on the same bulletin board.

A green poster with black letters: REPORT ANY PERSON YOU SUSPECT MAY BE A CARRIER OF POSTBELLUM DISEASE TO YOUR LOCAL HEALTH DEPARTMENT CENTER!

A black poster with orange letters: SUPPORT OUR GREAT NATIONAL RECOVERY. Beneath this was an orange drawing of a man, a woman and a child, holding hands.

He idly watched Kane's hair stir in the wind blowing in her open window. He closed his eyes and salty darkness took over. It wasn't until he had sunk his weary bones into the back seat that he became aware how exhausted he was. Dumping the week's dead was dreaded—the tons of limp weight that had to be moved to the truck, then to the furnace.

Glaser never seemed to tire. He talked endlessly. "I hear they're gonna plow down some of the old cities and put up some new projects. Looks like we're gonna be back on our feet soon."

"What if they start another war and wreck it all over again?" Underwood said.

"We got to take care of things one day at a time, Max. We get back on our feet, and we handle whatever comes next. It'll be a hell of a long while before things get back to where it was when the war started. The government's got to get back on its feet; the economy's got to get back on its feet—you're talking *years* from now."

"All right, *years* from now. Somebody's going to have to carry the load, like we're doing now."

"Like I said, man: one day at a time."

"Coming back from the slaughterhouse, eh, son?"
Underwood hit the counter.

The Chinese food was spread out on the table between them, releasing steam and exotic aromas. Underwood emptied a block of rice on his plate.

"Why is it that you don't like frivolities like having a place to live, or knowing where your next meal's gonna come from?" he asked his father.

"Look, it ain't that I don't appreciate good living, but I've spent too much of my life eking out what morsels of existence I could for the both of us, out there in the death zone. I'm not going to suddenly go for all this airy-fairy bullshit about the 'new civilization' the government is hyping. They could damn well do it all over again."

"What's your alternative: living out in the ruined cities again? Where the plague is?"

"Most people didn't get the plague. It's only a few, that you're knocking off so you can have clean hands."

Underwood put down the fork.

"You never liked my being a trashman anyway, so what's the point?"

"The point is responsibility. The powers-that-was were stupid enough and irresponsible enough to foul their own nests; now they hire a bunch of shits to clean up the poor motherfuckers they caused to go crazy. It's bad."

Underwood stared at J. P. His father looked down, bit into an eggroll.

"Yeee-hahh—" Glaser disappeared under the crystal-blue water. He had been at the center of everything, hands on hips, ruddy-skinned and paunchy. Underwood chuckled, holding a cocktail, wearing a multicolored shirt, white slacks and dark glasses. It was a million miles from the green coveralls, the combat boots, the caps of the trashmen. The sky was clear, deep blue and sun-bright. He lifted the dark glasses to observe the tall, tawny young woman who stood at the other side of the pool, holding a drink, talking to a tanned middle-aged woman. His eyes trailed from the long, straight hair that fell down her back, the skin-tightness of the white swimsuit, and the curve of her round hips, down to the long, shapely legs. Nice.

J. P. stood next to him, wearing a white short-sleeved shirt, black pants and a black beret. He leaned closer, said, "So *this* is modern man. Tell me more pretty stories."

"Why don't you relax, get a beer, a hot dog, and enjoy it?"

"While you're off chasing tail."

"There you go." The man is equipped with radar, Underwood thought, as he walked around the pool.

Night came, and the guests lounged around the lighted pool area, laughing and drinking. It had been quite a while since Underwood had been friends with a woman. He and Kane were casual acquaintances, but it was mainly business.

The tall woman's name was Carter, and she worked on the Health Department committee that tried to unearth plague-bearers within the new settlements. She looked like a teenager, and although there was a certain low-pitched seriousness in her personality—like someone who was taking a brief vacation from a charnel house—Underwood could see her arousal at meeting someone she could get into interesting conversation with. When he raised the drink to his lips, he glanced at her small breasts. It was going to be an interesting night, yes it was.

Then he noticed J. P. having a fairly loud argument with Glaser. He looked like a white-bearded gadfly buzzing around the tall, relaxed, probably high, bare-chested Glaser.

"Come *on*, Mr. Underwood, you can't be serious. Let them live in a colony? They'd be at each other's throats—they'd kill each other in a week."

"Then leave it up to them. You're starting out on the same double-handed mentality as you did before. The same disregard for human life."

J. P. can't relax anywhere, Underwood thought, turning back. He caught the observant expression on Carter's face.

"Your father could get in trouble talking like that," she said. "I wouldn't report him, but somebody here is bound to."

The maniac had a tight grip around his throat with a strand of wire, pulling back as if he had a grip on the devil. Underwood's head felt like a swelling red balloon; the sun shone in his eyes, isolated in a dark blue sky. Rough animal noises squeezed through his throat. He cursed himself for keeping the knife in his boot. The second maniac, scaly, fish-grey in the tattered remains of a suit, waved the iron-smelling bar under his nose. Living in the death zone, Underwood had never learned fear. J. P. had taught him how to be tough.

He drew the last moisture from his throat and spat it on the bug-eyed scaly face before him. The maniac's mouth rose in a grin; he swung the bar into Underwood's groin.

That was it. The ropes were cut and Underwood slid down into a red place where pain filled everything. The grip loosened and he felt himself dropping, his legs sagging under him. He balanced himself with one hand on the stony ground as he clutched at the knife; he jerked it up and plunged it into the thigh behind him as deep as he could. He felt it hit bone.

The grip broke and the ground hit his shoulder as a long, agonized tenor chewed raggedly at the air above. He heard scuttling footsteps, then something fell into a pile of junk. The other one kicked him in the ribs, raising the bar for a smash. His silver head exploded, showering Underwood's coveralls with red paste. Small hands and big hands helped him up, but he had trouble finding his feet. Kane and Glaser, at that moment resembling angels, helped him to the van. Fireflies buzzed behind his eyes but he could make out Kane's worried squinty grimace; he felt himself being lifted back into the darkness of the van.

"Just come back from the slaughterhouse, eh, son?"
"And I damn near got slaughtered."
"You'll live."
The doorbell rang. Underwood opened the door to two men in dark blue suits and hats.
"Mr. Maxwell Underwood?"
"Yes."
"We're from the Health Department," said the one with a small, neat mustache. "We have to see your father, Julius Underwood."
"Come in."
"Thank you." The two men faced J. P. when they entered the living room. The other man, tall, with a loose necktie, said, "Julius Underwood?"
"That's right."
"You are requested to appear at the Plague Center for routine analysis and psychiatric tests this evening."
"Hear that, Max? Word travels fast. Well, I don't have the plague, so you're wasting your time."
"We're not asking you for your diagnosis, sir," said the tall one. "You are requested to come with us."

"To hell with you *and* your request," J. P. said, turning away. Underwood took him by the elbow, whispering angrily, "I want to talk to you," then, back to the men, "We'll be just a minute."

In the kitchen. "Are you trying to get yourself suspected?" Underwood asked J. P., trying to keep his voice below screaming.

"You're too young to know what's going on; this is a *witch hunt,* Max. And during witch hunts, people look behind their backs; and they *burn* people, Max. Soon enough they won't be able to tell the plague bearers from neurotics."

"Look, the demented element will undermine the new civilization, if you let them in."

"Believe in man and you're done for; to hell with them, Max."

"You're not going to blow it by casting aspersions on us! Trashman is third-highest-paying position in the new civilization, and you ain't going to blow all I've busted my *ass* for. You'll be fine, J. P. If you don't have the plague, then what danger are you in?"

"I see. You're selling me out, huh, Max?"

Underwood's mouth was connected to nothing; he had run out of words.

They went outside and the men escorted J. P. to a black four-door automobile. Underwood watched it drive off down the quiet, cobblestoned, tree-lined avenue.

Underwood idly watched Kane's hair stir in the wind blowing in her open window. It had been a week since they took J. P. What the hell were they doing? He had called and a woman told him J. P. was being kept under observation at the center.

Underwood answered the door and found Carter on the doorstep. She was wearing a trenchcoat.

"Come in."

"I thought instead of them sending you the notice through post-shuttle, I'd bring it to you, for what it's worth," she said quietly.

Underwood took the brown envelope, dug into it, read on a green sheet of paper:

TO <u>Maxwell Underwood</u>:
YOUR <u>father, Julious Powell Underwood</u>, HAS BEEN FOUND TO HAVE <u>extreme mental distress, resulting in subversive tendencie</u>s. HE WILL BE REMOVED TOMORROW AFTERNOON. WE OFFER YOU CONDOLENCE AND ENCOURAGE YOU TO CONTINUE TO SUPPORT THE NEW CIVILIZATION AND OUR NATIONAL RECOVERY.

                                            HD
                                      DIRECTOR

"It hurt me too when my brother and mother had to be removed, but when you realize that it's necessary for the national recovery—it's almost encouraging," Carter said, idly fingering a coffee cup.

"Yeah, but it's hard when it happens to you, you know," Underwood mumbled. "I told him what he was doing. You can tell someone what he's doing wrong, but you can't live his life for him, you know. It's his fault."

Carter stood up, moved around behind him, began to stroke his head. "I don't mean to be disrespectful, but he *was* becoming irrational and must have been suffering great pain. And one person mustn't be allowed to stand in the way of our recovery. But why don't we get our minds off the uglier aspects of progress?" she said, hugging Underwood around the neck.

Underwood idly watched how Kane's hair stirred in the wind blowing in her open window. The car was silent save for the radio, turned down low. A small bubbling was happening in the pit of his stomach. After today J. P. would be dead, taken to the special center in the ruins of the Eighth District where the demented found in the new towns were gassed.

If he couldn't keep up with progress, he had to go.

Underwood stood in line to punch the clock. His eyes ran over the same posters on the same bulletin board. There was an announcement tacked up, about the interdistrict trashman softball games.

The filthy bodies slid down into the hatch, tumbling and landing with thuds. The scream of the machines filled his head, pushing out all other thoughts but work.

Underwood pushed down his glove, looked at his watch. It was one o'clock. Removals took place at two and seven, weekdays. If he concentrated on his work, he would never know the time had passed.

He wasn't going to worry about it any further.

It was a good spot on the roof of what had been a pharmacy, fifty yards from the entrance of the removal center. When the man in white coveralls brought J. P. out of the green van, Underwood took aim.

The shot took the top of the man's head off, and he fell in the street, leaving J. P. standing there in a straitjacket, looking stupid. When the driver got out of the van with a rifle, the next shot knocked him up against the front, tearing a ragged hole in his chest.

Underwood dabbed at the sweat on his brow, then climbed down the fire escape to the street. J. P. was still standing there.

"What took you so long, Max? You think this is comfortable?"

"Oh, stop noodjing me, I got here as fast as I could."

Max untied J. P., and they walked off down the wrecked street in the other direction.

"You know what it cost for me to come here, don't you? The job, the house, decent living?"

"It ain't all that bad, we'll manage," J. P. said.

"You really *are* crazy, like they said."

"Watch your mouth. You killed a lot of innocent people, son, and I'll see you do some penance for it. But you'll be okay."

"Terrific. I can hardly wait."

HOPE

Lelia Rose Foreman

Aunt Kiloma was brushing my hair with a wooden comb. I was still numb and didn't really notice the patches of hair she pulled out.

"But why did she die, Auntie? She was getting better."

Kiloma stopped pulling at my hair. When she spoke there was a catch in her voice. "I don't know, honey. I guess she gave up. I guess it's hard to keep fighting when you don't believe you'll be rescued anymore." Then she attacked my hair savagely. "But we will be rescued. God will see to it Earth gets our message!"

That was forty-five years after the crash. Forty-five years and sixteen days, the day my mother died of some virus that further yellowed her skin, eight days after my thirteenth birthday. My father had died forty-three years and three hundred eighty-nine days after the crash, when a dread-for-all caught him as he foraged. I grew up with death (as a way of life, so to speak). Of course, most of the people died in the first five years. They died of night-bites, diseases, food poisoning, and missteps around ground-joints and anemone-thorns. After my mother died, there were thirty-one of us left on this yellow, dusty world.

Gregory stepped inside the doorway. "Are you ready? Would you like me to read the Scriptures for you?"

I didn't look at him as I answered. "You're not a believer. You never were and you never will be. I will read them."

"I thought I could help you out, Hope." Gregory's scarred face furrowed with concern. He was only two years older than I, an old and beaten fifteen, but he took charge of most things, like funerals.

"I'm sorry. I . . . Let's go."

We went outside and walked past the circle of huts to the cemetery. Aunt Kiloma held my shoulders and said, "Just remember, honey, it won't be like this forever. It won't be like this forever."

A few months later a night-grunt suddenly squealed in terror. I lifted the door flap and stared into the night even though nothing could be seen by the murky light of the planet's rings.

"I think we caught one, Auntie."

"*Shh.* I know, honey. Close the door before a night-bite gets you."

Knowing that we would eat well tomorrow made it hard to go back to sleep. I lay on one side, then the other. After turning, I don't know, maybe ten or twenty times, I gave up, got up, and trimmed a candle. Fumbling about in the wavering light, I found a writing stick. I pulled a box of dirt close to the light and began to diagram an antique analog multiplexor. It was simple and I enjoyed the symmetry.

Kiloma rolled over like a sack of hard-get grain. "What are you doing, child?"

"I'm—"

A buzz-whine swooped and smacked into the leather door flap.

"Night-bite!" I screamed. We both hit the candle at the same time. It fell to the ground and winked out. We hugged each other as the night-bite scrabbled against the door-jamb. It scratched down to the ground, where it snuffled and dug against the joint of packed dirt and doorsill. I began to shake. Auntie pulled my head down into her bosom and covered my ears. But I could still hear the creature probe and scratch at every seam in the door. At last it grew discouraged and flapped away. I sobbed and panted and hiccupped.

Auntie stroked my hair. There was a terrible smell on her swollen hands. "Child, I wish you weren't always so afraid," she sighed. "Now what does it say in the Bible?"

I choked out, "Jesus is always with me, even to the end of the world."

"Calm down. It also says, 'What time I am afraid, I will trust in thee.' You say it."

" 'What time I am afraid, I will trust in thee.' "

"I want you to lie down and say it to yourself fifty times."

I did, and must have gone to sleep, for the cold dawn found Aunt Kiloma nudging me. I flashed awake.

"Oh! Let's see if we still have the grunt!"

"Don't worry, child. I know it's there. Come and see what I have."

I rolled out of my mat and followed Auntie to her corner. She lifted her pillow. I stared at what lay under it. It was a chunk of rottenwood with a hole carved in it. A crude carving of a night-grunt was jammed into the hole. When I pulled it out, one of the crumbly rottenwood legs fell off. The rotten-egg odor of it hit my nostrils.

"I'm sorry I ruined your sculpture."

"It's not sculpture, honey. It's prayer." She pulled her hair back from her puffy cheeks and temples as she sat back to smile at me.

"Huh?"

"It's true. We covered that pit over a week ago and haven't caught a blessed thing. Yesterday I decided to do something about it. So I carved what I wanted, put it under my pillow, and prayed about it all night. And it worked!" She hugged her knees and laughed.

"But that's idolatry."

Her face changed. "No, it isn't, honey. It's to help me concentrate on what I want."

"But—"

"Look, honey, I know you can't help it, not knowing the deeper things of the spirit. If it works, then it's right, isn't it?"

Now I was mad. I could hear the other people shouting excitedly as they raced toward the game pit. I didn't want to join them until I had calmed down. After washing, I climbed a many-trunk tree and remembered the dusk when my mother had looked at me and burst into tears. She wouldn't tell me why she was crying, and after going to bed I crept back in the dark to listen to her sobbing to my father.

"Jim, I don't think I can stand it anymore."

"All things work together for the good of—"

"I know it! But some days I can't handle knowing Hope could have been a genius if it weren't for her iodine deficiency. If she has children, they'll be cretins!"

"*Shh, shh, shh.*"

"I'm tired of being dirty. I'm tired of being sick. I'm tired of being hungry. We live like savages!"

"*Shh,* darling."

"But what do we have to look forward to? We'll never be rescued after this long. We'll have idiots for grandchildren!"

"We know the Lord's hand is upon us. I can't stand to see you cry."

"I know it, but there's nothing left to do."

My mother cried for a long time. I didn't know what cretins were, but I knew what idiots were; and suddenly I understood why I was shorter and uglier than the pictures of my cousins on Earth, and why I sometimes couldn't understand the lessons my parents gave me in the dark night hours. I had hair the color of mud instead of shining red like my parents. My blue eyes were dull and weak. We were all dull and weak from lack of iodine, lack of medicine, lack of food on this planet we called Sulphur as a synonym of Hell.

The next morning we had family devotions as usual. My parents never mentioned their conversation. I never did either. I thought about it, though, every time my aunt said I couldn't help it if I didn't understand. But there *was* something wrong with her rottenwood carving. If I thought about it long enough I would figure it out; but I was calm now and wanted to watch the excitement too.

When I arrived at the pit, Gregory was arranging the archers. Suzannie rushed up to me and grabbed my arm and danced.

"Think of it, Hope! Steaks and cutlets and fat!" She whirled away to gape at the grunt pawing at the splintered logs. Aunt Kiloma hobbled up and joined her.

"Look at that!" shouted Gregory, and pointed. "That log there didn't break. The grunt could have climbed that and gotten out if its leg weren't broken. Next time, we'll build the pit better." Most of the people looked and nodded.

My aunt smiled at me and mouthed the words, "Its leg is broken." I thought of the rottenwood carving and felt sick.

After the grunt was killed, Gregory strode over to me and slapped me on the back. "Listmaker! What day is it?"

"Forty-five years, one hundred forty days since the crash."

He slapped me again. "Good girl! Mark our success on your calendar tree."

"Okay."

He watched the people hack at the carcass for a moment. A buzzfly settled on his cheek but he waved it off. "Why did it take us so long to build a good game pit?"

I don't know why he asked the question. Our parents had been able to salvage so little from the crash: a family Bible, a few clothes, grain seeds that died of fungus the first year, shards of plastiglass, jagged bits of metal we used for knives and spear-tips. It's hard to dig a deep pit out of clay and rock when you're sick, when all the daylight hours must be spent in foraging, when you have improvised shovels that are constantly breaking.

When the butchers were finished, we all hoisted leaf-wrapped bundles of meat onto our heads and marched single-file back to our huts. We skirted the patch of grand-daddy ground-joint. The banshee trees quivered as small creatures popped in and out of the slotted bark. Suzannie swung the grunt's ten tusks on a loop as we sang and joked. Yellow dust clotted on the blood-soaked leaves, but what did we care? We were going to eat!

It was my turn to forage while the others prepared the food. When I went into the hut to get my basket, I saw Kiloma showing her carving to Suzannie and Francis.

A week later it was time to wash the bedding. When I gathered up my aunt's pillow, another carving dropped out. My parents had drawn pictures for me in the dirt, so I recognized the shape.

It was a rocket. I hesitated a moment, and then shoved it under a pile of stinking baskets.

I carried the blankets to the river that wound down from the crash-site plateau and jumbled hills. ("Actually, it's only a trickle," my father had said. "Now calculate the minuscule volume of water passing this point in twenty-four standard Earth hours.") I slopped them into the pond. A shadow fell over me. I looked up at Aunt Kiloma.

"All right, honey. Where is it?"

"Where is what?"

"My prayer ship."

I looked down, ashamed for myself and Auntie. "Under the baskets."

"What's wrong, honey? Why did you hide it?"

"I don't understand why you're worshiping idols."

"It's obvious you don't understand. It's only to help me pray. You saw how I got us that night-grunt. Now I'm going to get us home."

"It's God who has to do all that."

"But I have to pray first. Here, honey, sit down."

We sat on the water-smooth rocks by the river. A faroff wind-gaunt hooted. A slight breeze ruffled our ragged hair and made the banshee trees wheeze. It was easier to talk to Auntie sitting, because I was only three-quarters as tall as she.

"Child, I've been thinking. It's going to take a few years for an Earth ship to get here and rescue us. We have to start praying now if they're going to get here in time for our golden anniversary."

"Golden anniversary?"

"It won't be long until we've been here fifty years. What better way to celebrate than by going back to God's green Earth?"

Gregory clattered up with some buckets in his hands. "Watcha talking about?" He dipped a bucket into the sulphurous water. A mottled waterbug swirled in and scooted out again.

My aunt stiffened. "I'm going to pray and we're going to be rescued—fifty years after the crash."

Gregory shook his head. "Don't you know prayer is talking to yourself? That's time wasted, time you could spend doing something useful."

I winced. Gregory sounded just like his mother Accie when he talked that way. His father had died trying to find new edible plants to expand our food supply. His mother had been a hard atheist ever since.

Aunt Kiloma snorted, "Those who don't believe, get nothing!"

Gregory shrugged and hauled his full buckets away, sloshing water on the dusty path.

Auntie turned to me again. "I'm not the only one praying. Francis, Harley, and Suzannie are too."

I was shocked. You could expect Harley, since he was a Theosophist, to do any weird thing. But not Francis.

Auntie patted my hand. "A ship will come and take us to a glorious place. You'll see, honey."

I dreamed of Earth that night. I awoke in the black night and listened to Auntie's soft snoring while I tried to remember the bright images. When I was littler, I used to mix up the stories about Heaven and Earth. Now that I was older, I knew Heaven was the place with streets of gold, a metal that glows like the sun; and Earth was green all over. I tried to imagine trees that were green all over instead of just on the leaves like the ones here. I had dreamed of elephants with noses that touched the ground and people in orange robes bowing before carved statues. I decided I had to talk to Suzannie. I tiptoed to the doorflap and lifted it carefully. The huts were lighter humps against the black. The stars glittered. I didn't hear the buzz-whine of a night-bite or any obvious sounds of a predator. Dirt-frogs moaned. Something made tiny rustling noises in the whittle-berry bushes on the other side of the barren field; a slither, perhaps?

I ran, I hoped, in the right direction, found a doorway, and scuttled in. I felt around in the dark until I felt Suzannie's mat. "Suzannie," I whispered, "wake up!"

"Huh?"

"It's me. Move over," I whispered.

She did and let me lie beside her. I could smell the rottenwood under her pillow.

"Who's there?" grunted her father.
"Me, Mr. Martins."
"Anything wrong?"
"No, I'm just going to talk to Suzannie."
"All right. Keep it quiet." I could hear him shift under his blankets. He and his wife were agnostics, maybe. They refused to talk about it. They had had five children but only Suzannie lived. I knew many wished she hadn't, but I liked her even if she couldn't keep her mind on one thing for very long. Her parents didn't care that she was a Christian.

I brushed her hair behind her ear, put my mouth next to it, and whispered, "Why are you praying to a rocket?"

"I pray all the time, like you say."

"You're supposed to pray to God."

"Auntie gave it to me. Are you mad?"

"Yes. And I'm not allowed to talk back to Auntie. But it's wrong."

"Auntie said I might lose my faith."

"Where are you going to lose it? Under your mat? If Jesus has you, he's not going to lose you."

"I'm not going to talk to you anymore." She put her hands over her ears. I tried to pull them off, but she buried her head under the blankets. I gave up and wondered what I was supposed to do now.

I was pounding hard-get grain on a stone a few weeks later when Gregory sat beside me to sharpen some spear-tips.

"Hey, you know what your aunt is doing now?"

I knew. My cheeks turned hot.

"She carved another night-grunt and said we're going to catch one tonight." He scratched around one of the ulcers on his legs. "Isn't she funny?"

"No, she isn't funny. She took care of Mother and me whenever we were sick. I took care of her when she was sick. She's not funny."

Gregory rubbed metal against whetstone in silence for a few moments. Then, "I suppose you'll have your little carving like her and Francis and the Ables and Kadish too."

"No, I won't."

"Will you talk to your aunt?"

"I already have."

"There's a lot of people getting upset about this."

"Like your mother and you."

"Like me and my mother and the Martins and Halverson."

I threw my pounding stick down. "Well, what can I do?"

Gregory looked at me. "I don't know. But I'll think of something."

Yellow-grey light seeped into our hut the next morning. My aunt threw a blanket over her bulky body and struggled to get up. "Let's get our dinner, honey," she croaked.

"I didn't hear anything fall in the pit."

Her voice strengthened. "Have some faith, child. Help me out."

She leaned against my shoulder and hobbled out into the pale morning. I saw Suzannie and a few others picking their way back from the privy. My aunt nodded at them and started toward the pit. Everyone followed quietly. Gregory passed us, looking determined.

My aunt called out, "Child, haven't you forgotten your arrows?"

A look of disgust crossed his face, but he went back to get them.

We reached the pit. It was broken in.

"See, O ye of little faith?" said my aunt.

"Meat!" squealed Suzannie.

We drew closer and peered in. At the bottom lay a land-lobster, its claws and teeth and pedicles clicking slightly. Apparently, it had broken its back. A slither had crawled down there and was feeding on it.

"See? There's no grunt," I whispered.

"That is a grunt!" she shouted, and glared at me. "Don't tell me that thing hasn't eaten grunts. That's a hundred grunts down there that we could have had! Now that this predator's dead, we'll have lots of grunts to eat."

"That's true," said Suzannie in a tiny, frightened voice.

"You could look at it that way," said Francis slowly.

Gregory ran past us and shot the slither. It writhed a long time before it died. The slither's meat wasn't any good to eat, but its scaled skin would make nice bags and its many ribs would make needles. Gregory laughed all the while he was peeling the sandpaper skin off the land-lobster.

"Are you happy, child, that we've broken through on how to survive this planet?"

Gregory shook his head. "This is the funniest grunt I've ever skinned."

Cicero Able waved a hand at Gregory. "It's as good as a hundred grunts. Because it's dead, we're going to have more to eat." He winked. "I just hope I can chew all the food we're going to have now." He grinned and showed all the gaps in his teeth.

Every day it seemed another person would decide to carve a rocket, a night-grunt, or a bowl of hard-get grain. Soon there was a heap of stinking, crude rockets near the central cooking fire. Every nightfall and sunrise the growing body of "believers" stood in a circle around the rockets and prayed. I prayed for rescue every morning and night too, but I could not join with them. Soon they were chanting in unison and swaying. My aunt exhorted the people to more faith that things would get better, since they were concentrating right.

One morning after a hot and restless night, I woke to hear my aunt groaning. I rushed to her side. "Auntie, what's wrong!" I was terrified that she might be dying.

She heaved herself up to a sitting position and rolled her head from side to side.

"Auntie, tell me what to do!"

Her eyes focused slowly on me. She said feebly, "Honey, what day is this?"

I had to stop and think. "Forty-five years, one hundred eighty-nine days."

"Mark this on your calendar tree, honey. I had a vision."

"A vision? Like in the Bible?"

"Yes, ma'am. A vision of things to come." She struggled to her feet and smiled down at me. "Honey, we're going to be rescued."

I said nothing.

"Did you hear me? We're going to be rescued. On our fiftieth golden anniversary. God Himself is going to send us a ship. Then you know where we're going?"

"Earth."

"Nope."

"No?" I had grown up reciting every day that I wanted to go to Earth.

"No. Earth is good, but this is even better. I remember Earth and I know it has some problems your parents never told you about. Problems that made us colonists in the first place. Where we're going is perfect."

I was thoroughly frightened. "Maybe it was just a dream you had."

"How unspiritual can you be? It was a vision. This planet we're going to has fruit trees. There are no animals that can hurt you, no poisonous food. We'll have cars and electricity. In only five years, Hope!"

I knew it was wrong, but I didn't know why. I grabbed a basket and ran outside to forage by myself so I could think.

When I returned at noon, Gregory met me by the river. He shouted angrily, "Do you know what your aunt is telling everybody now?"

"It's not my fault!" I shouted back.

He breathed deeply a few times. "I'm sorry. We're having a meeting at our hut. See if you can get your aunt there."

After he left, I began to wonder *who* was having a meeting. I found my aunt in the rottenwood grove gouging at another limb. Her hands stank with curls of the yellow stuff under the fingernails.

We entered Gregory's hut and in the dim light I saw Gregory, his mother, Accie, and Mr. Goldstein. Mr. Goldstein wasn't a Christian either, but he was the kindest man in our group and I liked him.

Gregory's mother never was the type to waste time. "Kiloma, this nonsense has got to stop."

My aunt drew herself up. "Accident, I don't have to listen to you. I listen to God."

I was embarrassed. Accident was born the year after the crash, and her name was supposed to signify a lot of things. Nobody dared call her anything but Accie or Mrs. Colewell.

Her nostrils flared. "You have got to stop fomenting trouble."

Mr. Goldstein interrupted. "Please, Kiloma, consider how we will feel if we believe something will happen on a certain date, and it does not happen. We shall probably be rescued, but we cannot set a specific date."

I tugged at her hand. "Please. He's right."

She pulled her hand away. "Are you taking a seat among the scornful?"

"You must deal with reality, not fantasy," said Accie.

"This is very real. But you, poor child, can't be expected to understand the deep things of the spirit."

Accie snorted, "Myxedema madness!"

"Your goiter's as big as mine, dear. How can you say I'm mad and you're not?"

A terrible look came over Accie's face. "Maybe you're the first. Maybe we'll all become like you." She glanced at her dwarfed son and ran sobbing from the hut.

We found her body by an anemone-thorn. This time I arranged the funeral. That left thirty living, and three hundred fifty-six mounds in the cemetery.

After that, nothing was ever said again by either side to persuade or dissuade. Gregory went about his chores, but it was plain the heart was out of him. A few more became believers. I clung to the beliefs my parents had taught, but I had always been held as of no account, so no one cared. Surprisingly, things did get better. We learned how to bait the pit and caught many grunts. Mr. Goldstein experimented one last time, and found that the root of the common lacy-leaf was edible. And that, out of the dozens of plants we had tried, was cultivable. No more people died. One year, then two and three passed.

On the forty-eighth year, twelfth day after the crash, I was weaving an overblouse. The sun was setting, and we were all hurrying to finish what we could before it got too dark. I looked up to ease a crick in my neck. Sparks flared in a line across the purpling, star-sprinkled sky. A meteorite shower? I started to calculate their trajectory before I remembered again that Father was not here to check my answer.

"Did you see that?" called out Mr. Goldstein, leaning on his broom. "I remember watching those on Earth." We looked to see if there would be any more. There weren't, and we went to bed.

The next morning I saw a white line grow across the sky.

"Auntie, what is that?"

She stared up for a long time, puzzled. Suddenly her face brightened. "It's a vapor . . . it's a contrail! Glory to God and concentration, it's a ship!" She shouted and waved. "Look at the reward for our faithfulness! Our ship's come early! Look!"

Everyone stared up and shouted, "We're going to be rescued! We're going to be rescued!" Suzannie threw rocks, leaves, anything, into the air.

I stared at the growing white line. All the history, alphabets, science, culture, and science fiction we had been taught as children seemed to coalesce into one glowing point: a ship was coming to rescue us.

"Hurry, honey. After forty-eight years, you don't want to be late."

It hadn't been forty-eight years for me, but I didn't want to be late. I looked around the hut one more time, trying to decide what to take with me. I didn't want the moldy blankets or the flat pillow, and I had so little else. Finally I grabbed my other overblouse and the straw doll my father had made.

My aunt carefully wrapped a rottenwood ship in a square of cloth. "Well, dearest, do you still call this rocket an idol?"

"No." I had had time to think it over as I watched the rituals develop for three years. "The carved ships are not idols. Your concentration is."

"Oh, you poor child. But you can't help it." She crushed me with the magnanimous hug of a winner. "You're going to love where we're going, honey. After I'm gone, they'll take good care of you." She rose and went outside to lead our little band to the crash-site plateau.

If a ship were looking for survivors, it would come to the plateau. Great chunks of metal had gouged dark furrows in the thin yellow soil. Radioactive residue formed another beacon. Once a year we trekked up to the plateau and polished all the skyward metal surfaces to make another glittering signal.

We moved slowly. Aunt Kiloma, Mr. Goldstein, Mr. Kim, and Mrs. Lutti, the original survivors, were very old, and no eagerness could make them young. Marylee was shivering from another illness. Glad had lost the use of one leg.

We skirted grand-daddy ground-joint for the last time and jeered at it. Suzannie grabbed a rock and swung back to throw it at the ground-joint.

"No, don't!" I said, and held her arm.

"How come you're always afraid of everything?" said Gregory. He bent down to look for a rock.

Mr. Goldstein enfolded Suzannie's hand and mine with his. He said softly, "Grand-daddy's old, and I'm old. Let's respect the aged, eh?"

Gregory dropped his stone and shrugged.

We walked past the pit, pausing when Mr. Goldstein carefully laid a packet of spoiled meat on the edge.

Auntie hooted, "Don't you think they have food on the ship?"

"Now, now, Kiloma," said Mr. Goldstein. "We may want to give them a dinner before we leave. A predator like land-lobster might be a treat for them."

"Suppose it takes them a week to find us?" said Gregory.

"God sent them. They'll find us. Let's sing!" The believers chanted until they ran out of breath as we clambered up the rocky cliff.

The plateau was a windy place, with stunted plants spaced about eight meters apart. Broken spaceship walls rose jagged against a flat horizon. We walked to the shade of one wall and sat down to rest. The believers joined hands and chanted, "Come, come, come, rocket. Come, come, come, starship."

My aunt began to cry. "Think of it, dearly beloved. Fruit trees!"

"Amen," moaned Able.

"Foam rubber beds!"

Suzannie clapped. "Soft beds! Soft beds!"

"We'll have paper and pens instead of dirt and sticks!"

"Concentrate on it!" shouted Francis.

"Aspirin and antibiotics!"

"Amen, amen."

I turned away and prayed by myself. The other nonbelievers grouped in the densest part of the shade and pretended to ignore them. An hour dragged by. So did another hour. Mr. Goldstein and Gregory had been the only ones to think of bringing any food, so all of us shared their meager meal of hard-get crackers and dried lacy-leaf root.

The sun crawled across a sallow sky. The air hung like a heavy curtain. The sun was nearing the rim of the world when a spear-point streaked across the sky.

"They're here!" screamed Suzannie.

We leaped up and poured into the open. The spear-point banked and slowed. It seemed to float toward us. We burst into tears and shouted and hugged each other.

Mr. Goldstein took my hand and said deeply, "Thank God."

The craft touched down in front of us. Fear rose in my throat and choked me. Some mechanical sounds came from the ship. I turned and ran away.

"What's the matter with you? Afraid to be proved wrong?" shouted my aunt.

Yes, I thought as I skidded behind a thrust-up wall, I'm afraid to be wrong!

I peered through a rent in the tortured metal as I cried to myself, What's wrong with me? Help me, Jesus! They won't leave me behind, will they?

The door opened. A ramp slid out. A figure about two meters tall appeared in the shadowy doorway.

"Thank God you've come!" shouted my aunt.

The figure stepped out and everybody froze.

The creature had a rat's pointed nose and lustrous auburn fur. It walked upright and wore a compartmentalized belt, nothing else. Four more creatures followed it.

"Angels!" Auntie shouted. "They're angels come to rescue us! Get down, everybody!"

The believers flopped down and the rest stood uncertainly. The lead creature walked down to where my aunt was groveling in the dirt. It looked at her and chittered something to its companions.

"This is ridiculous," said Gregory. "They're aliens and we need to communicate with them." He snatched up a stick for writing in the dirt and strode toward them.

An instrument was in the creature's hand. It pointed at Gregory. And there was a hole in his chest. His mouth opened, his eyes glazed over, and he fell down.

Suzannie jumped and flung her hands into the air and screamed. It shot her down.

My aunt looked up—"Why?"—and her chest exploded.

The other creatures took out instruments and began to point them. Down went Mr. Goldstein, Able, Caruso, and Fortune. The rest scattered, screaming. Down went Marylee and Edgar.

I ran toward our camp, not able to think of anything but the screams. I threw myself over the edge and slid down the cliff, dust and rocks clattering after. I ran between boulders and into the forest. I ran.

I reached the pit, panting and snorting. There was a hole on the far side of the covering. I stumbled around and fell beside it, crying, to see the meal we would never eat.

My heart froze with another terror. Pacing the bottom of the pit was a dread-for-all. Its tentacles above each clawed limb curled and uncurled in animal wrath. Its broad jaws opened and shut like traps. A sixth sense caused me to look up and roll at the same time. The ground smoked where I had been and I saw the alien point at me again. I fell behind a many-trunk. The creature ran after me. It saw the change in ground color too late, and plunged into the pit. The alien's shriek was strangled.

The sound of footsteps told me another alien was coming. This time I knew where to go. I broke off what leaves and branches I could as I went. When I ran around the circle of grand-daddy ground-joint, I dropped the leaves on the path so the alien would not see that we never walked near the small puckered thing in the center of the clearing. I waited on the far side.

The alien came around the grove of banshee trees. I threw a rock at it and ducked behind a boulder. The boulder scorched. I dared not look for fear of having my head burnt off.

The alien walked into it. The ground-joint's radial ribs crackled up and sliced the alien. The puckered thing enlarged to feed on the pieces.

I listened for a long time as a wind shifted through the forest and made the banshee trees moan. No one else came. The sun set and it grew dark.

"How long wilt Thou forget me, O Lord? Forever?" I cry silently as I shiver in the cold. "How long wilt Thou hide Thy face from me?" Everybody is dead. What will I do? What will I do?

It is too cold for me to sit any longer. If the aliens have gone away, I can start to bury the bodies. And then what will I do? I stumble along the path toward the crash site again.

"How long shall I take counsel in my soul, having sorrow in my heart daily? How long shall mine enemy be exalted over me?"

I reach the cliffs and find them hard to climb. It is now completely dark. Night insects sting my arms and face.

"Consider and hear me, O Lord my God: lighten mine eyes, lest I sleep the sleep of death."

I reach the plateau and plod toward the crash site. I come close, and stop. The aliens are still here. The aliens have lights!

I hide in a curl of metal and quietly place whatever I can reach in the entrance. Now I wait. . . .

Because the lights are on the plateau, it takes longer than it would in the forest. The three aliens pace (nervously?) the perimeter of their brightly lit field. One takes out a flare and shoots it. Red sparks trail down like a fountain.

The swarm hits with a buzz-whine and hundreds of dark flitting bodies. Tiny razor teeth rip through auburn fur. The aliens snarl and bat at the night-bites. One alien stumbles into an anemone-thorn. The thorns pierce its leg. Its blood coagulates instantly and it falls under a flurry of black wings. One alien falls by the ramp. The last alien almost makes it to the doorway of the ship before its eyes are torn out.

I am fortunate. No night-bite notices me, huddled in my makeshift cave. While they gorge themselves on alien flesh, I fall asleep.

I wake in the morning, after the last night-bite has flown back to shelter. I see that I have no bodies to bury, only bundles of bones to straighten out and pray over.

Good-bye, Aunt Kiloma. May God have mercy and send you to His place better than Earth.

Good-bye, brave Gregory.

Good-bye, glad Suzannie.

Good-bye, kind Mr. Goldstein.

Good-bye, quiet and good Marylee.

Good-bye . . . Good-bye . . . Good-bye.

I wipe my eyes, for I am finished. I have nothing left but my name. I kick the alien skeletons off the ramp and enter the ship. After trying several combinations of buttons, I find one that makes the ramp slide in and the doors shut. I find the bridge. If this ship is like human ships, I won't have to fly it—the computer will. All I have to do is tell it where to go. I find a rack of circuits and randomly push them into slots. Once a screen lights up with a picture of a variety of ships and a human. It is a human not marred with scars, ulcers, dwarfishness, and swollen necks as we were. Did the aliens kill us because they are at war with humans, or because they are allies and we didn't look human? I take a break, scrounge around, and find a huge locker of food. If our nutritional requirements are the same, I won't starve for a few months, anyway. Then I go back to work again.

At last the right circuit connects. The ship races across the plateau. Its nose lifts and up we go, the ship and I, to see what we shall see. I can die only once, and I need not fear God's judgment. Who knows? God knows. I may find Earth. I may find the perfect planet. I may find death in an orbit too near the sun. But nothing shall separate me from the love of God, and I am content.

I recite out loud the end of the Thirteenth Psalm, "But I have trusted in Thy mercy; my heart shall rejoice in Thy salvation."

THE MOTHER OF THE BEAST

Gordon Eklund

Because her children were special and so often misunderstood, Hera believed it was her duty not only to teach them the ways of the universe but also to shield and protect them from its more malevolent aspects. For this, their first excursion away from the Moon, she had chosen the planet Kraton, a virgin world, newly discovered, quite devoid of danger. Hera had wanted it that way, for the sake of the children. The landscape here where she had scanned was dominated on all sides by jagged cliffs and crags. With her head tilted at an awkward angle, she could observe a fleet of dark clouds darting like demons above the tall pinnacles. Kraton—what she had so far seen of it—was a dark, brooding planet. She felt pleased; this place was exactly what she had sought.

The children scanned one by one. Hera counted as each materialized in turn before her: eight . . . nine . . . ten. Cady, staring in wide-eyed wonderment at her instantaneous trip through twelve parsecs of interstellar space, made eleven.

But time passed. Too much time.

"Now where's Ares?" she finally asked. "We can't possibly have lost him already."

"Peekaboo!" cried Ares, the horned child. He darted suddenly out from behind a tree and waved his arms gleefully. Nine E–

years old, Ares wore pale green shorts and no shirt. His horns protruded stiffly through a pile of unkempt black human hair. Because of his hoofed feet, he limped as he walked. "I got here even before you, Hera. I was the first—the very first."

"No," she said, her breath coming short. "Never do that—never." She had intended to speak to all twelve children, but several had already gone romping into the woods. "Now, you come here," she cried, slapping her hands. "I mean everyone—right now—I mean it. We have a lot to do. We'll need a camp and a fire. It may be dark soon."

"And the wild animals?" asked little Cady, nestling close to Hera's knees in search of protection. Her upper lip, a loose fold of fat skin, dangled an inch past her lower. She was young, fragile, a new student; the other children frightened her.

"We'll see about exploring tomorrow. Remember, except for the scouting team, we're the first humans ever to come here. We'll see about the animals tomorrow."

"And they'll tear us apart," said a boy, Dangel, growling fiercely.

"No, no!" cried Cady, shying back even farther.

"Yes, yes," said Hera, patting the child. "Dangel is just being funny. The animals here are very peaceful. You'll see."

"Does that mean we've got to climb those big cliffs?" asked another boy.

"Unless we intend to stay in this valley." Hera grew impatient. "Now some of you please get to work. Unpack our supplies, start the tent."

"What I want to know," Ares said, glancing around, "is where are the aliens? You know they're here—all around. When they catch us, that'll be the end."

Cady began to sniffle in fear. Hera said angrily, "Ares, that'll be enough of that nonsense. There are no aliens on this world and you know it. If there were, we'd hardly be here. Now be quiet and stop frightening Cady."

"I'll be quiet if the aliens will."

"Ares."

"Yes, Hera, dear."

Darkness fell suddenly on Kraton. Fortunately, both tents had been inflated and the lantern cast sufficient light to allow the children to gather wood from the forest.

After heating their dinners over the fire, the children ate greedily until Hera rose and ordered them off to bed. She undressed in her own tent and then came down to visit. Cautiously, she counted heads and bodies: nine . . . ten . . . only eleven.

"All right. Who's missing this time? Is it Cady?"

"I'm here, Hera."

"Patria, get back in your own pouch and leave Cady alone."

"But, Hera, she—"

"I said no. Now, please."

After Patria had sullenly complied, Hera addressed the twelve: "I want you children to get as much rest as possible tonight, as it's my intention to move out shortly past dawn. We'll hike northward and scale the cliffs there. The maps indicate a series of finger lakes in that direction and we ought to uncover a good deal of native wildlife."

"Big ugly fierce growling monsters," said Ares, "who'll gobble us up and spit out the pieces." Of the children, only he was part of a second generation—three-quarters human, in spite of the horns and hoofs. Hera went away. As soon as she left their tent, the children began whispering.

Hera paused just outside and cocked an ear. She heard, "Hera, Hera." Her own name. Damn them, she thought. Hadn't she warned them—no talking tonight? Their damned whisperings followed her everywhere. Feeling rage inside her like a flame, she shut her eyes and clenched her fists. She hated them when they whispered like this, when they talked about her.

Ahead, on a gentle slope, her own tent stood. The lantern gleamed and flickered through the open doorway.

Curled naked inside the sleeping pouch, Hera wondered. How long could she lie like this without moving? One hour, two, three, ten? Their damned fathers. Hera tried to imagine such men. She saw them strutting, wild-eyed, long-limbed, big-muscled. In harsh reality, a scout might stand four feet, ten inches, and be fat.

The women were much worse. How could anyone bear to mate with something unhuman? They always said, no, we're all one, descendants of the original longships that peopled the galaxy in millennia past. There are no aliens; everything is human, the same stock: Cady with her long lip; Samuel with his distended sex organ; Bruto with his reddish fur; Ares with his horns and hoofs. Still, evolution on alien worlds had turned wonders, created new breeds. To mate with such a being, overpowered by a vicious beast as lusty as a stag, was an ultimate desecration of the soul. And yet it happened. Twelve children testified to that. Hera heard their incessant, whispering voices.

Naked, she slipped free of the sleeping pouch, grasped the lantern, padded across the ground. At their tent she paused, then hurled open the flaps. "Now, please," she said, trembling. "Now, children, please be silent." The lantern cast crazy shadows on the inner walls. "We cannot—we simply cannot—"

"Damn it, we were," said Ares. "We were trying to sleep."

"You damned liar!" she cried. And then, with a start, she noticed that Patria had again left her pouch.

The second night, near midnight, while they were camped halfway up the face of the cliff, Ares entered her tent. She could see his figure only dimly, despite the bright lanternlight. He moved like a creature from a dream.

"What do you want here?" she asked coldly.

He limped forward, his eyes burning with a strange excitement. "Hera, I've found something utterly amazing that you won't believe. You've got to come and see."

"You ought to be in your tent, asleep."

"Oh, no, don't be silly." He crouched beside her. "Listen, I'm half-nocturnal, like Latone." He winked.

"I barely remember your father."

"No, of course not, but this doesn't concern him." He reached out and, with incredible strength, drew her out of the pouch to kneel before him. "I want you to come with me now."

She glared, neither frightened nor angry. "Don't you ever touch me that way again."

"I won't." His voice was a ghostly, disembodied thing. "Hey, Hera, come on, I'm not kidding. You'll want to share the credit for this, I guarantee you."

"What are you talking about?"

"Put on some clothes and I'll show you."

"All right." Obediently she dressed. "Now talk."

"Okay. It's a cave I found. A little off the trail and hidden by a couple of boulders."

"There's no cave indicated on any of the maps."

"So? It's not possible to map every feature of a whole planet in just a few E-years. Well, I went inside. To the very back. It was pitch black and wet along the sides but somehow I could just see. It wasn't empty. Something used to live there. I found alien artifacts. I mean real aliens, Hera, not longship humans. These things were monsters."

She stared at him. "Ares, don't tell stories."

"I think they're all dead now—extinct."

She was taken aback. "Ares, you're not making any sense. How do you know all this?"

"Because their coffins are in there. It's a burying place for alien monsters. Come on." He reached out to tug her arm, then thought better of it. "It's easier to show than tell. Everyone else is waiting, too."

"Everyone?"

When he admitted that he had roused the camp, she could not repress her fury. Outside, she found the children waiting in the dark, eager to be led. She ordered all of them to bed and stayed, watching, until they had drifted obediently away.

The cave was not far off. There was a malevolent air about the place, a feeling of rot and decay. Hera carried the lantern but saw nothing until they reached the back wall of the cave. There were eight large triangular metal boxes stacked in two piles against the cave wall. The vision appeared less than wholly substantial. She feared the boxes might vanish if she tried to touch them. She could understand why Ares assumed that each contained the body of a monster.

"Good God," she said softly.

Ares moved closer to the wall. "Shine the lantern over here."

She turned the light to illuminate a section of the damp wall. There were several small paintings here, crudely drawn, like obscene scribbles. Each showed an alien creature in the form of a triangular lump. Were these the beings who lay in the piled coffins?

"This is the most fantastic discovery in the whole history of creation," Ares said.

"If it's real."

"What do you mean by that?" He seemed suddenly tense. "Don't we have eyes? This is an immense discovery and we can't tell a soul for two damned weeks."

"I don't see how the scouts could have missed this."

"It's possible. Maybe this is all that's left. It could have been a million years since these things were alive."

"I wonder if—" said Hera.

All at once, she realized they were no longer alone. Ares sensed it, too. He ran to her and gripped her body.

"There," he cried, pointing frantically toward the roof of the cave. "I see it! Look! It's up there!"

Hera failed to raise the lantern in time to see anything. Ares kept shouting at her to turn this way and that until finally she stopped him. "No, that's enough. Hush up. You're frightening yourself."

"But didn't you see—?"

"No," she said quickly. "That's just enough of that." She drew him toward the cave mouth. "I want you to forget all about this. We can tell the scouts and leave it for them to study."

Late the next day they reached the edge of a broad plateau. While the children warmed a meal, Hera went to her own tent. She wasn't hungry. She prepared her sleeping pouch and climbed inside. In time, the children were resting, too. It was a cold night. Shivering, she touched her skin, silk-smooth after thirty-six E-years. Twenty-six on the Earth itself, then the last ten on the Moon. She believed in bodily care, saw it as a spiritual duty to the self. The lantern burned at high intensity. The thing in the alien cave. The shadow. Ares had insisted he had seen something corporeal. Who could know? She had felt it herself, and then today, while scaling the cliff, twice more, the same feeling. A lurking presence, never quite seen. Hallucination? Suggestion? Ares had told the other children nothing. It was only she and he who knew and thus believed.

Then she heard the scream.

"Oh, God, it's Samuel!"

The children, all eleven of them, clustered near the body. Hera forced them away. At twelve E-years, Samuel had been their eldest. After Latone, he had been the second crossbreed to fall into normal human hands.

"Don't look. Get back."

"I was just—" Ares turned away from the body. "He's been torn apart. God, what a mess."

She raised the lantern and saw what he meant. She gagged.

"Is there anything you can do for him? You used to be a doctor, didn't you?"

"He's dead."

"But we don't know how it happened," said Bruto, round and plump, red fur gleaming. "We just heard him scream."

"Ares, you tell me."

He dropped to his haunches and dug his hoofs into the hard ground. "It's just the way he said. We were asleep, and he must have gone out alone, maybe to pee."

"But how did you get here so quickly? I just heard him scream myself."

"I guess we ran faster."

"All of you," she said, "please get away from here. Go to your tent. There's no need to see this. It must have been a dreadful accident."

"Bullshit," Ares said.

"Patria, please. Take care of Cady." She pushed the clinging, sobbing girl away from her. "And be quiet, Ares. This is terrible enough already."

The children dispersed with unusual obedience. Only Ares

remained. "Shine your lantern here, Hera." He meant the neat pile of internal organs arranged beside the carcass. "Now, these are the lungs, right? And this is a liver. The heart. And all these are the guts. Now, no accident can do that."

"Then it must be something else. Some rare animal the scouts missed."

He nodded slowly and gazed at her. "An animal, yes. A beast. Some great, dark, terrible beast that's not going to let any of us live."

"Ares, please." She tried to meet his eyes. "Let's not make this worse than it already is."

Morning arrived without incident and Hera woke the children. She expected to reach the string of finger lakes within another two days.

"I think," she told the children, when they were ready to march, "we should decide about what happened last night. Clearly, poor Samuel died beneath the claws of some local beast, and it's our duty to protect ourselves from now on. Except for my knife, we aren't armed, but with sufficient caution, I believe we can all remain safe. No one will be allowed to go anywhere unaccompanied, especially at night. While we sleep, a watch will be maintained. This creature—this beast—it won't be strong enough to dare attack us all."

"Want to make a bet?" Ares asked.

She saw the necessity of exerting her own authority. "I'm saying this in order to save our lives."

"And yours?" he asked, grinning.

"Mine?"

"You said it yourself—nobody is to go alone. That means giving up your private tent, Hera. It means snuggling up with us freaks."

"No," she said quickly. "I appreciate your—your consideration, but I don't—" She made herself stop. He was mocking her openly. "I'm more than capable of taking care of myself."

"That's not good enough. Look, to get scanned home on time, we have to make it back to that valley, right? Without you, how are we going to pull it off? No, like it or not, you're necessary for our survival, and we don't intend to lose you to any roving monsters."

"My tent can be securely—"

"Not good enough. No tent." He glanced furtively at the others and must have sensed their solid support. "Either come to our tent or else we go to yours."

"I won't let—"

"Damn it, we're not kidding."

She glared at him. All night—with them. What would it be like? And their damned whispering. "All right," she said breathlessly. "I'll do it."

"And share a watch?"

She nodded, acknowledging defeat. "And that, too."

Crouched within the dark, Hera heard the children breathing. With the lantern extinguished, the tent was a vast, unseen arena, filled with sound. For most of the day, while they marched, she had sensed the beast. It didn't seem to be present now. The children had gone right to sleep—no whispering. Even Ares now was snoring. Latone, his father, had never slept a wink, but Ares was one-fourth more human.

"Hera?"

She jumped at the sound, reaching for her knife. "Who is it?"

"Me. Horace." He was a shy, stammering boy. "I need to go out."

"We already decided that you can't."

"But I have to—I—I have to eliminate."

She understood his need. He was younger than most of them, only one E-year Cady's senior. His hand suddenly gripped hers —five barbed fingers and a thumb. Like Latone, a blend of Zeus and Satan. How did these children live? "Then go. But don't stray far. Do it right outside the tent and hurry back." His mother's people, longship puritans, had gleefully torn her apart when her bastard son was born among them. "And take my lantern."

"Yes, Hera."

She slid aside to let him pass. He loosened the tent flaps and went straight out.

Later she heard: "Hera?"

The voice came from right beside her. "Ares?"

"You bet."

"What do you want?"

"It's time for my watch."

"Oh," she said. "Oh, good. I'm already tired."

At dawn the children woke, although no light penetrated the tent. Hera, struggling against lingering sleep, sat up and tried to find the lantern.

Then she heard Ares shout. Crawling over, she pushed open the unsealed tent flaps. Daylight momentarily blinded her.

The children, drawn by the light, pushed past her.

She heard Ares: "Hera, Hera, come quick—it's Horace."

She found him at last and fought the children to reach the body. The sight of poor Horace affected her even more deeply than Samuel. Had she forgotten the horror so soon?

"It's exactly the same," Ares said bitterly. He pointed at the neatly arranged pile of internal organs. "Do you still think it's an accident?"

"Get back," she told the children. "Go inside the tent and wait there. Patria, come and take Cady. Please go away."

When they were alone at last, Ares pointed to the lantern beside the body. "How did this get out here?"

It was the moment she had dreaded since Ares' first shout. "I gave it to him."

"You let him come out?"

"I—I—he had to go eliminate. You know how he was. It was the way he was brought up."

"You let him out and didn't say anything."

"I must have forgotten. I thought you'd notice."

"You let this happen. The beast was there."

"No, no." She wouldn't let him blame her. "It's just a wild animal, and you can't feel that."

"You've felt it yourself—don't tell me you haven't."

"No—never."

"You liar!" He gripped and held her. "Damn it, you have to know."

"I don't—I don't know anything." She jerked away from him and ran, fleeing back to her children.

They walked unsteadily through a delicate forest that seemed alive with shades of green, blue, and gold. This, thought Hera, must be how the ancient Earth had looked and smelled during the long eons before mankind arrived to spoil its beauty. God, she thought, how long has it been since I've smelled these leaves and felt this wind? She remembered as a little girl experiencing such serene hours as these in urban parks; but this was a whole planet. She had gone to the Moon to teach. The special children —only Latone and Samuel then—had required a calm guiding spirit to lead them toward real humanity, and she had eagerly volunteered to serve.

Cady walked at her side. She would never remember. Nothing ever impressed Cady—nothing lingered. She had forgotten last year, last month, last week; in her mind, the past was a gray shadow. Cady saw the trees and clouds, felt the wind, heard the incessant music of whispering leaves and grass. Cady was a simple child who perceived existence as if it were a sudden and spontaneous creation; she carried no preconceptions within her. And I? thought Hera. If I stayed here, how long would it take before I became like her?

She sprang ahead, abandoning Cady. Ares stalked at the head of a ragged line. "I think we ought to stop somewhere near. We can't reach the lakes today."

"If you want. It's back there, you know."

"I didn't."

"You can't feel it?"

"The children said nothing. I've been walking with Cady all day."

He laughed. "She knows a lot she doesn't tell you. And I've been thinking, too. About the beast—what it might be."

"How could you ever know that?"

"I think it's one of us. I think we made it. It wasn't alive before we came. It's a ghost, an ugly soul, but it belongs to one of us."

"That's superstition."

"No, it's not. We all know about the unconscious mind. And this is an alien planet. Who knows what can happen here?"

"You have no basis for making such an assumption."

He glared at her. "Don't I? Listen, you tell me one thing that makes more sense."

"A wild animal."

"Bullshit, Hera. Animals have feet and we've found no prints. Animals have bodies and we've seen nothing. The beast isn't a thing—it's a dark spirit, a soul. It's part of this planet but it's ours, too."

"Oh, shut up, shut up." She clutched her aching head. "Stop here." She pointed to a stand of trees emerging ahead. "I'm tired —sick."

She and Ares were struggling to inflate the tent when Patria rushed sobbing to her side.

"Hey, slow down. Dear, what is it? You can tell Hera—you can." She shook the girl to calm her. "Is it about Cady?"

"She's gone off," cried Patria. "I tried to stop her, Hera, I did."

"I believe you, child."

"She wouldn't listen."

"Went off?" Ares broke in angrily. "How the hell could you let her do that?"

"You shut up," Hera told him. She realized now that the beast had vanished. The air seemed freshly scrubbed. She repressed her sudden panic. "Just tell me, Patria. Where did Cady go?"

She turned instinctively to Ares. "You know how she can be. She must have just forgotten—about the beast. We were playing, and Jambal was with us. Cady was supposed to hide her eyes, except when we peeked, she was already running. We called and called—I did—but she wouldn't answer. Before, she kept saying how pretty the forest looked. I think she just wanted to see it better."

"Damn it, we'll never find her now," Ares said.

"No, I'll try," Hera said.

"But what if something happens?"

"Then I'll be there to stop it."

"In there," Patria said, pointing. "That's the way she went."

"Then that's the way I'll have to go. Ares, you'll be in charge until I return. Get the children inside the tent and keep them there. Darkness or not, don't ever budge."

He was trembling with some deep emotion. "Don't forget. The beast is one of us."

She touched the knife at her belt. "This will help me more."

"Cady! Cady! Cady!" She shouted as loudly as she could. A dim, diffused sunlight filled these deep woods. Hera traveled in a circle, keeping near the camp. "Cady!" she called. "It's me—it's Hera!"

Would she even wish to answer? Cady's strangeness set her apart from the others. Her father, it was said, had belonged to a longship race glimpsed only once. The scouts landed, found the people, and hurried home again with the news. When a second party followed later via scansystem, they found only an empty world. Cady's mother, part of the original scout team, gave birth soon afterward to a daughter. If Hera had for a moment seriously considered Ares' theory concerning the beast, she would have guessed it was Cady. Her personality was no more than a fragile wisp; her unconscious mind dominated her physical and mental being.

"Hera."

She spun. "Cady?"

"Yes. Yes, here."

"Where?" She turned and turned; had the light entirely vanished now?

"Here, Hera—here."

She ran toward the sound of the voice, plunging through a thick, unseen clutter of foliage. Fallen limbs and tangled vines blocked her path. She stumbled, never quite fell. "Cady, I'm coming—hold on." All at once she saw the girl kneeling beside a tree.

"Hera, here I am—right here."

"I know. I see you. Wait." Hera threw herself down, wrapped her arms around the girl, and kissed her lips violently.

Cady drew away, out of breath. "Hera, are you frightened?"

"Yes, yes. The beast. Come. Come, we must hurry."

Cady stood as if frozen. "But the beast won't harm me, will it?"

"I don't know." The girl was so ugly, with that distended lip. "I know nothing about it."

"But it likes you."

"No." She shook Cady. "Don't you ever say anything so silly. It's evil, black. It can't like me—it only hates." She tried to gauge the fastest way of reaching the camp. Finally she pointed. "We'll just have to go in this direction."

"Back to them?"

"To the camp, the other children—yes, of course."

"But they hate me."

"Cady, don't ever say that."

"But they do. All except Patria. And you. I don't ever want to go back to them. I like it better here."

"Cady, you'll die here."

The beast walked with them—near—very near. Hera felt its evil presence like a foul, trailing stench. She wanted so desperately to run, but it was too dark now. If she tried, she would fall, and then the beast would surely be upon them.

Cady said, "It's back there behind us, isn't it?"

"No. What?"

"The beast."

"No, it's not there."

"But it won't harm us, will it? It's just watching us, isn't it?"

"Yes, just watching."

"Will it follow us to the camp?"

"I don't know what it will do."

"Because I don't want the others to be hurt. I hate them but I don't want them to die. They hate you, too, Hera. Even Patria says she does. They think you want them dead because they're freaks."

If only they could reach an open meadow, she thought, any place where they could really run. She felt certain the beast would never catch them there. "Cady, I want you to take this."

"What?" The girl held out her hand.

"My knife."

"Oh, I won't need that."

"No, take it." She tried to force the weapon into the girl's hand, but she still refused. "It's as sharp as a surgeon's scalpel. It'll protect you."

"But I'm not afraid, Hera."

She stopped.

"What—what is it?" For the first time, fear entered Cady's voice. "Hera, what's wrong?"

"Listen. Can't you hear it? It's the beast. It's coming. Cady, run!" she cried. "Hurry—run!"

"Not without you, Hera."

"I said run!" Hera hurled herself forward, dragging Cady's hand, but the girl dug in her heels, and both of them went sprawling.

Stunned, Hera looked up.

The wind suddenly howled with the rush of the approaching beast. Hera stared into the sky. She screamed, "Cady, get up and run! I love you! I do—I do!"

But it was late—too late.

The beast came thundering out of the tall forest behind. Hera thought at first it was just a great featureless shadow—a black blot on the sky. The beast swept down upon them. Hera wanted to hide her eyes but could not. The beast rose, then fell. At last Cady screamed. The beast had her.

Hera felt the violent sweep of displaced air as the great beast rose to seek its lair once again.

Hera bore Cady's body into the camp, where a fire burned, jagged flames reaching toward the midnight sky. A hard, swirling wind sent the smoke huffing through the air. The stink of the beast went with her. Ares, running frantically, darted forward to meet her. His eyes filled with tears, he said, "We knew it had to happen. We could feel it prowling out there all the time."

"I loved Cady. If she had been my own daughter, I could not have loved her more."

"I believe you, Hera."

"They all think I hate them, but it's not true."

"No, you don't hate them."

"I wish we'd never come to this dreadful planet."

"Isn't it too late for that now?"

"Well, what else can I do?" She lowered Cady's body to the ground. The survivors gathered around. Hera counted eight: Dangal, Jambal, Ulan, Patria, Jace, Bruto, Germania, Mendalio. But he was right. It was not they whom she hated.

"Now look here, Hera," Ares said, "it's just no use now. If we stay here and try to fight this thing, we'll die, one after another. We've got to run and try to hide. Separate—every man for himself."

"But we can't go back. The scansystem has to be worked from outside. It's not set to bring us back for days yet."

"I said hide."

"From the beast?" She could not help smiling. "I thought you said you thought it was one of us."

"I said that was a possibility."

"You said you thought it was Cady."

"I never said anything of the kind. It could—" His voice grew very hushed. "It could be you, Hera."

"Or you," she said.

"But don't you know?" he asked plaintively.

She shook her head. "No, not yet."

Hating these children as she did, she would not have hesitated to wish almost any of them dead. The feeling was one she attempted to conceal. The outsiders—the agents in charge of the school, for instance—were not aware of her real feelings. They loathed the children, too, but assumed she was different. Latone had made them think that. When she came and confessed he had raped her, they had been willing at first to accept her statement, but when she refused an abortion and bore him a son, they had changed their minds. They believed she had opened her thighs and allowed him to penetrate her. If Latone had been a cross between Satan and Zeus—perverse mating of devil and god—then these others were simply wrong. Sometimes, seeing their extra fingers, sagging lips, colored fur, distended organs, beaks, horns, and fangs, she felt a physical revulsion, a symptom of spiritual disorder. The agents at the school had ordered Latone put to death for a crime of which they believed him innocent. Yet they carefully fostered these bastard children born of ungodly unions. Why? Was it merely human sympathy? She knew it was not. The true human race, bound in its purity to the Earth and a few sister worlds, feared those longship pioneers scattered on a hundred worlds. Who were they? What fantastic powers might they possess? To find out, the agents studied their halfbreed children. Hera knew them better than anyone. They were different—they were not superior.

Ares approached her where she sat gazing upon the sun as it cleared the distant hills. "Well, do you agree with what I said? Should we go and try to hide?"

"No."

He shrugged. "Then what, Hera?"

"We'll go back. To the cliffs, the valley."

They stopped at the edge of the plateau, with the cliffs dropping below them to the green valley beneath. Hera said, "It's too dark to go farther. We'll have to wait till tomorrow."

Ares shook his head. "I still don't see any point to this."

"Can you suggest an alternative?"

"No. No, I suppose not."

"Then go help the others inflate the tent."

She sighed and watched him limp away. All these last days, the beast had stalked them, but it had never drawn near. The cave was close now. Whatever was hidden there would provide the final clue she needed to solve the riddle, and for that reason she was certain she would not be allowed to reach it. The beast, despite its own deep fear, would surely kill tonight. She bowed her head. Was she ready?

She did not stir until a fire was burning; then she rose and sat down beside Ares, a little apart from the other children. She saw the scars his hoofs had made in the soft ground. "Well, so far, so good," he said. "The thing hasn't touched us yet."

She nodded. "Yes, but it's there."

He shifted uncomfortably. "The others feel it, too."

"Are they afraid, do you think?"

"They don't want to die."

"Them?" She felt herself losing control. "Why do you always speak of them? Why not us, Ares?"

"You?"

"Or you. What makes you so sure the beast won't kill us, too?"

He stared at her, then suddenly tried to get up. "Don't say that, Hera. Don't twist my words."

She pulled him down with one powerful hand, then threw her arms around him. "Ares," she whispered in his ear, "please tell me now. The beast—it is real, isn't it?"

"You've seen it, haven't you?" He squirmed in her grasp.

"I've felt it. I've known it. And it's you, isn't it, Ares? You are the beast."

"No, no!" he cried.

"There was no alien cave. That was a dream you made me have. No cave and no beast. It's just you, Ares. You and your father—Latone. You've come to kill my children."

"No!"

The beast rose into the air. She sensed it beating against the high sky. "You killed them," she said. "Horace, Samuel, Cady. You killed them and you know why."

"No, it's not me. It—it's you. I knew it all along. It's you, Hera."

She slapped him as hard as she could. He fell back and she stood over him. His nose was bleeding. "You hated them, but most of all you hate me. Why? Because I let him die? Because I let them kill him for the act of bringing you into this universe?"

"Stop it. Don't say it." He hugged his ears with his palms. "Please don't."

"Why?" She pulled his hands away and shouted. "Because you

don't already know it's true? Yes, I'm your mother, goddamn it! Yes, I let him do it! Yes, it was the only time in my life! I wanted him to. I liked it. I loved him. And you knew that. You knew all along and you killed them for it!"

"Stop it. No." His words came in tired spasms. "Make her stop it. Please." Tears ran with the blood upon his cheek. "Come and please stop—" He sprang to his feet, his eyes widening in shock. "No, no, don't do that! No!"

She embraced him. "It's too late, Ares. You've told it what to do. That's what you wanted all along. It was me you wanted dead —never them."

"Don't, Hera," he begged.

But the beast had risen. It plunged toward them, a black charging shadow. Ares squirmed free and rushed toward the forest. Waving his arms, he cried at the beast to go back.

Hera sprinted after him. "Kill me!" Ares screamed. "It's me you want—me!"

The beast came down upon them.

At the last moment, Hera drew her knife from her belt and drove the blade upward. Ares howled. She dropped the knife and put her arms around him. Their faces touched and she could see nothing. The beast—the beast engulfed them.

She kissed her son. Her lips smothered his and her tongue plunged inside his wet mouth. She felt his hard, bestial thighs.

Then he twisted away. "No, not me," he said. "You thought it was me, Hera, but it wasn't. It was him. The one who made me. It was that beast all along. It was Father, Mother, Father. We found him in that cave. We woke him up. *Oh, God, please take me.*"

And Hera watched as the beast took and tore the child apart. She saw his organs burst and his bones crack. It was over in a moment; then the beast rose into the sky and was gone forever.

ROBERT FRASER:
THE XENOLOGIST AS HERO

Sydelle Shamah

You think you know about the cravies. The dregs of human society, you say. There is no lower form of life. What do you know? Do you know about the cursed Kestan drug melsedrine? Do you know what draws them to it? Are they lured by the brief peak, when the drug acts as one of the most powerful aphrodisiacs the human species has ever known? Or the rumor that it can induce telepathic powers? Can anything be worth the plunge, the monumental depression, during which the body functions slow down and eventually reach the freeze stage: a deathlike coma? If they survive the freeze, the cycle begins again: the need building up until they must have the drug or die, then peak, plunge and freeze. The effect of the drug on the body is cumulative, and eventually fatal. They die with it or without it.

My first sight of Dr. Robert Fraser was a shock. I had expected my hero to be a giant, not a small, frail man of seventy. In his most recent tapes, he had seemed at least twenty years younger. I supposed the tapes had been retouched.

He had silky white hair that sparsely screened his pink scalp. His face was dominated by bushy eyebrows and a long mustache. His eyes were washed-out blue, but alert.

"I'm pleased to have you with us, Ms. Carson," he said, extending his hand.

"My pleasure." He led me to one of four metal desks. There was a computer post, with keyboard as well as microphone.

He spoke slowly, carefully enunciating each syllable. "Every department of the University of United Earth is participating in the cultural exchange program. Our department is responsible for the translations." He explained how the material was being processed and reorganized for translation into other languages. I liked him immediately. I'm sure that it was the man I liked, and not the reputation.

Fraser had been ill, and did his work at home for two days. When he returned to the office, he seemed to be in better health, more cheerful, and not as slow-moving, although he did seem to be in pain. The pain seemed to bother him more each day. He would wince, and sit very still with his eyes closed. Then I would see him straighten up, draw a shaking breath, and return to the work before him. He would work awhile, then pull into himself again. There were tremors along the left side of his body. The others in the office pretended not to notice. One day, after he left, I asked.

A woman at the desk across from me answered. "He has a neurological disease that he picked up on Deneb Three."

"Yeah, and that's not all he picked up on Deneb Three," added the associate xenologist, Ed Jacobs. "Freak-lover."

"What?" I asked, looking from one to the other.

The woman looked at Jacobs coldly. "Dr. Fraser is an exceptional person. He has no prejudices toward other life-forms."

"No prejudices, sure," returned Jacobs. "I'm not prejudiced either, but I wouldn't have sex with an alien, and neither would any other normal human being."

I maintained a casual pose with some difficulty.

"That's enough," said the woman. "Dr. Fraser is a sick man who is trying to carry out his responsibilities to this group. His personal life is his own business."

I realized that they could not possibly have known about my personal life. I wondered what they meant about Fraser. I knew that he had been married, and then separated soon afterward, more than forty years ago. From what I understood, the experience had left an unpleasant taste with him, and he had never again been interested in women.

"Neurological disease" explained his condition, I felt, and I didn't consider any other possibilities. Even his bulging, red-lined eyes didn't alert me. Not until I saw him drinking coffee with four spoons of sugar did comprehension hit me. There are some things that the mind finds difficult to accept. Like the fact that the universally known and respected Dr. Robert Fraser, the xenologist who stood virtually alone in the field on nonverbal literature, was a cravie.

Soon now, I thought. Does he have someone, or is he going to try to solo? I didn't think he was strong enough.

I knew that he had waited as long as he could. I followed him home to his apartment and raised my hand to knock on the door. What if he has someone, I thought. I might be walking in on them. I almost went away. Then I thought: But what if he doesn't? I knocked.

"Who is it?" The voice was weak and slurred.

"Sheila Carson. Could I see you a minute?"

"Perhaps some other time. I'm not well." I could hardly hear him through the door.

"It's very important. Please."

I heard him take a deep breath. "All right." He opened the door. His eyes were wet; left shoulder jerking, both hands trembling. "Yes?" he asked.

"I know," I said gently, touching him on the shoulder.

He looked at the hand, then at my face. "What do you know?"

"I know . . . about the malt."

His face did not change. "What exactly is your problem?"

"You need help," I said. "You need someone. I don't think you're strong enough to solo."

"It has been done." Telling me that he'd already tried.

"Anyone who has soloed knows the risks." I looked at the man, in pain, at the limit of his endurance, and yet holding his eyes steady on me. "I can fly with you. Let me. I've done it before."

"But you are not now addicted, although how that is possible, I do not know."

"It is possible, and what I have done, I can do again." Who do I think I'm fooling, I thought. Myself? Luck, and accident. I could not expect to come through again.

"Ms. Carson, if you cannot withdraw from the drug, you will die. I am an old man, and will die soon, in any event."

I looked at the trembling hands and shoulder. "Then you really do have a neurological disease."

"Block's Syndrome. I will not live more than a few months. The risk of your life would be for nothing." I wondered if he had taken to melsedrine to relieve the pain. But why melsedrine? There were plenty of legal and nonlethal drugs that would have been preferable. He must have had some other reason for taking malt.

"I'm sorry."

"Thank you. Now, if you will leave, I can get on with the offensive necessities." He started to shut the door.

"Listen. I can sort of fake it, or if I have to, take a tiny dose and make it work like full measure. Let me try." My face and my tone of voice told him that this wasn't the first time.

"You will not be in danger?"

"No." I shook my head and smiled cheerfully.

He saw that I wouldn't back down, and knew that he did need help, not just for tonight, but for the distance. "Very well," he said, "and may God have mercy on your soul."

If ever I had a soul, surely it would have left me the first time.

Twelve years ago, during my first year at U.U.E., I met an exchange student, Cor, who was so nearly human that he could pass. He wanted to teach me his language. I was a xeno major, I couldn't refuse. There was a way, he said, to really learn the language. Learn it from the inside.

Cor didn't have much imagination. He had hoped that Fraser's study of his home world, *Myth, Language and Culture on Kesta*, would inspire him. When it didn't, he had thrown the book at me with a sneer. "How can a *human* presume to tell us about ourselves?"

Fraser had written in their own language, analyzing their myths structurally, in the old Levi-Strauss technique. Studying their mythology had provided Fraser, and through his book, me, with a "window into the mind," that is, an understanding of the personality mechanisms, categories to think with. The categories are the same for myth, language and fantasy. I doubt that the clues I found were evident to the Kestans. No one ever sees himself. Perhaps the message was meaningful to me only because it was transmitted from one human thinking in Kestan to another. The material in Fraser's book often made it possible for me to run fantasy with Cor without sparking. By limiting the amount of malt I took, that book may have saved my sanity, even my life. Fraser gave me understanding, insight, hope, and not only a tool, but pleasure as well. If only for that book and no other reason, I owed Fraser anything in my power.

I saw Fraser shudder as he swallowed the capsules. I had raised my hand to my mouth. He couldn't know whether or not I had taken anything. Before he shut his eyes I heard him whisper, "I wish there was some other way."

I cued with what I knew about Deneb 3, knowing that Fraser's thoughts would carry him back to his experiences there. The natives are a beautiful, seemingly gentle people. Avian, bilaterally symmetrical, standing upright on graceful, slender legs that tuck under when they fly. Their bodies are ovoid. Strong musculature sweeps back and away from the breastbone. The wings are brilliant, like a butterfly's. Iridescent patterns ripple as the sunlight plays on rich colors: silver, peacock, ultramarine, emerald. Small but functional arms extend from under the wings. They have three-fingered hands and feet.

Fraser was not the first anthropologist to go native. The temptation can be strong.

And Arrl. Gentle, lovely Arrl.

Arrl, dainty in spite of her size; glittering, teal blue. Pale, nearly human face, with oversized warm indigo eyes. Long eyelashes. A flexible, almost human mouth close to the bottom of the softly pointed face. Where the human nose would be, she had a pale blue brush of olfactory and auditory tendrils.

Arrl, who had answered his questions when none of the others would. Who had told him about the literature, and finally shared it with him.

Arrl, cast out by her people for the shame of intimacy—the shared literature—came to live with him in his little shelter. He learned what his asking had meant, and what she had had to do, to be his informant. His carefully built defenses came tumbling down. At the age of sixty-three, unlooked for, almost unrecognized, love had come to Robert Fraser.

Then it's down, down, down. Fraser's remarkable discipline over his body helped conceal the effects of the drug. He forced himself to compensate, by moving at what was, to his perception, high speed. His movements, though still slower than normal, were accepted as a symptom of the neurological disintegration associated with Block's Syndrome.

Fraser looked up from his notes. "Will you be able to finish this section? The notes are complete, but I won't have time to integrate them." He was tired, used up, like a crumpled tissue. He had taken nearly a minute and a half to say those two sentences. He would fall into freeze tonight.

"Yes, don't worry," I answered. "I'll finish the translation. Try to get some rest." His blue eyes continued to look at me. I thought I knew what he wanted to say. "In the morning, I'll activate the tape you prepared. The office will get a sick call from you. I'll ask the right questions for the answers you've recorded."

He slowly raised his head, as if its weight were unbearable, and let it fall. The equivalent of a "Yes, that's all." I watched him get into bed. His thin arms and skinny legs, with bumpy, gnarled knees, hung out of his nightshirt like a pipe-cleaner doll's. Neat, sparse white hair, and that scruffy mustache. Clean face, with deep parenthetical lines around the mouth, and pits below the cheekbones. There was strength in that face, even now. As the approach of sleep relaxed his control, his eyes showed incredible weariness, as if to say, ". . . Just let it end."

My heart went out to him. I would do anything for him not to have to suffer, but I knew that his own strength would have to carry him.

The phase after freeze is the easiest part of the cycle. That is, until the need for more melsedrine becomes unbearable. Fraser's eyes regained a sharp, steel blue. Color returned to his face. He stood straight, and carried himself firmly, in spite of the pain.

For the next two weeks, he taught, and I learned, cross-cultural analysis, structural components, and fundamentals of nonverbal literature. I was fascinated with the material he was developing. I suggested that he withdraw from the cultural exchange project and devote his full attention to the literature of Deneb 3. For the ghost of an instant, I saw a softness in his eyes, and then his mouth tightened and he said, "I must finish my term. I have an arrangement with U.U.E. On the completion of my three years with this program, a grant will be provided to establish an ongoing field situation on Deneb Three. Students in xenology, linguistics, exobiology, and so forth, will train there. Perhaps someone will be able to continue my work." He shook his head. "That grant is very important to me."

I thought of Deneb 3 and Arrl, and remembered that her people had excommunicated her. I knew some of Fraser's most private thoughts, and I didn't want to pry any further. I hesitated, then asked, "Would it be possible for you to use some of your own money?"

"I don't have any."

I must have looked puzzled. He had written, taught. Royalties, retirement funds. I knew he didn't spend much.

"My wife. The divorce."

My God, I thought. I lowered my head and walked over to the wall to pick up some papers.

"Would you please bring me the green folder?"

I brought him the notes for a lecture he was to give at the main auditorium of the university.

He looked through the folder, then began dictating. "The literature of Deneb Three will probably become the paradigm for the concept of separation of sacred and secular language. Such separation is seen almost universally, as stylized or archaic usages reserved for sacred literature. There are cases, and even in Earth history, where an entirely different language was used for secular speech, as, for example, the European Jews of the nineteenth century. They used Hebrew for sacred speech and literature, and Yiddish for everyday matters. However, Deneb Three is the only known culture where the individuals have separate organs of speech for sacred and secular matters." He stopped and closed his eyes.

He was due for his medicine.

Gentle breezes wrap around him. Arrl comes close, reaching out with her tiny, three-fingered hand to touch his mustache, thinking that his facial hairs serve the same functions that hers do —among them, communication. Waves of oscillation pour over him, but he doesn't understand. She draws him closer; the vibrations become stronger. Then she speaks, and explains that this *is* the literature, and this is how it is shared by the people. In this society intimate contact is religious, rather than sexual. (Or is it both? A human could never know, could never be completely objective about intimate experience.)

On Deneb 3, the individuals share their literature intimately, and it is passed on from generation to generation, by direct experience, through the organs of sensation. And these waves of perception have been translated into words by the only man in the galaxy who could have done it. He designed and built an implant, by converting one of his translation devices into a highly sensitive receiver, that could amplify the energy waves that radiated from Arrl, and translate them into something that his mind would read as sensory perception. Fraser had had extensive biofeedback training, in order to prepare himself for the hazards of living away from medical help. This sense of what was happening in his body, and the control over his nervous system that he had learned, helped him conduct the impulses that were the

Denebian literature to his brain. He showed Arrl how to implant the device into the ganglion between his shoulders. He taught her to use that as a receiver for her loving communication. Then he translated by successive approximations—first with the implant, from impulse to sensory perception; then from color into sight images. By drawing on their close relationship, Fraser had some intuitive sense of what the transmissions meant to her people. Finally, he was able to set some of the material into written literature.

Work at U.U.E. doesn't stop for people with cyclic disorders. You make yourself fit, and you go to it. The period following peak is depression, but if you're disciplined enough, you handle it. Fraser would need malt again, though, within three weeks. I hoped that I could skip that dose, shade, and hold out until he was ready for the next one. There wasn't much malt in my body, yet. I'd managed before, but that was twelve years ago, when my nervous system still had recuperative ability.

Fraser had three months and eleven days left of his term as director of the cultural exchange program. I didn't think he would make it. Either Block's Syndrome or malt would get him before that.

He worked every minute he could on his Denebian material. I had taken over most of his share of the department work. As the days went by, Fraser grew weaker and slower, past the point where he could compensate, and he had to stay at home. The pain of his deterioration seemed to grow unbearable as he approached freeze. At times he was too weak even to cry out. For the thousandth time, I asked myself, "How much longer?"

I hated to leave him to go to the office, afraid that he would fall into freeze and injure himself as he lost consciousness. I wanted to strap him into the life-support system, but he insisted on working until the last minute. There would be times in the weeks to come when neither of us would be capable of work at all.

I walked into the office and stacked Fraser's finished work on his desk. I riffled through the new folders and tapes.

"If he can't do the work, why doesn't he step down?"

I turned. The remark had come from Ed Jacobs. He was supposed to be Fraser's assistant. "He's done his work," I said, "and he'll do these, too." I put them in my briefcase.

I did my own work as quickly as possible and prepared some of what Fraser was supposed to do later. I hated the close green walls and the same dozen or so tunes someone kept replaying.

By now, Fraser was probably in freeze. At least he won't be suffering, I thought. Then I realized. Freeze. That was why Fraser was taking the malt. Not to soothe the pain, or alleviate the suffering; not for the thrills or the fantasy, but to gain time. During the plunge phase, when body functions slowed down, the deterioration of his nerves would also be slowed down, and virtually halt in the freeze phase. His nervous system was being destroyed, but he would be able to function for a little while longer as the effect of the drug compensated for that of the disease. Melsedrine destroys nerve cells by increasing sensitivity, killing by overload. Block's Syndrome weakens the fibers until they eventually dissolve. Fraser's solution, using malt to prolong his life, was clever in a bizarre sort of way.

Robert, poor Robert. A week, eight days. He won't survive longer than that without it, I thought. And how many more doses can his body tolerate, for all his stubbornness? He's going to need four more after this one to meet the deadline. (Deadline—what an awful word.)

Arrl—and her child. Fraser's child, not biologically, but socially. The tenderness he feels as he watches her fondle it. Male, isn't it? And would its name be Frrzrr?

Arrl hadn't said that he could go, but she hadn't tried to cover her tracks through the tangled brush. The chill night smelled of evergreen. Fraser wondered why she didn't fly, or walk around instead of through the rough terrain.

He understood, finally. Their mating ground had originally been an eyrie, but upheavals through the centuries had all but buried the mountain. The pattern of walking to reproduce had evolved the upright posture needed for the development of larger brains.

He was aware of others approaching, and stayed out of sight. They gathered in a rock-strewn clearing. Arrl was treated like the others. Thrashing wings whipped strong currents past him. Moonlight unleashed kaleidoscopic patterns changing with sets of partners.

Arrl fondles the egg. She has no one to help her nurture the embryo. Fraser does as much as he can, but even though he knows about their sensory communication, he can't transmit to the embryo. What he can do, and does, is to give love to Arrl, in as many ways as he can, and hope that she can love the offspring enough for both of them. And she does, extraordinary creature that she is.

Fraser, who would be stygmatized by his own people if they knew the extent of his involvement. Fraser, living a dream that not another man could have had. Fraser, coming back to his people to share what he had learned, so that we would learn, too.

—and Fraser, dying a little with each milligram, who won't live to see us learn.

I can't take it anymore. Never feeling that I belong anyplace except among other species. I'm a field worker. I don't want to sit behind a desk. I want to be somewhere where the sun shines on unspoiled primitives frolicking in the clean grass.

Aw, malt always makes me cry like a baby for my crib, I thought. Snap out of it, girl. You're going to take those four more doses, and then get untangled, somehow.

I had to work harder now, but I could still hide my symptoms, and my freeze lasted only a couple of hours. Fraser's freeze lasted four and a half days. One day he isn't going to come out of it, I thought. That's how he's going to die, because he's too stubborn to give up his life when he's conscious.

Fraser wakened at last. I was beginning to think that this time he'd had it.

"Sheila," he said in a raspy voice.

I went to his side quickly. "Are you all right?"

He closed his eyes, then opened them. "Yes." He took my hand

and smiled. "If I don't get another chance to say it"—his voice cleared a little—"thank you."

I tried to think of a joke, a throwaway. I wiped the back of my hand nonchalantly across my eyes.

"What will happen to you?"

"Not to worry," I said with my all-weather smile. "I told you in the beginning that I beat malt before."

"How old were you?" He was still holding my hand. "If you were very young, the damage to your system might have been minimal."

"Sixteen, what's the difference. Maybe my system is immune."

"No."

"Do you feel like working? Shall I get the tapes ready?"

"Mmm." He carefully untwined himself from the life-support system and got out of bed. He started walking slowly toward the bathroom.

"Do you need any help?" I asked as casually as I could.

He turned to me and smiled. "Thank you, but I think I'm still capable of washing myself."

When he came out of the bathroom, I put some makeup on him. He sat at his desk. His hands were resting neatly, the right on top to steady the left. He delivered parts of the lectures he had been preparing.

It's just not possible, I thought. A whole course, forty lectures, he'll never be able to finish. I watched his face as he spoke. The material means so much to him, and the field of nonverbal literature will never develop without it. He can't finish the series, but maybe I can. Matching background, cut, splice. If he plans the structure, if I have enough tape of him speaking about the material, enough words.

We worked all that day, and most of the night, until Fraser was too exhausted to speak. Then I taped him, looking tired, muttering that he didn't feel well, and would work at home today.

Fraser managed to appear at the office for a few hours each day for the next ten days. Sometimes we stayed late at the office to use the reference materials there.

Ed Jacobs looked through some of the notes and watched as Fraser did the presentation.

"What is this stuff?" demanded Jacobs. "Animated drawings, disconnected sentences, staccato bursts of color, atonal music?"

"Those are my translations of the literature of Deneb Three," explained Fraser.

"But which is the translation—the color, the pictures, the words, the electronic pulses, which?"

"Any, and all. They are all equivalent. What I am attempting is a total experience. A special area will be constructed, in which the observer can see, feel, hear and smell materials which I have prepared. The total effect will be an approximation of what this literature is to the people who share it."

I don't know why he wastes his energy trying to explain to Jacobs, I thought. The man is too ethnocentric, and even egocentric, to appreciate any of this. And anyway, he thinks translation means word-for-word equivalence, with no regard for the meaning of an entire piece.

"I see," said Jacobs. "And what is the point of wasting all this time and effort?"

Patiently, Fraser continued. "The development of language was the last important evolutionary step on the road to homo sapiens. Using equipment that he already had, nose, tongue and lips, man began to speak, and natural selection favored larger brains that in turn could better deal with language, which in turn led to selection for larger brains, and so forth."

"I know that, and also that the development of language increased the ability of men to work together, and transmit knowledge. But what does that have to do with this incoherent junk?"

I winced. Fraser continued, "By studying preverbal and nonverbal material of other cultures, we get a better understanding of our own history and nature. I thought that much would be obvious to anyone who had learned grade-school xenology."

"Fine," said Jacobs. "But you did more than understand. You were inside their heads. There is only one way that could have been possible." He made an ugly face, looking straight at Fraser. "Certain drugs."

I made myself busy with my papers. Fraser looked at Jacobs levelly. "Possibly. However, since that method was not available to me, I used an implant." He explained how he had built and operated it.

Inside their heads . . . Jacobs' words called up a memory from my undergraduate days. A psychology professor, who had invented what he called a transfer cap. It had worked fine when he switched the minds of a cat and a mouse, but when he had tried to throw his own mind into that of a rhesus monkey, he had had to be carried away in a straitjacket.

Jacobs was still harassing Fraser. "School's out now," I said. "Could we get back to work, please?"

"And you, too." Jacobs whirled to confront me. "Who made you his nurse?" As he said those words, his face whitened and his mouth stayed open. He looked again at Fraser.

Oh, I thought. Mr. Jacobs has finally realized, but how much has he realized? His "certain drugs" remark was probably a wild guess. Fraser has tremors, watery eyes, but he's been like that for months now. A malt pair is such a bizarre concept that I don't think even Jacobs could guess the truth. He probably figured out our sleeping arrangements, that's all. I hope that's all.

As Fraser's melsedrine-starved system kicked him around, he became too weak to work at the office. I had to run some of the tapes we had made of him. There was still almost two months until the end of Fraser's term. I didn't think his body could stand more than one more dose of melsedrine, if that.

I watched him suffer, night after night, thrashing around on the bed, trying to convince his body that it didn't really want what it was clamoring for. I watched him, eyes and nose running, face soaked with perspiration, knees to his chest, looking as if he'd shatter with each convulsion.

Enough. I brought the capsules. Forty milligrams would kill him, I knew, and his body probably wouldn't respond to less. I measured out thirty for him, ten for me.

The rippling wind of hundreds of wings fans against me.

The sky glitters ultramarine as the Sons of the Mountain burst forth . . .

Even with the powerful stimulation of melsedrine, Robert's body was too weak to respond. I knew that the agonizing need for physical experience would strain his nerves to a point where the pain might kill him.

I wipe out the Sacred Mountain and take him instead to the Sheik's Garden. Velvet grass for a couch. Exotic string sounds of the zither and the *oud*. Rhythmic beating of the clay *derbeke;* a husky voice with thick consonants and throaty vowels extols the virtues of *Bint Ilgiron,* the girl next door. The tinkling of swaying fringe, as dancers slowly swirl their hips in a figure eight, bending backward toward the ground. They sway faster and faster. On old Earth, the girls had worn fringed breastplates and gauze skirts, banded with metallic fringe below the navel, but this is paradise, so they wear only the fringe.

Wine rains down in soft, warm droplets. The air is heavy with the sweet woody aroma of hashish. A thousand tiny fingers, and hundreds of lips and tongues augment what I am doing to Robert's body, but to no avail.

I take him instead to the little grass hut where Krishna and Radha share love eternal that flees and pursues through all the centuries. Bedecked with flowers, their love, like a flood, transcends heaven and earth.

Robert had always liked these verses intellectually. He is able to use them now to pull himself into the experience. As compassion and tenderness explode inside me, incredibly, a response catapults from him.

Time, time. I hated time, and I hated the laws that men had made. The absurd archaic laws that had given Fraser's wife everything, forcing him to start all over. I hated Arrl's people, too, for their stubborn rigidity, casting her and her son out. The proposed field situation on Deneb 3 was the only way that Fraser could ensure Arrl's future. He had hoped that she could work with the Earthmen as an emissary, and perhaps regain status among her own people. She was able to trade minerals that Fraser sent to her to her people for the other things that she needed. And now, if he didn't live to finish his term, there would be no field situation, no more minerals for Arrl, and everything until now would have been for nothing.

It's not fair, I kept thinking. One tired and sick old man against the galaxy.

Time sped by, or crawled, I couldn't tell which, and one night I dreamed of snow. Dali's clocks were chasing me through a storm. I was shivering, both from terror and cold, as ice crystals cut my feet and my thin shift beat against me in the cutting wind. I ran until I couldn't breathe. The clocks stopped, melting into the dirty, punishing snow.

I woke up knowing. I ran over to the life-support system. Fraser had been in freeze for nineteen days, but now there was a difference. I checked the instruments and found that the slight pulse and respiration were gone. There's a mistake, I thought, check again. I checked again, and again, but the dials wouldn't move.

Thank God, I thought then. His suffering is over. I just stood there looking at him until tears came.

After a while I washed my face. I knew that I should be using this little time when I was relatively clear-headed to plan my actions. In a few days, in addition to covering for Fraser, I would have to cover for myself. I kept thinking about Robert Fraser, the way he had been, the way he was at the end, and the things I wanted to remember. I wanted to remember every detail. There wasn't anything else.

It's been nearly three weeks since anyone saw Fraser in person, I thought, and there are three more weeks until the end of his term. Could I possibly carry off the deception? What if someone demanded to see him? And is this life-support system really going to keep the body preserved until I can safely pronounce him dead? Robert, I thought, we've been through so much, just a little more. Those weren't malt tears that I had to keep washing off my face.

I had another problem, too. Crave nagged at me. I pushed it out of my mind and left the apartment.

In the office, I concentrated on the work in front of me, wishing I could integrate myself into the printed page, and detach from the awful screaming of my body. I am in control, I told myself. The body is my servant.

The day was endless, endless. I drank my tenth cup of coffee, adding more sugar, and looked at the clock. My eyes watered, my nose was runny; well, the dust from the old books was irritating. The most difficult thing I had to do was converse with "Dr. Fraser" on the viewer. He looked so real, so alive. I could see the muscle in his left hand twitch just at the edge of the picture. We hadn't wanted that to show, and yet the tremor, nearly under control, was what made the image real.

The day ended at last and I went back to the apartment. Crave was screaming at me. I looked at the small figure in the net of the life-support system. I walked over to the controls and checked the readings. I lowered the temperature a little. Nothing to do but wait and see.

I forced myself to work on Fraser's project, then on the department work. I had to do as much as I could now, before . . . Before what? Before I died from need? Or from overdose? Don't think about it. I got coffee and poured half a cup of sugar into it. I did deep-breathing exercises. I worked a page, fought for control, and worked again.

The next days were worse. I couldn't stay at the office. I knew I was going to need at least a little melsedrine to pull through. But not now, not yet. I was a crazed, caged animal, trapped in that room. Once in a while I managed to look at the life-support system and check what the computer was sending to the office from me. I couldn't have reset it if I had wanted to.

Hell with it, anyway. I reached behind the drawer. I looked at it while my blood raced. I watched my hand raise it to my mouth. I closed my eyes and counted, ten minutes till it hits.

I tried to lift, but it wouldn't come, and I couldn't even create my own fantasy, as I had done when I hadn't taken the drug. I needed a partner, a flesh-and-blood one.

I lay there for hours, burning, aching for release. I thought of Cor, the bastard who taught me this, and I wanted to shrink away into a corner as I felt his eyes on me.

Cor wouldn't go away for a long time. The smell of him, the slight tinge of ammonia that indicated annoyance, then the hot smell of man, and then the heat would bring out the acids that body catalysts make from malt. The acid odor in his perspiration, and faintly on the breath that started even trace amounts of melsedrine in the blood of another humming in resonance, until crave became a tidal wave sweeping me under. I'd spark then, and he'd laugh, leave me beached, solo; and bastard that he was, he'd watch.

Need crave, worse than malt crave, intensified by malt crave, crave that wanted contact, any kind at any price. Endless repetition, of bodies and limbs and knotting ugliness, and all the while my sensuality, betraying me mindlessly, loved it. But it wasn't enough, couldn't be enough. I arched and contorted as my body shook with spasm after spasm of meaninglessness.

Cor, laughing. Damn you, Cor, you're dead. Cor, laughing, reaching. Me, using fantasy to hold him from lifting, making him think he hadn't sparked, so he took more, and more.

I looked at the calendar. Eight more days of Fraser's term. I had to stay alive, stay functioning that long.

I managed through the next week, even getting to the office once in a while. The malt I had taken was enough to give me something to fight with. The knowledge that the end was so close did the rest.

Then, on the last day, a man came to the office looking for Dr. Fraser.

"He's not well, could I take a message?" The familiar words came out easily.

The man seemed upset. "I'm from the committee. We're to establish a grant for his research program. We need his thumbprint on the document."

"I see," I managed. My thoughts raced. Nothing. "Well, perhaps I could call you later, if he's feeling better." I smiled weakly.

The man gave me his number.

One more day. One more idea. If only I could think of something, anything.

I excused myself from the office. All for nothing, I thought, as I walked back to the apartment. The planning, the phony tapes, his life, mine, and now we've lost it all.

I looked at the frail little body. The machine had preserved him, but what was the good, with nobody inside? They wouldn't fall for a thumbprint from a dead man. Fight, argue? Appeal? To whom? The computers, bureaucracy? He hadn't finished his term, and that was all they would understand.

There must be something, anything. One more crazy idea. If I could get inside his head . . .

The crazy psychology professor. The transfer cap. I tried to remember. When they carried him away, did they get the cap?

I held the cap in both hands. The notes had been clear enough. This is suicide, I thought, death or insanity. But I'm dead, anyway. Nothing to lose.

I called the man, told him that Fraser was very weak. Fraser would see him, but only for a few minutes.

I disconnected everything, and slid the life-support equipment out from under and around him. I carried everything to the bathroom and locked the door behind me. I arranged myself comfortably on the floor. I fingered the timer that the professor had used, the one that was supposed to break the circuit and bring him back.

Nothing to lose, I told myself. My throat started beating, choking me. Fear held me rigid, a cold fear, older than the history of man.

There was a knock.

"Come in, it's open," said the tape slowly, in Fraser's voice.

I pressed the switch.

Darkness, and cold. Pain, pain, worse than I had thought. I heard a sound. He must be talking to me, better answer.

"Hhhh." I forced eyes open. Shadow moving toward me. "Hh." I realized that I had to draw breath. "Hello."

I heard more mumbling. The shadow moved closer. I raised a hand. I felt pressure.

". . . admire . . . work."

"Th—thank you." I exhaled deeply. The body shook. Inhaled. I tried to smile reassuringly.

The shadow backed away a little. I felt pressure again, cold this time against my hand. The document, I hoped.

"Not well," I said.

The shadow retreated. ". . . pardon . . . cooperation . . . thank you. . ."

Pain, dulled by six weeks on life-support, but not dull at all, pulled me, pulled. I saw a well with no bottom, a howling cavern; felt cold, cold. Must be time to switch back. Darkness, whirling. I had forgotten to breathe. Forced the lungs, nothing. Opened mouth, gulped empty. Blacker, roaring, oh God, not like this. Cold, cold.

Cold smooth, sound of water inside, cold shivering against my skin, light against eyelids. Squeeze tight, open slow, white tile.

Tile! I ran my hands along the bathroom floor, closed my eyes, exhaled. I started to laugh. I took a deep breath and checked my body. I hadn't dared hope.

Tears ran down my face. Robert, Robert. I used you. I climbed over your dead body, and now I'm free.

I'll repay you.

I already know the spoken language, and I know about the literature.

Arrl, and the child, too, as informants, but . . .

Jacobs *was* right. Objective understanding isn't enough. You have to be inside their heads.

There's the implant. There's the transfer cap. And if all else fails . . .

There's always malt.

PERSEPHONE

Rhondi Vilott

Chrystan watched the long staggering lines of soldiers against the snow as thermal charges flared behind and below them, illuminating the ice caverns. The soldiers cut their way toward the surface, their yellow snow-gear giving them the appearance of ichor-stained entrails thrusting from the wound that gave them birth. She felt sick, and repressed the feeling. The retreat was painfully slow. She knew her husband would be expecting a report from her so that he could coordinate shuttle liftoffs, but she did not wish to talk to him just now. Weeks ago when she left for the front they had said all she wished to hear. The military would fill in the gap she left. Someone else would be giving him the reports. Yet, as she watched the lines, she wondered who was going to fill the gap in her, the ache of watching everyone else go home.

She gathered a closer mindshield on her twenty-kilometer front, feeling the exhaustion of her troops as they climbed out of the planet's winter-locked interior. In her mind she saw them as flames banked in a deliberate fire. It was her job to keep the spark of each soldier shielded from the icy breath of the enemy Bharan. When the men and women were gone, there would be a fresh set of troops, and then another, and another.

A soldier wavered and fell in the line straggling across the foot of her knoll. His companions, numbed by frost, fear and hunger, bunched around him as Chrystan plunged through the crust. They pulled back when they saw her. He lay on his back, his cheeks whitened by the summer snow. She felt his flickering essence when she took his hand.

"Don't leave me!"

"No, no," she told him. "We won't leave you." She put cold fingers on his forehead, fingertips slipping on the clammy sweat of his fear. She fed back into him the sensations he was pushing out violently. She talked soothingly as she did so, impressing images of green grass and light blue spring water. His pulse steadied.

"You're going home. You can't quit now," said Chrystan.

He took a deep breath. "It's a rout back there—we're the first coming in from the nests. I don't think the others will make it."

She removed her hand. "Just as long as you do. A little further, and you'll see the shuttlecraft. Come on now, stand up and get moving."

Ignoring his protests, Chrystan shouldered him to his feet. She lifted her shield on the rest of the battalion long enough to feed the individual spark within him until it flamed. He took his weight off her and straightened his weapon pack.

"Just keep your eyes on the back of the man in front of you, soldier," she said as he moved away. The binding intimacy of that last contact forced her away abruptly. She never could say goodbye.

She was struggling in the snow pack to regain her vantage point when a large hand clasped her forearm.

"Here—let me break a path for you," the officer said as he passed in front of her, not waiting for an answer. His big ungainly frame forced its way upward, the hard crust cracking aside. He waited for her on the boulders. Chrystan recognized his face then, and an unexpected flush warmed her cheeks. This was one of the men in the Seventh with whom she had slept in order to force acceptance of her shielding powers. It happened occasionally, but it was not a practice she enjoyed: to force her brain patterns through a gateway created by the most intimate of moments. Usually the man broke down and cried, and she would cradle his face to her bare chest as the shards of his façade flooded away.

With this one, this huge and homely yet gentle man, she had been the one who wept; and he had held her close through the night.

He did not leave when she gained the boulders, but stood to block the wind from her. Summer on this world meant forever a place of rock, snow and ice. The oceans held a promise of teeming life a million years beyond, if the Bharan could be driven out of the interior.

A faint queasiness invaded her again. Pushing the feeling aside, she looked at the man beside her. Though his being was imprinted deeply into her memory, she had never known his name.

"Who's coming in behind us, lieutenant?"

"Second and Third Battalions," he answered. "If they make it."

Chrystan shuddered. They had waited too long to bring in fresh troops. Damn them! How long were they willing to let the infantry fight a war both physical and mental?

As if signaled by her thoughts, a moan started in the jagged grottos below and worked its way up the line of soldiers. Chrystan threw her power full force along the limits of her battalion, creating a vortex to draw in the attacking power. Beside her, the lieutenant opened com lines. Faintly she heard him say, "Get me Commander Rodriguez. This is Seventh Battalion, under First Wave assault."

A crackle, then, "Rodriguez. What is your position?"

As she spun the shining vortex that was the molten psyche of all of them and none of them, pain wrenched her at the sound of his voice. *Manny,* she thought. *Help me.*

"We're the first lines coming in, sir, about five kilometers northwest of the base," answered the lieutenant.

Her husband swore. "That means Rand has buckled. All right. We'll be airlifting two shields in for replacement."

"Make it three—sir," the lieutenant said sharply. He cut off transmission as Chrystan swayed.

Her mind became a battleground where she stepped upon silver ashes and crackling bones, and grey and ebony death surrounded her. Rocks melted and leathery growths stubbed upward. Normally she would swing the vortex of power about in her hands, dump it on the ground to see what she had captured, and deal with it, but this assault was different. The hairs on the back of her neck prickled. She advanced into the strangeness. *Dear god, Manny, I don't want to be here again.*

A shadow stirred at the far end of the valley. With the odd lumpy shuffle of its manylegged walk, a white-robed Bharan approached. It stopped, cowl-hidden face toward her, with the violet aura of the Queen surrounding it.

Chrystan's heart fluttered. Beneath that tall and humped robe was a being who commanded thousands upon this world: a queen intent upon sucking the marrow from human bones.

A violet bolt sizzled at her while Chrystan shaped the vortex. At the last second she flung up her half-formed shield. She staggered back as it deflected the bolt. Heat dissipated about her, and she saw the Queen through wavery light as she completed the shield. Rand used to talk about fighting the Bharan in mindspace, encapsulating his power with shining silver wings and missiles. Others thought in terms of dogfighting biplanes. She preferred the imagery of shield and sword, though it meant a heart-stopping closeness to the aliens. Chrystan swallowed as she shaped a fiery blade in her hand.

She deliberately took a defensive stand. First Wave assaults were short, concentrated efforts to break the physical and mental barriers of the troops, and they cost the Bharan a tremendous expenditure of effort. If she could hold on . . .

"When she falls," the Bharan said hollowly, "she is to be left for me, as First Meat."

Chrystan heard the chilling words as she had been meant to. The violet aura speared to her right and then left, feinting before the bolt fired. She sliced it aside. Then blows rained upon the shield, melting upon contact, sparks sizzling about her ears until she crouched nearly deafened. When it stopped, Chrystan rose. She leaped, closing the distance between them. She struck with the sword, felt it deflected by the Queen's own bodyshield which hung about her like a second robe. The Bharan seemed confused by her attack and gave way.

The alien's presence was a dark and crushing fear that threatened to break her. With her shield arm, Chrystan wiped sweat off her forehead. Where was Manny? Where was her relief? She darted aside as violet fire grazed the armor, and again she withstood the attack.

The veins stood out on her arms as her muscles cramped and trembled under the weight. She faltered. She threw the shield up, going to one knee, sword hand and hilt pressed to her side. *Dear God, not again!* The cramps lanced her stomach like a mortal wound, and within the agony flickered a spark of life fighting its own battle. She staggered to her feet.

Driven, Chrystan advanced on the Queen. She swung the blade recklessly, caring only that the Bharan gave way once and then again. Women among the stars were mainly sterile; conception was difficult, full-term carriage nearly impossible. She had lost two unborn in these desperate battles before and she would not lose another.

The Queen took the defensive now; her cowled head bobbed uncertainly. Chrystan drove in on the advantage. In the last burst of her strength, she knew she could end it all here. There was a flicker as the Queen disappeared and left Chrystan plunging past. She missed the final blow, swinging at empty air, and pitched forward onto her face. The taste of ashes filled her mouth.

The lieutenant held her tightly about the waist as she heaved bitter bile and fear into the snow. When she finished, he set her down on the rocks and gently wiped her mouth with clean snow. He brushed her tangled hair from her eyes.

Hot tears rolled down, the icy wind turning them brittle. The nausea and cramp continued, then slowly eased. Chrystan laid her trembling hands on her lap. Below them, the straggling lines of soldiers pulled upward as though nothing had happened. She took a deep breath. Manny hadn't come in time. Again.

The lieutenant took her hand in his, concern on his broad, open features, saying, "You're cold."

"What I am, is pregnant."

He flushed. "Is it . . . could it be mine?"

The world stopped, except for a buzz in her ears. She thought of the day Manny had said reluctantly that they could try again, and if they were successful, she could return home to carry his child. Home to green hills and deep drinks of blue world air. To spring.

She looked at the lieutenant, and saw the reflection of her shocked realization in his face.

The sound of hovercraft cut off his words. He helped her aboard carefully as the other shield disembarked. Hands, all about her: seating her, buckling her in, cutting off her view of the lieutenant. As the engines revved for takeoff, she leaned to the door.

"Your name! Please . . . your name?"

"Hartwell. Lieutenant Steven Hartwell," he shouted.

She saw his upturned face follow her line of flight until the mountains separated them.

Manny met the hovercraft at the base, his military maps shoved under one arm. She took a long look at his compact, middle-aged figure in uniform, his naturally browned face, gray sprinkles in his black hair.

He helped her out and dropped his hands from her as she stood trembling in the snow. "The other shields here told me you put up one hell of a fight. Good girl. Bharan operations stopped all over the planet. You nearly had her."

"Nearly? Only nearly? God, how I wanted to put her down!"

"Why didn't you?"

Chrystan stammered, "I tried. I missed. I've been shielding for three weeks. Where the hell were you?" *Hold me,* she thought. *Tell me it's all right.*

His gaze dropped from hers. "Come on," he said, taking her arm. "Come inside. You're upset."

In his office he handed her a cup of nucoff and put a blanket about her shoulders.

"I need to go home, Manny."

He sat down carefully. "Only two of those shuttles will be hooking up for home. The flagship is headed to another defensive quadrant where we'll get a few weeks' rest before being reassigned. I've been promoted, Chrystan! I was right about their nesting grounds. Now we have a clue to their swarming patterns." Manny's face lit up with happiness.

The coff burned her lips but she gulped it down. She tried the phrasing out internally first before she said, "Manny, we agreed that you were retiring. That we were going home. That I could have children."

"That would be difficult to plan now, wouldn't it? Or do you want to become like the Bharan female soldiers—producing mindless litters of babies for troop consumption? With your role as a shield, you wouldn't even know who the father was!" His lips whitened.

"We agreed—"

"What we agreed when we married was to avoid the mistake of my first marriage and remember that my career comes first! You're just a volunteer, but the years I've put in are important to me, and if you think I'm going to give it up just when my potential is being realized—" He stopped suddenly and took a breath.

In fear, Chrystan put out her hand to bridge the distance between them. Manny did not take it.

She pulled her hand back, saying, "As a woman of childbearing years, I have the right to request home passage anytime after two years' service. That's *my* potential, Manny. You used to say that my being with you was what made this hell livable. Well, it's not livable for me. I'm tired of death. I want to go home because I'm pregnant, and I won't lose this one too by being on the wrong world while it tries to grow!"

He tried to look at her, but found his desk top easier to deal with. "What will you do?"

"What will I do?" she repeated. "I have my therapy work, back pay, my painting and the baby." She stood up, dropping the blanket from her shoulders, and left her husband sitting there.

Chrystan hunched her shoulders against the bitter and barren cold as she made her way to the shuttles. She lay down in a berth, pressing her hands to her stomach for a moment. She felt the coursing of a tiny spark along wire-thin nerves to a mind still forming. Then she reached up to attach monitor strips and begin the coldsleep setting. She thumbed in Manny's transceiver on her com lines.

"Good-bye," she said. There was no answer.

Chrystan lay back and closed her eyes. The abduction was over.

THE SMELL OF THE NOOSE, THE ROAR OF THE BLOOD

John Barfoot

An aeroplane flew along the Strand at a height of one thousand feet. When it reached Trafalgar Square people began jumping from it. Bystanders found it difficult, later, to describe the sound they made as they fell, but many found great significance in the fact that some had actually bounced on hitting the ground. This detail was repeated many times, with relish or revulsion or awe, to friends, police, mediamen.

To Frank, however, sitting on a damp bench in the Square, hands thrust deep in pockets, lazily pondering spectacular methods of exterminating the grimy pigeons dipping and bowing at his feet, the most significant point concerning this unexpected event was that it had no style. Something like fifty bodies lay about the Square, smashed and broken, crumpled and bloody. Some had hit buildings on the way down and rags of flesh were daubed along parapets and balconies; some, amazingly, were not dead, and were now moaning and crying. It was . . . messy. Personally, Frank would have tried for something memorable, like impaling himself on the upraised arm of Nelson, atop his column; but then, of course, he would never have involved himself in such a vulgar mass stunt, in which there could be no individual recognition.

He heard the sound of the aeroplane again and looked up. It had turned sharply, somewhere above Knightsbridge, and was now heading back for the Square. More people jumped, and the scene was repeated. No point, muttered Frank; once achieves the effect. He looked hopefully up at Nelson's arm. Nothing.

The aeroplane made two more passes, on the last of which the falling bodies were joined by a snowstorm of white leaflets. Frank picked one up.

It was headed, CHURCH OF UNIVERSAL DESPAIR.

Brothers and Sisters! Look around you! Do you like what you see? No? Then WHY do you put up with it? What do you think God feels when he sees you wallowing like PIGS in the mess you have made for yourselves? Isn't it obvious? He thinks, How can they Love Me when they have turned the world I made into a PIGSTY and wallow in it like PIGS? How can they turn their eyes up to Me when they are so busy rooting in the SLIME they have created? And God is right, Brothers and Sisters, you know He is! You must prove to God that you Love Him, you must show Him that you have nothing but contempt for the world you have created. And how is that done? Brothers and Sisters! It is done by rejecting the PIGSTY you have made, by treating it with the utter contempt which is all it deserves! You know, Brothers and Sisters, in your heart of hearts, that the only sane response to the PIGSTY we have made for ourselves, is to leave it! To give ourselves to God in pure faith, to prove to Him by our rejection—

Frank crumpled the leaflet and threw it to the ground. It made him sick when people joined themselves together like this, so that they were indistinguishable, one from the other. What was the point of them all killing themselves together like that, for some stupid cause? They might as well have thrown a couple of hundredweight of guts from an abattoir out of that aeroplane.

Police sirens were approaching from all directions, and the Square was rapidly filling up with people, running from one smashed body to another. Some were collecting souvenir smears of blood on handkerchiefs, some were rapidly clicking cameras, some stood frozen in some powerful emotion, staring at the scene. The pigeons were hovering in a great cloud, but some were landing now, pecking daintily at the pools of blood.

Frank found the scene pathetic. The way people were able to be so completely, so shamelessly . . . themselves . . . the way they were able to ignore what others might think of them and just behave exactly as they felt—fighting and shoving to catch a glimpse, stupid wet mouths open, hands anxiously clutching and pushing. After all, the scene was no more bloody than the gang fight in Hyde Park last month between the Punks and the Lords —when the cleavers and hatchets had stopped swinging, the Park had looked like a butcher's shop. And of course, when the Mob had an outing, the city streets were piled high with torn corpses. And yet they behaved like this just for some pointless religious stunt.

Thinking of the Mob, he realised that there was every chance a nucleus would form here shortly—people were already coalescing into groups and several fights had started—and he had no desire to be locked in when the riot barriers slid into place. He walked quickly away towards Lower Regent Street, as the Square began to fill up with police lorries and resound to the rise and fall of sirens and loudspeaker announcements.

These public scenes were something he tried to remain aloof from, and he had seen plenty of them in the four days he had been wandering backwards and forwards across the city. People would be moving along quite normally and quietly, then something would happen, and it would be as if, suddenly, strange animals with flashing eyes and teeth jumped out of their bodies and turned their faces into savage masks. Not that Frank minded the savagery—it was usually so real that it could only be honest —no, it was the inconsistency that upset him, the way people could change completely from one second to the next and not even be ashamed or embarrassed that the flimsy cardboard of their façades had been torn away for everyone to see inside. He liked people to be one thing or the other, but he could not bear it when they were both. He, personally, never let his mask slip. He was always himself.

He paused at an Instapape slot, inserted a coin, and carefully folded the flimsy yellow sheet as it emerged.

C.U.D.'S MOST SPECTACULAR STUNT YET

The Church of Universal Despair today chartered a Hercules airfreighter which was used in a mass-suicide demonstration by the Church's disciples over central London. Two hundred men and women jumped from the aircraft over Trafalgar Square in what was described as an evangelical gesture. The Church, which considers suicide the only acceptable response to the modern world—

He stuffed the pape in his pocket. Evangelical gesture! No one would ever know the names of any of those two hundred, they would forever be as anonymous as the remnants of their bodies, probably even now being sucked up by the police waste-vacuums for eventual consignment to the Ilford rubbish-tip. Stupid! Dying for nothing.

He had just passed the end of the Haymarket when the rush-hour warning lights came on and the klaxons began to rise and fall. The iron gates of the office buildings swung open all at once, and almost in the same instant, riot-barriers began to slowly creak and grate out of their housings and across the streets which led to Trafalgar Square. The first office-workers to come tumbling blindly out of their buildings saw this and sprinted madly for the slowly narrowing gap, briefcases bouncing on their wrist-chains. Some made it and continued running across the Square to Charing Cross Station, skirting the fast-growing Mob on the left. The others were too late and after kicking the barriers in frustration, began the long roundabout walk which would eventually bring them to the Station. The street was full now, of pushing, stumbling, elbowing people, all completely single-minded, and as Frank had been unable to get into a Shelter before the rush began, he was forced to shuffle along with them. This was a much better area of the city than the one in which the Department of Unemployment, where he worked, was situated. These people were probably going home to single-unit houses out in the country: three, or perhaps even four rooms, tended day-long by neat wives, fingers always on the button of the Dustmaid, or the Airkleen, or the Dazzlewash. They did not look at Frank, they did not look at each other, they did not raise their heads at the steadily growing howl of riot behind them. They were secure. They knew where they were going.

Frank realised that he had been carried well past Lower Regent Street, and had to push and shove vigorously against the unyielding, uncaring wall of bodies around him before he could join a cross-flow going up to Piccadilly. Once out of the main stream, the crowd thinned a little and he was able to make a small space to walk in untouched. The flow took him to just short of Piccadilly Circus before it lost its identity in the strolling crowd. A boy with piled-up blond hair smiled at him. A woman wearing only shorts and high-heeled shoes looked at him and lifted her breasts in the palms of her hands. A man beckoned at the doorway of a club offering the torture of live animals on stage "in the half-round." He ignored them, only sank deeper down into himself.

There had been women in his life, he'd known women. He wasn't a boy to be excited because a whore flaunted herself at him in the street. No, sex exerted no power over him. He thought of Julia. He had never made love to Julia, never even touched her . . . anywhere. He had given her no reason to think him base, like other men. He had struggled to hold her above the filth, the way he had excluded those he loved from his adolescent masturbation fantasies. And she had left him, of course. Yes, she had left him.

He turned into Shaftesbury Avenue and walked past the Thrill Palace. A scaffold projected from its roof with a body dangling from the rope. MAN HANGED ON STAGE EVERY NIGHT! screamed the posters. A small knot of tourists was already forming a queue to book for the evening performance. A busker, stripped to the waist, and obviously drunk, was trying to attract their attention. A young man accepted his challenge to make him sick by punching him in the stomach, and after handing over his five pounds, rolled up his sleeves. The punch was short and vicious and the fist almost disappeared in rolls of flesh. The busker staggered backward, fell, but picked himself up, pale-faced and bent double, to prove that the five pounds was his. Frank moved on.

Next to the Thrill Palace was a sex-shop. He dawdled at the window, looking at the finger-breakers, branding-irons, eye-gouges. Cellophane-wrapped magazines with titles like *The Execu-*

tioner, The Torturer, The Pain-Object. FULL-SIZE IRON MAIDEN, said a poster, ASK INSIDE.

He walked on slowly. In a street off the main road he found a small café and had a coffee, pretending absorption in his pape while he drank it. In fact, he was thinking of bodies falling from the sky, spinning and twisting, the expressions on their faces caught by telephoto lenses at the beginning of the descent and held through the long fall in detail, faces distorted in the rush of air, limbs out of control, eyes fixed on the earth turning below, jerking upward with sickening speed, down and down and down until they rammed into the earth like bullets. He felt his teeth being smashed through his lips, his skull crushing into pulp, his spine telescoping, his legs splintering, and clutched the pape convulsively.

A detail which had not been prominent appeared before him vividly: falling beside each body, slamming and banging in the slipstream, had been a briefcase, held in place by a wrist-chain. . . .

Outside, he wandered back the way he had come, and stopped when he reached the Thrill Palace. The actors' queue was already forming at the top of the narrow alley at the side of the theatre. The busker had changed his act. He was now making shallow cuts on his body with a razor blade. A crowd of grinning Japanese tourists were dropping five-pound notes in his hand and pointing out the spots where they wanted the cuts to be made. Frank watched absentmindedly for a moment or two, and then, as if suddenly remembering an urgent appointment, broke away and walked up the alley at the side of the Thrill Palace, pushing his way through the group around the vacancies board.

WANTED:
    ACTRESS: ROUGH HANDLING AND INTERCOURSE WITH
        ANIMALS
    ACTOR: SEVERANCE OF RIGHT HAND
    ACTOR: CRUCIFIXION (HANG FOR MINIMUM ONE HOUR)
    ACTOR: SEVERE BEATING
    ACTOR: SEVERE BEATING WITH BROKEN LIMBS
    ACTOR: HOMOSEXUAL ACTS WITH SEVERE BEATING

There were over thirty entries on the list. At the bottom, in large capitals, was the entry:

ACTOR: STAR PART: *DEATH BY HANGING*

He joined the queue, looking disdainfully at those beside him. In front of him, a hunchback with sharp delicate features ran his fingers nervously up and down the strap of the tape recorder slung from his shoulder. A fat man wearing a tentlike white djellaba continually licked his caricature cupid-lips. An intelligent-looking woman wearing a fur coat smoked cigarette after cigarette, sucking smoke deep into her lungs, closing her eyes often.

"Hat-trick tonight if I'm lucky."

He looked round. A little man behind him gave an apologetic smile. His face was covered with bruises and his bottom lip bore a scab from a recent cut. "Hat-trick tonight if I'm lucky," he repeated. "Got a severe beating part last night at the Theatre of Terror, a prolonged interrogation with slapping at the Roxy Squealdrome matinee this afternoon, and this'll be my hat-trick if they take me on tonight."

He turned away and heard the little man say, half-defensively, but almost without interest, "Fifty pounds so far . . . seventy-five if I get it tonight. . . ." His voice took on feeling again: "Mmmm, wouldn't mind if *he* administered the beating . . ."

Frank was thinking about the Cross. Hanging by nails through the palms of his hands and the soles of his feet in front of an avid audience. Moaning occasionally, hearing answering moans from out beyond the footlights; gasps from the spectators as he moved his body sensually in a vain attempt to find a less painful position. He relaxed his left leg, unconsciously adopting the slouch he remembered from mediaeval paintings of Christ on the Cross. The Cross. Rough pine, splinters, wood-smell . . .

Up ahead at the end of the alley the stage door opened and a man wearing denim emerged. A pair of sunglasses was pushed up on his forehead. Accompanying him was an earnest young girl with a harelip, carrying a clipboard. The man in denim nodded at her.

"Actress—rough handling and intercourse with animals," she called out.

There was a short silence, then the woman with the fur coat stepped forward, looking defiantly ahead, her cigarette held carelessly between two fingers of an extravagantly dramatic right hand. The denim-clad man glanced at her and said, "Hired."

His assistant ticked her list and called out, "Actor—severe beating." Several men stepped forward, including the hopeful bruised one. The director studied them and chose a short, stocky man with an impassive face. Frank watched the bruised man as others were chosen for "severe beating—broken limbs" and "homosexual acts—severe beating," and saw his pulpy face fall into dejection. He went up to the director, pulled his sleeve, and said urgently, "Listen, I can do a novelty torture, always goes down well, got my own gear, really unusual . . ." but he was ignored.

"Actor—severance of right hand," called out the harelipped assistant. The bruised man hesitated, then stepped forward. No one joined him. The director looked at him for a long time. Then he yawned and said, "Hired." The little man sagged. It was not clear whether he was weak with happiness or with shock.

"Crucifixion," called the girl, "minimum one hour."

Frank stepped forward, feeling a cut above these primitive masochists. Twenty others stepped forward with him.

He hid his surprise, but his pride suffered. He had thought he would be the only one, the only one with enough subtlety to handle the exquisite pain of crucifixion.

The director studied the applicants for some time, his gaze moving impassively over Frank's expression of studied boredom. He chose a tall emaciated man with straggly hair. Frank felt humiliated that he had put himself up for hire and been refused. An evening's martyrdom was something he would have liked . . . someone . . . to feel responsible for.

But he did not leave, stayed instead to listen to the calls for subjects for flogging, branding, partial flaying. He felt a mounting excitement as the end of the list was neared.

"Star part," called the girl, "death by hanging."

There was complete silence in the alley. Traffic-noise drifted in from Shaftesbury Avenue. A pigeon coorooed from its perch on the wall above them. The girl cleared her throat.

"Star part—death by hanging."

Frank stepped forward.

"Hired," said the director.

At a small booth just inside the stage door the actors and actresses were registered and made to sign formal contracts for the temporary use of their bodies. Numbers appropriate to their parts in the show were stamped on the backs of their hands in violet ink. The old man in the booth stamped Frank's hand much harder than was necessary and refused to look at him. Frank was not asked to sign.

In the theatre basement they sat on long benches in the communal dressing room. Moisture dripped down the brown-painted walls. A conical enamel lamp shade swayed gently in the breeze from a street-level ventilator. Some were in a state of barely-suppressed excitement, others apparently impassive. They did not look at each other.

Frank felt euphoric. He was not thinking about the reasons he was here, but he could feel excitement building in his chest. At this time he would normally have been at home, sitting up in bed watching television, steadily smoking ready-rolled joints. He put the palms of his hands together and clasped them between his knees, saw that his legs were shaking, began to hum tunelessly to himself.

A fat man entered the dressing room. He was wearing white trousers and a white t-shirt with sweat stains at the armpits.

"Will you please all go along the corridor to the wardrobe room at the end," he said. "Those of you who need costumes will be fitted and those of you who have lines to say will be given crib-sheets and any necessary instruction. Refreshments are available at the kiosk near the stage door, but do please be back here thirty minutes before showtime."

They began to shuffle out. As Frank passed him, the fat man gently grasped his elbow and said, "Please step into my office, will you?"

Frank followed him through dingy corridors, fascinated by the multidirectional movements of his fleshy body. They entered a large, comfortably furnished room. Thick rugs covered the parquet floor; there were potted plants in a large free-standing box. On the wall were objects Frank did not recognise.

"Ah, yes," said the fat man, "those are relics from a less literal age than ours. The small plastic sacs are blood capsules—a small explosive charge discharged their contents when a blank cartridge was fired. The knife above them is spring-loaded—it was used to stab without harming the actor. In the box are plastic scars and wounds, madman's foam made from egg-white, tears of water in plastic vials fitted with easy eye-applicators. There was a certain amount of artifice in pain in those days." He looked directly at Frank. "The leather harness to your left was used to simulate hanging," he said, waiting for his response with slightly amused curiosity. When there was none, he continued: "The actor would strap it on beneath his clothing and the noose was unobtrusively fixed to that small hook at the back there. Swing for days in that thing without coming to any harm."

Frank heard someone walk rapidly along the corridor past the room, saying, "—and now the bloody Spanish Mare's got a broken leg . . ."

"Sit down," said the fat man. He gestured to a chair upholstered in green velvet. Frank sat down and crossed his legs, rested his elbows on the arms of the chair and clasped his hands over his stomach. He was starting to feel more himself. Here was someone he could react to, someone to whom he could justify his actions, or choose to leave ignorant. Amused condescension appealed to him at that moment, and so he raised his left eyebrow and allowed a faint smile to ever so faintly twist the lines of his mouth.

"Never been in this line of work before, have you?" said the fat man. He smiled momentarily. "Won't get a chance to be in it again, that's for certain. Still . . . you'll have your . . . moment of glory . . ."

Frank was trying to think of something to say that would instantly convince the fat man that the choice of death before an audience was an existential decision meaningful only to him, which automatically excluded puny sarcasm on the part of others, but nothing came. He cranked his smile up a centimeter or so and attempted to look inscrutable.

"Sure you wouldn't like to tell me about your, er, reasons? Might as well not indulge in games at this late stage . . . if you want to tell, get it off your chest . . . you won't get a chance later . . . no one'll be interested. . . ."

Reasons? Frank smiled to himself. The fat man was just like the commuters who came to see his shows: laughably sure of himself, never realising just how small was the circle his power illuminated. His patronizing attitude was not insulting. Only amusing. How could he ever understand, anyway, that the "reasons" were not apparent even to Frank, that his act was like that of the quiz contestant who presses the buzzer as soon as the question is finished, hoping that the answer will occur to him before the cameras close in on his face? Unless . . . this was not an unusual attitude. Perhaps it was more common than any other . . . his stomach went cold as he felt his uniqueness threatened. He realized that he had not spoken for six days. He decided that it would be bad luck to break the silence now. He was funny like that.

"Oh, well," said the fat man, putting his hand to his mouth to cover a yawn, "please yourself. Not important. Probably a woman. Or anything else."

He became quite suddenly businesslike and, going over to a large mahogany desk, began rummaging in its drawers while continuing to talk.

"Payment will be made if you wish it. The rate is a hundred pounds and the money will be paid to a nominee of your choice when your act is completed. You will sign this contract ninety minutes before your appearance and will from that moment be legally bound to fulfill your obligation. In order to ensure that you do not break your contract once signed, you will be guarded, and should you show unwillingness to participate in our spectacle, the guards will forcibly ensure your appearance on stage. It's of no importance, really; many audiences prefer a little, er, coercion—but some actors have a great regard for such things as dignity and pride. . . . Oh, yes, and I'm obliged to tell you that individual funeral requests cannot be met—the Greater London Council insists that all waste biological material from the shows be reserved for the recycling vats." He smiled and gently laid the contract on Frank's knee. "You are due to sign in two minutes. Please use my pen."

Frank had not been impressed by the obviously prepared speech. He was familiar with the use of sadism from a position of power, was in fact quite adept at the practice himself, and he saw the cold description of impersonal death as a weapon hurled at him by the fat man in a battle of personalities, rather than as a factual account of his own impending demise. He signed, and, unwilling to perform for nothing, entered Julia's name and address in the nominee box.

The fat man took the contract and the pen from him. "Oh, in case you're wondering," he said, with the air of someone imparting interesting but not essential information, "about the significance of the ninety minutes? . . . er, that is the minimum time in which we could find another actor for your part . . . less time than that would not make the task impossible, but it would certainly be more difficult." He smiled. "You see . . . men like you are very rare . . . very rare indeed . . . after all, we only use one a night. Admittedly, that *is* every night of the week, and the show *has* been running for thirteen months . . . but what is that compared to . . . say, the population of India? . . . a drop, a mere drop in the ocean . . ."

He smiled.

Frank was fitted with white stockings, black breeches that buckled at the knee, and a loose-fitting white shirt with frills on the chest. Black shoes with large silver buckles completed the outfit.

It was the costume of his fantasies, it was what he had seen himself wearing on the nights when he had stood opposite the Thrill Palace, hands in pockets, staring at the posters and the crowds and the gibbet and noose and dummy body swinging high above the street. It was as if he were being clothed in his dreams. And the costume helped him to approximate his dream-self, for his back stiffened, his shoulders straightened and his determination not to soil himself with speech increased.

As he entered the big dressing room, the raucous opening music of the show blared out. Even filtered by distance it was strident and harsh. The hunchback jerked his head up at the sound. Then he returned, after a brief, embarrassed glance at Frank, to the rapid speech he was making into the microphone of his tape recorder.

An attendant followed Frank to his seat. He adjusted his truncheon in its leather holster and said, "You taking a fee, mate?"

Frank meant to ignore him, but nodded when he saw the small cold eyes.

"Assigned it?"

Frank nodded again. The attendant stared at him a moment, twisting the thong at the top of his truncheon between his fingers, then he grunted and turned to face the room.

"Numbers one to twelve, stir yourselves, numbers one to twelve." He grinned as eight men and four women stood up and looked at him nervously.

"Your big moment has come," he said, "this way, if you please . . . ladies and gentlemen . . ."

He led them out. At the door he said something to the second attendant, who looked over at Frank and shrugged.

Frank had just realized that he had nodded only twice in answer to the guard's questions. Two was not a complete number. He nodded once more to make three. Then he nodded in two more sets of three just to make sure. Three threes was unbeatable.

"Opening's a demonstration mass-beating number, I believe."

Frank looked up and saw the little man with the bruised face.

"They always get the run-of-the-mill stuff out of the way first." He smiled at Frank and tried to look into his eyes. "You and me, now—we're novelties—we're what the public comes to see. We're something special."

Frank stared straight ahead, expressionless.

"Be about an hour before I'm on," said the little man. "Got a tableau part all to myself, costume too . . ." He indicated the badly-fitting cloth leggings he was wearing and the shapeless peasant's jerkin with its big front pocket. "Even got a line . . . I have to say, 'Nay, Lord, I am no thief.' " He beamed. "Yes, that's it: 'Nay, Lord, I am no thief.' " He looked down. "But they don't believe me, of course, and I, er, I get punished."

Frank did not speak or move. The little man coughed. "Of course, the only reason I do this is for the money," he said, "wouldn't do it otherwise." He coughed again. "I suppose you've, er, nominated someone? . . . for your fee, I mean? . . ."

Frank turned slowly and stared at him. The little man blushed bright red and hurried on: "Yes, of course you have, of course . . . don't worry, I'll pass it around, you won't be bothered."

Frank turned away, enjoying the control he was exercising.

The little man looked doleful. "Be nearly an hour before I'm on . . ." he said. He moved slowly away, massaging his right wrist with his left hand.

What would Julia do when she received the check for a hundred pounds? Without allowing himself to indulge in the humiliation of hope, he decided that the fee would be sent with a brochure for *Punishment Follies* and an offer for cut-rate seats. His name would be prominent on the note attached to the check. There would be no doubt in her mind as to what he had done. How would she feel then?

His fantasy faded into darkness. So what? What did her feelings matter? He knew now that she was not important. Four days ago, when he had risen from his desk in the middle of Monday morning, cleared his papers neatly away, put on his coat and picked up his briefcase; four days ago, when he had ignored the puzzled questions of his colleagues, walked calmly out of the room, held the door open politely for Mr. Whittaker as he left; four days ago, when he had quietly waited for the doorkeeper to draw back the great bolts, ignoring his exasperated mutterings, and finally stepped out into the vast shining street; four days ago . . . he had thought he was doing it because of her. For an hour or two he had walked the streets in a vision of golden crucifixion, each grimace of pain mirrored in Julia's repentant face, looking up at him from the foot of the bloody cross.

But he soon forgot about her. She slipped his mind. No, she was not important; he was not doing this for her. It was more as if she were the last insignificant piece of a jigsaw puzzle it had taken him all his life to solve.

"Hello," said the hunchback, delicately perching on the bench next to Frank. "I'm a reporter for *Yellow Sheet*. Do you mind if I talk to you?" He had been fitted with a specially tailored jacket which emphasised his hump, and subtle makeup made his thin sharp features even sharper.

Frank was fascinated by the makeup, which gave extreme heights and depths to the face, and by the great swell of the man's back.

"Oh, yes," said the hunchback, "it's makeup and padding, they had to do it for my spot."

Frank looked blank.

"My spot . . . it's one of the most popular parts of the show apparently . . . it's, er, it's where someone who's, er . . . afflicted . . . is, er, beaten up. If they don't think you're, er, unusual enough, they, er, try to help out a little . . ." He looked suddenly ashamed. "It's for the paper, you see, only way I could get in to do the article. Authenticity, you know?"

Frank turned away. Even if the interview had been for the *Sunday Times* with perhaps a full-colour double spread, his vow of silence would have prevented him taking part. But with this crippled cub reporter and his toilet-paper rag . . . it was ridiculous. Feeling his carefully built-up aloofness threatened, Frank moved farther along the bench and stared stonily into space.

But the hunchback was lost in his own little world. He set the tape moving and with the manner of a man addressing millions, began to speak into a small black microphone:

"I'm sitting here in the actors' dressing room of London's famous Thrill Palace, where *Punishment Follies* has been playing to packed houses for over a year, and I'm about to talk to the actor filling tonight's star part. Why do these men submit to commercially-staged punishment, and some even to death? Is it the money, or is there some deeper reason? Perhaps our star for tonight will enlighten us?" He looked expectantly at Frank, moving the microphone under his nose.

Frank found himself wondering what the medical term for a hump on the back was. He felt a strange urge to run his hands over it. He would have liked to be one of the men who would administer the hunchback's beating tonight.

The hunchback coughed and looked nervously at the guards. "Er, I'm sure our readers would be very grateful for anything you'd care to say, er . . . sir . . . er, anything you'd like to add as to, er, exactly, er . . . exactly why you're here . . ."

The directness of the question panicked Frank, and he began a complicated game which involved pressing the knuckle of his right thumb five times with his left thumb and then the knuckle of his left thumb five times with his right thumb, the whole being repeated five times until five sets of five had been achieved. But it was not enough. The question hummed in his head. The thought of dying pointlessly, like the C.U.D. suicides, filled him with horror.

He imagined the hunchback talking nervously to a C.U.D. priest, holding his microphone up to the clean-shaven face, backing slowly and reluctantly to the wide-open door of the air freighter, hesitating momentarily on the lip of the booming space, and then, in helpless response to the bland, emptily smiling face, ruefully stepping out into air, falling like a sack of brittle sticks towards the wheeling ground, talking, talking into his microphone, apologizing to the telephoto lens with his smile. The image was so persuasive that Frank almost smiled to himself.

The audience roared above him and there was a spate of wild clapping and cheering. "Number twenty-six," called the attendant. The emaciated man with the crucifixion part stood up and left the dressing room. Frank stared after him, ignoring the hunchback's nervous questions. Presently the sound of hammering floated down from the stage. The audience was silent.

Frank turned his attention to the hunchback, and saw that the guards were standing behind him, grinning. One of them tapped him on the hump and said, "You're on next, mate—severe beating, aren't you?" The hunchback smiled sickly and made to unhook the recorder strap from his shoulders. "Oh, that's all right," said the guard, "we'll take care of that for you . . . wouldn't want any of this lot to nick it now, would we?"

They led him away, walking so quickly that he was almost running between them.

Presently a storm of applause floated down from above. Frank had a sudden vision of faces composed of wet slabs of flesh with ears and lips stuck on like lumps of modelling clay, saliva dribbling over stubble and face powder, eyes bright and blank and unblinking, limbs of monumental heaviness stacked against each other like lengths of waterlogged timber. And hands, great soggy puddings of hands, colliding damply with each other, dumb and contented in the warm darkness. Pigs away from the sty for a night, sitting upright and snorting. The old hatred built within him, blistering, bringing tears to his eyes, grinding his teeth together. He wanted to rampage among them with an axe and kill until his whole body was red with blood, he wanted to break and maim and chop and slash until the pieces of the broken bodies could never be fitted together again, he wanted to kill them all and stand triumphant on a mound of severed heads.

But the anger died in his chest as it always did, as if he were filling up with ash. He had never been able to release his hatred because he knew that he would be unable to control himself if he did; he knew that only the destruction of the world could satisfy him. Standing up to his knees in a river of blood, bodies floating and turning like drifting spars as far as the eye could see, the last man left alive on earth, hands covered in blood . . .

He was trembling violently, and he clasped his hands tightly together between his legs in an effort to still himself. The guards returned to the dressing room and he quickly picked up an Instapape someone had left on the bench and forced himself to read, quickly turning the flimsy yellow pages:

MILLIONAIRE SHOT DEAD BY HIS OWN DOG

Armaments millionaire Johann Kreuz was today shot dead by his own dog, a three-year-old bull-terrier named Nicki. Kreuz, who was out hunting, left his loaded double-barrelled shotgun on the back seat of his car with the dog. Nicki's lead tangled in the trigger-guard and when she jumped out of the car to greet her master—

The guards laughed as they smashed the hunchback's tape recorder. Frank turned the page:

TRAFALGAR SQUARE RIOT SPREADS

The riot which began earlier today in Trafalgar Square, scene of a C.U.D. mass-suicide demonstration, has spread down Whitehall to Parliament Square where riot troops have just begun to use automatic weapons on the mob. A smaller riot, started by commuters unable to get to Charing Cross Station because of the riot-barriers which were closed on the south side of the Square, is under control, but the barriers have had to be closed on the Shaftesbury Avenue side of Piccadilly Circus—

"Goodbye," said the little man. He smiled at him as he was led from the room. Frank was alone with the guards. No escape, he thought.

MORE TO BE SQUEEZED INTO HACKNEY HIGH-RISES

The GLC announced today that the density quota of the Hackney high-rise estate is to be increased by 50% to cope with overspill from inner-city areas. This will mean dormitory accommodation for most of the estate's 48,000 tenants, but Mr. Albert Cooper, spokesman of the Tenants' Association, threatens that—

The smell of soggy cabbage and urine was heavy in Frank's nostrils. He was one of the tenants of the Hackney estate, and the article had instantly created for him its powerful all-pervading smell. Fifty percent increase! As it was, his room was only a partitioned section of an access corridor, barely large enough to lie down flat in. But even that was preferable to sleeping in a dormitory with pigs.

Things were going to get worse. It was clear to him now. Soon the world would consist of armed camps, and after that, naked savages in mud-pits. Somehow, gradually, quietly and powerfully, life had become unbearable; a threshold had been crossed and the long slide into coldness and darkness had begun. The only salvation was to go inside and carefully lock and bolt all the doors, shutter the windows, turn out the lights, douse the fire, and wait in perfect quiet, alone. His retreat into himself was complete. There was nothing outside worth seeing. Only endless vistas of pale molluscs jerking back into darkness as sunlight swept over their undersea depths.

He felt that his actions were being endorsed, and when the hand grasped his shoulder, he was ready.

"Wake up, mate," said the guard, "You're on next."

Frank stood. He adjusted the waistband of his breeches. He coughed.

The guards took his arms and led him out of the dressing room. He saw the dingy corridor in absolute detail: olive-green paint, bubbling and cracking; grey concrete floor where his footfalls created eddies of sluggish dust; white ceiling where islands of paint were surrounded by seas of bare plaster, fed by spidery cracks. One of the attendants had blood on his toe-cap, the other had tiny spots of blood on his trousers. A black beetle edged into a crack beneath the skirting board as they bore down on it.

Applause broke out wildly above and the attendants grinned at each other. Footsteps ahead told them that someone was coming along the narrow corridor, and they stopped opposite a room with an open door and moved close in to the wall. The interior of the room looked like a medical tent set up in the middle of a field during some bloody Civil War battle. Two men in white overalls were swabbing blood from the surface of a large wooden table; a man with a white mask over his face was threading a large surgical needle with black cotton. Actors and actresses sat on benches around the walls. Some were unconscious, some moaned softly, some were rocking backwards and forwards as if comforting themselves. One man was slowly licking his lips, his eyes fixed on the opposite wall. Frank saw the hunchback. His face was bloody. And elated.

The little man with the bruised face came along the corridor, supported by two attendants. He was barely conscious. A red stump protruded from his right sleeve. Something was sticking out of the long pocket of his costume. It was a finger. The pocket was slowly staining red. He was taken into the medical room and laid out on the table. Frank imagined him painfully raising himself on one arm, waving his stump, and saying, "Hat-trick—got my hat-trick." But the little man simply lay there, breathing heavily. The doctor began to tend to the stump.

They continued along the corridor and came into the backstage area. Skirting two glowing braziers in which branding-irons rested, and a long upturned blade mounted on wooden trestles, one of which had a damaged leg (". . . and now the bloody Spanish Mare's got a broken leg . . .") the attendants brought Frank into the wings and stopped him. He could see the stage clearly. It was covered with sawdust, stained red. Instruments of pain and torture hung from iron racks. A wooden gallows was being erected in center stage. On a large cross stage right, the emaciated man hung from coach-nails driven through his hands and feet, moaning softly.

The lights went down and a white spotlight played on the black-clad men working on the gallows. A dim red spot focussed on the face of the crucified man. A voice rang out from the speakers, the kind of effortlessly patronising voice used on popular educational programmes on television. It said: "Since man began to walk upright, he has found it necessary to punish those members of his race who do not conform to popularly accepted Law. In primitive times the tribe would simply stone the lawbreaker to death, but as man became more sophisticated, so he created more sophisticated methods of execution. The ancient Egyptians, for example . . ."

The voice faded from Frank's consciousness. He had often felt that many hidden doors would be opened to him if he could release his hatred, that he would be made new in the clean flame of revealed desire. That his desire meant death and pain to others seemed nothing now, although it had always kept him sealed like a blast-furnace before. Always the anger had been turned inward, until the gnaw of self-inflicted pain was second nature to him. Now the ultimate self-hurt. And by some strange reversal he realised that his pain would be felt by the others, his death would spread through the world like a cancer, turning blood into powder, bones into dust. By killing himself, he was killing them, every one. He was about to snuff the world out of existence.

The gallows was complete. A man in black tights and a black mask was standing on the platform, slowly knotting the noose.

"The Spaniards," said the narrator, "have long favoured the garotte . . ."

Frank felt a glacial calmness—a motionlessness of the spirit that was almost frightening. He stood alone, in the safety of his own body, unassailable and perfect. No one was connected to him, there were no decaying memories of people in the corners of the little fortress in his head from which he observed the world in darkness and silence. I am one, he thought, whole and indivisible.

He drew himself up and squared his shoulders. They tied his hands behind his back and tried to put a black bag over his head. He refused it, and began to touch each of his teeth with the tip of his tongue, first from the back, and then from the front. Three threes before they took him on stage.

". . . in regular use in this country until twenty years ago. Tonight we re-stage an execution by hanging for your entertainment. A man will die here before your eyes. The hangman is a direct descendant of Pierpoint, the last great artist of this method of execution, but remember—should he fail to gauge the weight of our victim correctly and shorten or lengthen the rope accordingly . . . death will be a long time coming . . . the hanged man will kick and jerk for some time before slow strangulation causes his heart to stop beating. Of course, we all hope that our hangman will be efficient . . . but only the next few minutes will tell. Ladies and Gentlemen: I give you—*death by hanging.*"

The lights went down. A drum-roll began. The hangman jumped heavily on the trap and then beckoned to the wings.

And suddenly Frank was on stage, smelling the bloodstained sawdust, and off to his right was a great emptiness that drew in its breath and waited. His bowels loosened; his penis stood suddenly and painfully erect. They dragged him up the steps. The smell of the pine overpowering, misting vision, fainting in anticipated pain. Before him the noose, rough and hairy. The nose-tickling smell of the rope. Ah, around his neck. Blood roaring, roaring in his ears. A sudden bang. A feeling of lightness.

I never touched her.

I can't remember her name.

Light spinning, sound throbbing, and the emptiness was faces; ah, yes—faces all looking at

The emptiness sighed.

AND THE TV CHANGED COLORS WHEN SHE SPOKE

Lyn Schumaker

The sky was gray. Harris walked quickly, her skirt clinging to her knees. She could feel the hole in her stocking as a ragged circle of cold. Cold touched her through her blouse; her black overcoat was too large and loose. She looked forward to the small pleasure of the next day, when she would wear the jumper over the blouse. She couldn't wear it more than twice a week; it might be taken as a sign of discontent. Once, at the factory, one of the silent women had been found wearing two sweaters. Nothing had been said, but she had not come back the next day.

Harris walked mechanically, trying not to hunch her shoulders against the cold. In the street were other people dressed in black walking home from work. They did not look at her; she did not look at them. The clouds were full of snow, but none fell.

(it had started with a touch, or the memory of a touch, gentle, unexpected. you are not to be touched, not gently, but she had been touched.)

She turned onto a street in the factory district. At the corner near her building was a small open plaza where the bonfire was set each week. In the center of the plaza was a monument to the end of war. Small sickly trees grew in brick planters at the edges of the plaza. Harris walked past a tree with a blackened crown. The night before, a cat had run screaming from the fire and climbed into the branches. The watchers had leaped back, shaking the sparks from their clothing and laughing.

(it started with a touch, but it became a hand, resting quietly upon a windowsill. the rest was blurred, except that sometimes she could see stars shining through the window.)

Harris lived in a women's building near the factory. She had lived in a nursery five years, in school ten years, and in this building seven years. She remembered nothing else.

(except in dreams.)

Her building was a warehouse that had been converted to rooms. It had bay windows on the upper stories, but all the rooms inside were windowless. The bay windows had been walled off to reduce the loss of heat. Day and night, the seven years she had lived there, Harris's room had been lighted only by a bare bulb in the ceiling and the glow from TV.

(the glow, day and night. It would invade the dreams if it could. she buried her dreams deep.)

At the door of her building she paused to straighten her coat and tuck her hair under the scarf. As she was about to step into the view of TV-at-the-door, a small, catlike cry stopped her. She looked around but saw nothing. She composed her features, stepped in front of the screen and said her number.

"Woman . . . or witch?" TV asked.

"Woman," she answered. She heard a noise at her feet. The screen remained white, and in a moment the door clicked open. She hurried in.

After the door closed she looked around to see if a cat had slipped in with her. She had not dared to look before; TV might have noted her inattention and begun questioning. On her way home one night, a man had taken her by the wrist and pulled her close to him, roughly opened her blouse and begun fondling her breasts. She remembered his eyes gazing impassively down the street. There had been a blemish on his lip. She had been unable to move, unaware of any feeling other than the fear that he might kiss her with his blemished lip. Other people had walked by without looking. At last he had shoved her into the street. Her legs shaking, she had buttoned her blouse and walked to her building. TV had noticed that her top blouse button was missing. It had asked questions, the screen changing color at her answers from angry reds to cold browns and blues. Women had lined up behind her, muttering.

(the cruel colors. if only the eyes could be closed. but don't close them. make the mind blank, safe. nothing happened, nothing happened. face the screen, don't move, don't think. and the colors fade, the door opens.)

She did not find a cat inside the door. A rank smell of cooking floated down to her. At each landing the smell of the communal bathrooms combined with the smell of food. She turned down the hall to her room near the front of the building. She unlocked her door and switched on the light.

(first came the touch, then the hand, then movement—movement like the movement of thoughts in the back of the mind. she could hear it when the wind blew—soft, furtive sounds—behind the wall where the window was.)

Harris left her overcoat on while she made dinner. After a while the room warmed from the cooking, and she took the coat off. On the coldest nights she would pull the overcoat over the single blanket on her bed. She had had two blankets, but one had been stolen. Blankets were scarce; she would not get a replacement. Whatever her discomfort, she dared not complain. The war against physical illness had been won. Only the last and greatest war remained: the war against mind-sickness.

Harris remembered times in her childhood when all the energies of the city had been turned to eradicating the witches and the madness. Bonfires had burned night and day, graying the sky and forcing down the snow from the clouds in a sooty blizzard. Many witches had been burned, along with the cats that spread the contagion. The authorities did not really approve of such messy solutions. But they had benevolently allowed the people to vent their anger upon the mad ones.

(from the sounds and the movement grew a form, back between the wall and the window, away from the TV light. She could not see it clearly. there was a face and mad eyes . . . and a gentle hand . . . and the stars, behind the glass.)

After eating, Harris put on her housecoat and sat on the bed. She listened to the noises of the building, the creak of her neighbor's floor, and the wind sounds that came from the walled-off window. She sat on the bed, and the glow from TV surrounded her, reaching into her mind.

(but the glow did not reach past the wall. there was darkness behind the wall. there were stars beyond the glass. and there was a person.)

She was cold in the thin housecoat, but she did not put on her pajamas. She had not worn them since a night when the building manager had come into her room. It had not been the first night. For a time he had only come in and put his cot on the floor. He would lie there grinning and watching her in the cold light from TV. The other women had looked at her knowingly—it had happened to them. One night he didn't bring his cot, but simply got into bed with her. After a while he pushed her legs apart and tore her pajamas. He did something that had never been done to her before, something that hurt.

(in the space between the wall and the window, she could see the person. the person was a woman.)

The rest of the night she lay under him, breathing his stale breath. While she lay there, afraid to move, two cats met in the night and howled. Not knowing what that meant, she imagined them dying in pain at the hands of the men who walked the streets after dark, looking for witches, for cats. She never wore her pajamas again.

Room-TV came on. She faced the screen, but looked at the bare wall above it and tried to recapture the silence that had been in her mind before. But soon she was watching the screen. It showed a woman. TV was questioning her. "Woman or witch?" it asked. She said, "Woman." They always said woman; they always meant witch. TV knew. The woman panicked. How coarse she looked when she was frightened; how guilty.

The treatment began. With each question the woman screamed in pain, or sobbed. With each question, the colors changed.

Harris watched. She found she could make a mist before her

eyes by not blinking. She let the mist grow between her eyes and the screen. She shut out TV until she could hear nothing but the creaking of her neighbor's floor and the tiny sounds from the walled-off window, the reassuring sounds. When it was very late, the pictures faded and the voices receded into a soft hiss. She prepared for bed, hanging the housecoat on a hook. For a moment she stood naked in the faint glow from TV. The light searched into the crevices of her body as unrelentingly as the low hiss penetrated her head. She lay down under the single coarse blanket. The mattress buttons hurt her back. She tried not to think. It was so quiet that TV might hear. She shut her eyes.

There was a scratching sound. It was not a sound that she had heard before. It came again—from the walled-off window. Quietly she sat up and pried loose a board. She saw a dim shape between the walls. It moved, and shining eyes turned toward her. It was the cat she'd heard come in with her at the door. It stood at the far end of the narrow space, by the wall that closed off the window.

Harris replaced the board to prevent the cat from getting into her room. Then she lay on the bed, trembling.

(the woman sat down and the cat jumped into her lap. they sat in the narrow space between window and wall, and the window was like another wall, a wall of stars.)

After midnight the manager came in, slamming the door behind him. He was rougher than usual.

(behind the wall the woman stroked the cat. her hands were gentle, her hands were strong.)

Once, when the manager hurt her, Harris raised her fist over his head. Then her hand, not knowing its purpose, sank again to the mattress.

When he was done, he raised himself on one elbow, and cold air dried the sweat he had left on her breasts. He lit a cigarette. She lay very still, listening for noises from the window. After a while he went to sleep. The light from the screen allowed shadows in the corners of the room.

"Witch . . . or woman?" TV-at-the-door asked. She straightened her coat, composed her features.

(the woman behind the wall spoke. "what's the difference?" she asked.)

"Woman," Harris said, and gave her number. The door clicked open.

Nearing her room she heard hammering and men's voices. Sawdust was tracked into the hall. The manager came out of the room.

"Come here. Look at this," he said.

She could not move.

"Come on." He stepped out and pulled her by the shoulder through the door. The wall that closed off the bay window was being removed. The workmen stepped on her belongings as they moved from place to place, carrying hammers and two-by-fours.

(the woman stood with her back pressed against the glass. the cat leaped into her arms.)

The manager grinned at Harris.

"I'm moving in."

She nodded numbly.

A workman dropped a two-by-four. It crashed against the glass.

(the woman leaped out of the window, the cat in her arms . . . falling . . . falling . . .)

The manager grinned at her again. There was no room for her with the workmen in the room. She brushed a little sawdust off the bed, then went out into the hall.

(shadows chasing colors, the darkness welling up to break the surface. the shadows, the darkness, the dreams breaking out . . .)

She rushed downstairs and out into the cold. She stood in the street looking up at the broken window. The evening darkened around her. The window was like an empty eye gazing out over the city. The window was like a mouth pouring shadows out over the world.

There was a motion at her feet. A dark shape moved away from her, forming an indistinct shadow as it passed through the glow from TV-at-the-door. A cat? It moved toward the darkness, crying plaintively. It merged with the shadows. Harris followed it.

THE ONLY TUNE THAT HE COULD PLAY

R. A. Lafferty

Tom Halfshell was taking his major in Trumpet, his minor in Nostalgic Folklore, and his outreaching corollary in Monster-Morph.

"That isn't a perfect balance, Tom, my son," his father had said. "The selection is too soft. It's a soft art, a soft science, and a soft speculative syncrisis. My son, you had better introduce a harder and more manly element into your studies."

So Tom took up Hard Geography for his sustaining corollary. This gave him four fields of study beyond the basics, a heavy schedule for even an intelligent young man. And this got Tom where it hurt, because he was not very intelligent. He was intuitive, he was rhythmic, he was effervescent, he was enthusiastic; and he was a young man of tone and taste. But he just wasn't very intelligent.

Still, he got good acceptance by both his elders and his contemporaries. And the hard hand of friendship will help one through almost any course.

Tom and three of his friends, Cob Goliath, Duke Charles, Lion Brightfoot, manly boys all, talked about his deficiencies and advantages, and the varying joys of the world, as they hunted fierce hogs with spears from muleback one spring morning.

"You are an unmatched half, Tom," Cob Goliath shouted as

he doubled back on his coursing mule after a very tricky and tanglefooted hog, "and ours is a world full of matched wholes. Complete yourself, Tom, complete yourself!"

Anything to do with man's best friend the swine is a worthy occupation, and lance-killing is a particular joy. The swine is meat and leather. He is also ferocity and fun and friendship. Spilling hogs' blood is almost as tall a thing as spilling one's own.

"Complete myself, that's what I'm trying to do!" Tom howled as he killed the boar with an absolutely perfect lance thrust, from a bad angle, and already past the beast. And the other young men gasped in admiration.

Tom Halfshell wasn't as big or as strong as these other young men. He hadn't their tough intelligence, or their dedicated hardness, or their steadiness of hand. And yet he made more spectacular kills than any of them, with a real virtuosity of lance and mule-handling and boar-butchering. He was the least of the four in every element that should count high in boar-spearing, but he made the most kills, and he made them more dazzlingly than the others.

One of the things he had was trickiness, a quality not much understood.

"Unmatched Halfshell Tom," Duke Charles sang as he led the charge after more of the fierce and bristling porkers. The four young men had killed nine hogs, and they had three more to go this morning. "Halfshell Tom, it always seems that there should be another half to you somewhere. When they spun the naming wheel, it stopped just right for your name. You do so many things well, and still you are not complete. Why not? There's an OHAFA element in incomplete things. The rest of us are complete. Watch that porker!"

The porker, a solid tusked boar, cut back into the feet of Tom's mule and knocked the beast down. It cut back a second time on a shorter radius and charged Tom, who had barely found his feet after being thrown. It was in too close for Tom to use the lance blade, and he used the lance butt and spun the charge of the boar twice. And then the boar had him—

—but Lion Brightfoot had the boar then, with a slicing, almost backhand thrust of his blade, as Lion's mule, a clattering hack who enjoyed his work, brought him in exactly to "top kill" position on a long sweep.

Ten porkers killed. Two to go. And the shaken but talented Tom Halfshell was on muleback again and leading a new charge.

There was great friendship among these four boys, and they risked their lives and limbs for each other again and again. Their coursing area was only the hog-run behind a small slaughterhouse, and there were surely easier and safer ways to slaughter the hogs. But hogs should be slaughtered splendidly. All things concerning hogs, those totem animals, should be done as splendidly as possible.

Now there was a furious and fleet-footed sow among the porkers left, and she was super-dangerous. There were elements of hate and intuition among sows. Swine were man's best friend, but that didn't apply to the disappearing sows of the species. The sows felt somehow (for they could not really know, since the thing was never mentioned in their presence) that even the remnant of them would soon be replaced by clone-boars.

This fast sow was all the more deadly for being short-tusked and close-coupled. She was murder, challenging and charging murder.

"Thank all things that there is no analogy among men to these fierce carryover animals," Goliath called. "We'd all be better dead than have such savage things within our own species. Watch it, Lion! Watch it, Tom!"

The boys would rather find their eleventh and twelfth kills among the uncomplicated porkers, but this shrilling and squealing sow forced the kill upon them. She threw the mules of Cob Goliath and Duke Charles with charges so swift that those canny-footed animals could not cope with them at all.

But then it was the bloodied Tom on his own lamed mule who killed her with luck and trickery and curious desire. The other three of them did not like to be involved with the remnant sows at all; but Tom Halfshell liked it particularly. He had her in an exciting and bristly kill. His lance had a large gout of flesh on it when he was finished, and Tom for a moment had the notion of having a pet pig from it.

And then the ridiculousness of that idea struck him. It was only from bits of boars' flesh that pigs were ever cloned. Besides, Tom already had one little pet pig. He would wait till it was too big to be a pet before he requisitioned another one.

Then Lion Brightfoot killed the anticlimactic twelfth porker.

Oh, it was all simply hard and hot and bloody work that the boys had to do; but they would not have been boys of the species if they hadn't been able to infuse it with glory. They dragged the dead porkers to the tripods at mule-tail, and they had the first of them hoisted up quickly. They began to skin them to the tune of their own hog-skinning songs. Youth, youth, and the danger and death that it loves to bring to even the easiest task! This was fullness. This was completeness!

Except for Tom Halfshell. And they always joked that he was in some way incomplete. But there was something unusually important coming up this day.

"We are lucky that we will all take part in the Last Man Festival tonight," Lion Brightfoot shouted as he worked the skinning knives and tongs with strong hands. "There have been Last Man Festivals before, but this is the last of them all. This Last Man Who Remembers is a hundred and forty years old, and that doesn't even count the twelve 'given' years. My father says that we will invent other festivals, that we will never run out of festivals; but nothing like this one can ever be held again. It's the end of an era, he says. We will all play tonight in the bands, but only Tom will be with the twelve trumpeters. Will you play the brass trumpet, Tom?"

"No. I think I'll play the conch-shell trumpet," Tom said. "Anyone can play the brass trumpet."

"And no one can play the conch-shell like you," Duke Charles cut in. "You'll drive us clear over the hills with that conch-shell tune of yours, Tom. The way you play the conch-shell, it's *demanding* an answer."

"It is, yes," Tom said, "and sometimes I think that I can hear that answer from over the hills. Mine is one tune that's *supposed* to have an answer. I had a Butterfly Moon Shell once and tried to play it, but I could get no real music out of it at all. And the Butterfly Moon Shell is listed by the musicology museum as 'deceptive and nonmusical.' But I bet *someone* could play it. I bet someone could play the answer to my tune on it. Maybe, to some people somewhere, the conch-shell trumpet is 'deceptive and nonmusical.' No, I can't tell you in words what I mean. But I could tell you on the conch-shell what I mean, if you would only listen and understand it. I bet the Last Man Who Remembers understands it. I saw him yesterday, and he had a mighty deep look to him."

"The Last Man won't understand anything after tonight," Cob Goliath said, as he did fine and strong work with a butcher's saw. "He will die tonight, and he says that he's ready for it. His official title is The *Last* Man Who Remembers, you know."

"Who remembers what?" asked Tom, who was not quite as intelligent as the others.

"Oh, if anyone else remembered what it was, then he wouldn't be the last man to remember it," Lion Brightfoot said reasonably. "And when he is finally dead, then no one at all will know what the old secret was. It was a crumby thing anyhow, they say. And my father maintains that nobody now left would understand it even if it were explained to him."

These four boys had arrived on simultaneous requisitions just about two years before this. They were boys, as good as any you will ever find. And the fact was that men and boys, like everything else, were getting better all the time. Men now had a thorough understanding of what they were doing when they put in their requisitions for sons. They were more scientific about it than ever before. They understood the goal, and they got the results.

"The reason for the world is the enjoyment of the world," was a sound current ethical-scientific statement, "and the reason for men and boys is the fulfillment and pleasure of those same men and boys."

The men and boys did fulfill, and they did please themselves.

They lorded it over the universe and they brought it into accord and resonance with themselves.

These four boys who had come from the potting sheds at the same time were doing quick and hard pork work (the most meaningful and totemistic of all work). And after they had worked, they must go to their instructions. It would be that way all their lives: in the mornings, work; in the afternoons, instructions; in the evenings, enjoyments. Intellectuality and friendship and art and pleasure were the things that life was built upon, and not one of them must be slighted.

These boys usually took their basic courses together; and then they took their majors and minors and corollaries with others who followed the same specialties. But even in the specialty subjects, there were "cross-currents" meetings between the basic friends. And the instructions must be carried out as splendidly as the pig-killings and other things.

Boys came to their instruction years with explosive momentum, and the acquisition of knowledge and skill and understanding was supposed to continue at an explosive pace all their lives. The perfect balance, the passion, and (yes) the serenity, can only come at high speed, as a rapidly spinning top will have balance and surety and serenity. But when it slows down, then it wobbles, and sometimes it falls.

When the boys had been in the potting sheds (the flesh-pots and the mind-pots) they had developed great bodily and psychic and mental intensity, but *they had not been conscious* in any of those areas. They had been in the large, unconscious, amitotic environment of intense activity kept well below the surface. It was there that the requisitions for sons were fulfilled: it was there that the selections were made as to what things should rise above the surface, what things might be kept in harmless somnolence below the surface forever, and what things must be destroyed while they were still below that surface to prevent them from making trouble later.

So it was that the boys broke up through the surface of that environment with bright memories in some areas, and with gappy holes in their memories in other sections. Into the holes in their memories other sorts of things might be flowed during the instructions, things of unrelated substance. But all the boys broke through that old surface with great power, like porpoises leaping, like rockets riding on controlled explosions, like shouting stones hurled by spring-released catapults. And when the boys surfaced they became conscious, and they were all registered as having the "given" age of twelve years. (They might have been in the amitotic environment anywhere from six weeks to six months: but not twelve years.)

Tom Halfshell went at noon to his instructions in his major of Trumpet and related subjects. Horns were paramount in the musical part of the instructions. All boys arrived with the memory of blowing a sort of Triton's horn in the depths of a sea. Drums and gongs and bells and clanging iron were important in their music also, and the rattling and singing woods, and even strings and keyboards. But it was the horns, and their cousins the pipes, that were the royal instruments.

Tom Halfshell played the brass trumpet as formal instrument, and the conch-shell trumpet as informal instrument. And he was good, much better than any of his fellows, on brass or wood or shell or bone horns, or pig-tooth whistles or penny whistles, or even on that most royal of all instruments, the squealing pig-stomach bagpipe. And yet he was not at ease with the pig-pipe, nor it with him.

"You are much better than the other boys, Tom," the instructor told him, "but they are complete, and you are not. There is something amiss with your blowing. There may even be outlawed OHAFA elements in your tune. Your tune keeps looking for a missing piece and calling out for it. But, by the character of the world that we live in, there is no such missing piece. Do you understand that?"

"I understand it as a statement, but sometimes I feel otherwise as a feeling," Tom Halfshell said.

"You are not allowed to feel *too* otherwise," the instructor told him. "I am recommending that you change your major from the trumpet to the pig-stomach bagpipe. Your father is a piper and not a trumpeter, and his requisition for you was for a piper."

"No, I must stay with the trumpet and the conch-trumpet," Tom said. "My tunes will not talk right on anything else."

"You seem to have an endless repertoire of tunes," the instructor said. "You seem to have them, but you haven't. All the things that you play are variations of the same tune. Leave that tune, Tom. You play it well, but incompletely. Play other tunes, even if you play them badly for a while."

"No, I can't," Tom said. "It's the only tune that I can play."

"But it has OHAFA elements in it."

"I don't know what those elements are, and you can't or won't tell me."

"Ah, I always hate to see a boy chopped down before he ever becomes a man," the instructor said sadly. "Your blood be upon yourself!"

In his minor, Nostalgic Folklore, Tom Halfshell also had his difficulties, to go along with his splendid experiences. Nostalgic Folklore was full of holes: that was the best that could be said about it. There had been changes made. Once it had not been all swine Myth and solar Myth. Once, perhaps, there had been moon myth in it, and other things. But you could sure get yourself demerited if you asked why there were no moon myths now. There were quite a few areas that you had to avoid.

And the name of the course was the trickiest thing about it. Yes, it *was* very evocative of nostalgia: but there were so many sections of forbidden nostalgia. There were blood memories whose expression had been erased. And there was foolish stuff of poor quality that had been put in to fill the holes where something had been torn out by the roots. In particular was the land or plateau of OHAFA blocked out, and yet there was evidence that any tricky boy could see that the land had once been central to folklore.

Monster-Morph was a powerful course. It converged on man as its center. Man himself was the golden monster to whom all the roads and designs ran. And the primordial morphs of man were all interesting, trolls and boogermen, bears and apes and swine, lions—ah, and eagles, giants and ogres, cyclopses, and one-eyed pirates. The last was quite revealing, for man seemed to be returning to the powerful single-eyed vision that had once been his. Modern man was particularly accident-prone to the blinding of one eye (but not both). One man in three now wore a black patch over the blinded left (or sinister) eye, and it was a patch of honor. And Tom had learned that, as a thing quite recent, men were requisitioning cyclopean, or one-eyed, sons. And they were getting them too, now, for the first time, in this very season. There is much to be said for the power of the single vision.

The power of monsters was assumed into man, and what man or boy would not glory in such an accretion? But Tom Halfshell was bothered by a devious monstrosity omitted. There had to be complementary shapes to the power-monsters, and there weren't. There had to be complementary colors and after-images to the golden solar swine who was Man. But something had happened to the ability to see after-images.

Over the hills was a land named OHAFA, but it wasn't on the maps of Musicology, Nostalgic Folklore, or Monster-Morph. That is why Tom had selected Hard Geography as his sustaining corollary when his father had advised him to take an additional instruction. Tom wanted to learn some Hard Geography about one particular place.

And there was some semihard geography about the particular place, but not really hard. There was even the statement that OHAFA was a generic term and that there might be a dozen or so of such regions (none of them very big) in the world. There was also the statement that OHAFA might be regarded as an archipelago of many land-surrounded islands, showing the same (non-geographic) characteristics in every instance.

"There is something in the OHAFA Archipelago that has cut us off as sheerly as we have cut it off," was one statement. But was it a statement of Hard Geography? As geographical information, it was very frustrating.

There was only shadow information about the place in

Musicology and Nostalgic Folklore and Monster-Morph and Hard Geography. There were only fossil memories (having the shape, but not the content) of the place that came out of the pottery sheds and the daily world. But Tom found that it would not be possible to go to the place.

"You have already broken it by asking," the instructor in Hard Geography said. "A well-raised boy would not have the trickery to ask. No, permits to go there are not given to *anyone* now, nor have they been for many years. It is a sign of criminality even to ask.

"Ah, I always hate to see a boy chopped down before he ever becomes a man. Your blood be upon yourself!"

But sometimes Tom Halfshell rose late at night and went to the high Festival Meadow to blow powerfully on his conch-shell trumpet. He would blow, and then listen for an answer. He would blow, and then listen again. But the answering music-call (Tom had a fantasy that it would come from an unplayable shell-trumpet of the Butterfly Moon Snail) never came from that inland island beyond the hills.

Then, on the last night of them all for him, the answer did come briefly, in a briefness of only seven notes. But it came just a little bit too late for Tom to hear it.

That was on the night of the Last Man Who Remembers Festival. Tom Halfshell had been selected as one of the twelve high horn-boys for that festival. Really, he wasn't that good. He was better than any of the others in his instruction classes, but the dozen high horn-boys for this festival were selected out of hundreds of instructions classes. There may have been a hidden reason for Tom being selected to so high an honor. There were a lot of cryptic remarks bounced off him that final evening.

Even Tom's father said, as several of the instructors had said in the same stilted words, "Your blood be upon yourself!"

"Let it be in myself and on myself then," Tom said cheerfully. "My blood sings in me tonight."

"The only song that you can play, is that what it sings to you?" his father asked.

"Yes, it does sing that, and maybe some additional trumpetings also. Father, that is a requisition for a son that you are filling out there. And that is a cloning vial of your flesh and blood that you are packaging with it. That is not a legal thing for you to do. You already have a son—myself."

"It will be legal," Tom's father told him. "I am dating it tomorrow, and I won't mail it until after midnight."

The Last Man Who Remembered was a crowing, cackling little rooster of a fellow. He was a hundred and forty years old, and that didn't even count the twelve "given" years.

"Heh, heh, they weren't 'given' to me," he cackled to an audience of a million men and boys. "I came before that. I'm the only one left who came before."

There were about a million men and boys there. The people liked to invent festivals every week or so and flock to them. There was an eighty-acre festival ground between the city below and the hills beyond. The people watched one half of a football game. Then they had band music and speaking and short snatches from the Last Man Who Remembered.

"Heh, heh," the Last Man Who Remembered crowed to the people. "They ragged and they nagged. And what can you do with naggers and raggers? Get rid of them, that's all."

And an officer of some high station addressed the crowd briefly: "Ours is a world to be lived in. It is a complete world. It is the way we like it."

They had the semifinals of the regional pig-sticking tournament then, and some of the best riders and lancers in the nation took part. They had three hundred marching bands, but they often had more than that at their weekly festivals. They had thirty speakers, loaded with wit and wisdom, and limited to thirty seconds each. They had the second half of the football game then.

All of these things were carefully balanced and interspersed. And again and again they cut back to the Last Man for his remarks:

"Heh, heh," the Last Man Who Remembered cackled. "They thought that we couldn't get along without them. We showed them. There used to be the saying 'You can't live with them and you can't live without them.' And then there came along a taller saying, 'The hell we can't live without them!' "

"This Last Man Who Remembers will soon be on his way out of the world," an official announced. "He will be accompanied by a boy, and by the pet pig of the boy."

The select dozen horn-boys blew with such trumpeting power that there were, here and there in the assembly, burst ears and blood running down jowls. The boys blew superbly, but one of them, so it was bruited about by those who understood high trumpeting, blew incompletely. This incomplete trumpeter would have to be killed, the rumor said. But one always hates to see a boy chopped down before he even becomes a man.

There was a heavyweight prize fight, very good, and it ended in a knockout in four rounds.

"Heh, heh, they were always more trouble than they were worth," the Last Man Who Remembered was cackling to the assembly. "Well, we *did* give up something when we gave them up, heh, heh, but I'm the only one who remembers what it was, so it won't matter to the rest of you."

"There are still some few persons who are incomplete and unsatisfied," another high official announced. "There's about one of them in a million. They believe that they're missing something. Some of them even believe that the missing element lingers on the other side of the hills. But all of us who have our sanity and balance know that there is nothing worthwhile over the hills, that we're not missing anything. What could there possibly be that we don't already have?"

The twelve loud trumpets spoke again, and then one of them predominated. It didn't win a prize for loudness, or for excellence either. It won a temporary first place by the trickiness of its tune. There was shocking joy in that tune, but there was more joy in the knowledge that there would be extra bonus blood spilled that night.

"Hey, hey, 'tis said that some of them are still left in OHAFA valleys," the Last Man Who Remembered crowed. "I never believed it."

And now the action picked up pace and moved to the climax. Twelve trumpets shouted together. And then eleven of them fell silent, and a single one kept on with its strange tune that seemed to be requiring an answer or at least a counterpoint. "It's the only tune that he can play," people with special trumpet knowledge told their neighbors. Then the lone trumpeter with his conchshell trumpet still roaring and soaring came to the very center of the arena. His pet pig was at his heels; and the finest riders and lancers came to that same center which was really the coursing area.

The Last Man Who Remembered, wired for sound so that none of his observations might be lost, was brought to that central area.

"Heh, heh, we got rid of them," he cackled. "Good riddance. They kept the whole world in a turmoil. How is it that the trumpet-boy knows about them, though? Well, no matter. He'll be going with me."

Tom Halfshell, the trumpet-boy, still played. The expert pig lancers were in the mule saddles to make their kills and send the three creatures on their way.

"Heh, heh, they're well forgotten," the Last Man crowed. "They were one kind of fun, but there were so many other kinds of fun that you couldn't have when they were in the world. Why, you couldn't even have a pig-sticking pageant with them around."

A lancer got the old Last Man then. He was down, dead on the turf, with a self-satisfied grin on his face. And an era was over.

Tom the trumpeter blew powerfully and disturbingly again. A lancer killed the pet pig, a very tricky small target. The little pig was stretched out on the turf at the head of the dead Last Man.

Tom blew his powerful half-tune again. Then it was cut off sharply by a lance. He was down dead, and he was placed on the turf at the feet of the dead Last Man. That was the end of the pig and the boy and the man, and of any secret that they might know.

But an answer to the tune of Tom Halfshell arrived then, distantly, but clear and carrying, from "Over the Hills and Far Away," played on the unplayable trumpet-shell of the Butterfly Moon Snail.

This really *was* an answer to Tom's tune, a convincing answer, and it thunderstruck a million men and boys—while seven notes of it sounded—and then it was cut off sharply—by a murdering lance.

There is no faking a lancing.

SURVIVORS

Rita-Elizabeth Harper

I haven't wanted to write in my journal for a long time. Not since our town was attacked. When the fighting got close Momma decided we should run away and join the refugees hiding in the woods. We lived there for five weeks until Momma thought it would be safe to go home again. But when we came back to town the Citizen Protection Force had taken over. They said we couldn't live in our house or even in our town anymore. Momma says we have to do what they tell us because they are our protectors so we left our town.

We took the train to the relocation center in the city but we didn't ride in the passenger cars, we had to ride in box cars with a lot of other people. I hated riding the train like that. The toilet was a bucket in the corner hidden behind a blanket somebody hung from the ceiling. It was dark and smelly in the box car and the little ones cried all the time because they were scared. Sometimes Momma would sing to them to make them stop crying. And when she did all the people would listen and some of them would sing, too.

The relocation center was a big gymnasium. We stayed there almost a month. At first there were some people we knew from our town but new people came and the others left and after a while everybody around us was strangers. Every time somebody we knew left Momma would cry.

A few days ago it was our turn to leave. The protectors at the relocation center made us get on the train again. We have finally stopped but I am not sure where we are and we have come so far I wonder if Papa will ever find us. There are no telephones, there is no electricity. The train we came on has left and no one knows when it will return. But the protectors say we are safe here. They say they have been ordered to take care of us until peace comes and we can go home again. I hope it will be soon.

We are in the mountains in what is left of a town and after two days of waiting we've been assigned a living place. Momma says at least we have a home again. The protectors have given us an apartment on the top floor of an old brownstone house. There is a kitchen and a living room but the best part is the bathroom because the plumbing still works. We can use the toilet and Momma says even if we don't have soap anymore we can wash clothes and take baths. The protectors say we can drink the water, too, but it has to be boiled for a long time first. In the living room there is a sort of stove made from a big metal drum that sits on bricks laid on the floor. Ned, Carrie and I have a mattress and there is another for Momma, Jane and Baby Anna. There is an old blue armchair with a high curved back and cushioned seat. Carrie decided the chair will be Momma's throne and we will all sit on the floor at her feet like loyal subjects adoring a queen. Momma laughed and said she was glad Carrie remembered fairy tales but the chair was not a throne and she was definitely not a queen.

Momma woke us early. The protectors gave us food when they assigned our living place so we had bread and milk and cereal for breakfast. Then we went to work cleaning our apartment. Ned and Carrie dragged the mattresses out to the landing and hung them over the stair railing to air out. Momma said she would like to scrub them but they look so old and ragged she's afraid they will fall apart. While we washed the walls, Momma scrubbed all the clothes.

It is after lunch now and Momma has sent Ned to the protectors' warehouse to get firewood. Carrie saw a little girl playing in the alley and begged Momma until she was allowed to go out and play. I am stuck taking care of the little ones because when Momma went out on the landing to remind Ned to get matches she saw a woman on the stairs and decided to get acquainted. It always seems like everyone but me can just go and do what they want. I'm either watching the little ones or helping Momma.

The woman downstairs is Marie Christen. She came up to have supper with us tonight. She is very pretty and young, and she has a sleeping room all to herself, but she has to share her bathroom and kitchen with the man next door. Marie said the man expected her to cook and clean for both of them and to act like his wife. She refused and told him she was already married. Then he told her things being the way they were she was probably a widow and it wouldn't be long until she was knocking on his door. Marie said she was afraid of him and what he might try. Momma said she could understand the way Marie felt but that we should feel sorry for a man who was scarred inside and out. He is so ugly I don't blame Marie. The right half of him is normal but on the left side his face is scarred and puckered and he wears a patch over his left eye. There is no ear on that side either, just the hole that goes into his head. His left arm is bent at the elbow and strapped to his chest with a belt.

Tomorrow I am to go down and help Marie clean her room and the bathroom and kitchen. But I don't mind. She talks to me the same way she talks to Momma, like we are friends.

Marie has four dresses, two skirts and three blouses. And three pairs of shoes. She laughed when I got excited about her clothes, but in a nice way. She said that when she was evacuated she only had to carry things for herself and having pretty clothes made her feel good. She has two china plates and two cups with handles. And a soft blue towel and washcloth and a yellow crocheted coverlet.

Marie and I worked together all morning on her room, the

kitchen and bathroom. Her mattress is half the size of ours, her chair is only a wooden kitchen one, and there isn't a door on the closet, but we scrubbed the walls and floor, covered the mattress with the blanket and the chair with the coverlet and the room doesn't look bad at all.

Each day while Ned and Carrie take care of the little ones, Momma, Marie and I walk to Line. People in Line have started to smile and chat with each other while they wait and Momma says it is good for people to get to know one another.

Marie and I have named the protectors who give out our allotment. "Nextplease" is the man in the wheelchair who sits at the table and checks off each family's name. He does not smile. He says the name, checks it off his list, says "Next, please," pauses, glances up at the next person, says the name, checks it off, repeats "Next, please," and so on through everyone in the line just like a machine.

"Grayeyes" is next. Marie named him because she says he always seems to smile at her with his eyes. I've never seen it but Marie says I'm not looking the right way. Grayeyes has only one arm. The left sleeve of his uniform is folded neatly at the elbow and pinned to his shoulder. With his right arm he holds a clipboard, balancing it by pushing the end against his waist.

"Slowpoke" takes each family's allotment bag and fills it with the things Grayeyes reads off his list. After each item Grayeyes has to wait for Slowpoke to go to a box and get it. Slowpoke can't move quickly because his right leg is turned almost sideways and he drags it behind him when he walks.

When our bags are filled we walk back to the apartment and Momma makes lunch. Marie eats almost all her meals with us because she doesn't want to cook in her kitchen with the man around.

Marie is teaching me scavenging. There used to be a lot of houses in this town but nearly all of them were destroyed. The part we live in is downtown. Marie and I walk out to where the houses were and poke around in the charred wood and fallen stone. We have found dishes, pots and some silverware. It is funny how things are buried under the debris but aren't broken.

Yesterday we found some books in a cellar under what used to be a school. I brought them home and Momma spent an hour cleaning off the mud and smoothing out the pages. Two of them are partly burned but the third one is only moldy from the damp cellar. We now have copies of *Jane Eyre, Montgomery's Elementary English* and *The Encyclopaedia Britannica, "Extract to Gamb"* sitting on our closet shelf. Momma says we can read six pages every evening after supper.

Momma says we must think about school. She says she will teach us and we will study a few hours in the mornings and afternoons just like before. Marie and I have been scavenging all summer and we have four more volumes of the encyclopaedia and two other books. But there aren't any tablets to write our lessons on—even my journal is beginning to run out of paper and I can only write a little every few days. Momma says there is no reason not to have school, though. We will read and recite what we have learned out loud.

The protectors say the train will be here any day with more supplies and news. Momma and Marie hope they will be able to send letters when the train leaves again to let Papa and Marie's husband know where we are.

In October I will be twelve years old. I wish there could be cake and presents.

Today at Line the protectors cut our food allotment. We got one less can of soup and one less can of pork and beans, not as much cereal and we will only get one loaf of bread a week. They say it will only be until the train comes with more supplies.

There is snow now and the protectors say the train won't be able to come until spring. They have cut our allotment again.

Finally we can go outside. It seemed like winter would never end. The protectors say the train will probably come soon.

Momma says when it's warmer we can go into the woods and find nuts and berries.

Baby Anna can say her ABC's and count to twenty. I taught her how. Momma says I am good at teaching even though I get impatient sometimes. Momma says we will divide our little school in two parts—I can teach Jane and Anna in the mornings and Momma will teach Ned, Carrie and me in the afternoons while the little ones nap. Even Marie is helping—she is teaching us to draw. Momma was upset when Marie first suggested the art lessons because the only materials we have are charcoal from the stove and we only have the floor to draw on. But Carrie got so excited that Momma gave in. She said, "Everything washes." So twice a week we have art class in the afternoon. The little ones get to draw for half an hour before their nap but all they do is scribble and make a mess. Ned and I try to draw the things Marie tells us to but our drawings never look right. Marie says Carrie is the artist in our family. She can draw people and trees and houses. She even drew a picture of Momma sitting in her chair and it looked like Momma.

We have waited all summer for the train to come and the protectors have cut our allotment twice. Last night I heard Momma and Marie talking after we had gone to bed. Marie says some people are sick and yesterday the protectors caught two men trying to break into the warehouse. Momma said she couldn't blame them because they were only trying to take care of their families. Marie said there are ways of getting extra food but Momma said she wouldn't talk about it.

In six weeks I will be thirteen. Momma says there will be a surprise for my birthday. She says I'm starting to become a young lady, and that if Papa could see me he would be very proud. We don't talk about him very much. It's almost like we have forgotten him and the times before.

I am scared because I think Momma is dying. I noticed when she stopped eating with us but when I asked her she would say she hadn't slept well and had gotten up early and eaten then. But she seemed to get more and more tired. She made me start doing the washing, mending and cleaning in the apartment all by myself. Then she said I was old enough to teach Ned and Carrie as well as Jane and Baby Anna. Now she just sits in her chair and watches me. Sometimes she corrects me when I do something wrong. Or sometimes she will tell Ned or Carrie to help me.

Last week she told the protectors I would be coming alone to pick up our food. Nextplease made a mark by our name in his book and Momma hasn't gone to Line since. She sits in her chair and seems to get smaller. When we went to bed Momma would be sitting in her chair watching us, and when we got up in the morning, she would still be sitting there watching. Last night Baby Anna crawled on Momma's lap and Momma held her and crooned to her a little sing-song about Papa coming to find us soon.

Then this morning Momma was so weak that Ned, Carrie and I had to lift her from her chair and lay her on the mattress. I tried to make her eat and she did have a little soup but in a while she threw it up. She seemed to sleep then.

I know she has stopped eating because there is so little food and our allotment is so small. But we can live on it if she will only try.

When I came home from Line Momma told Ned and Carrie to take the little ones out for a walk. I knew she wanted to talk to me but somehow I was afraid of what she would say. I went into the bathroom and took a long time using the toilet and washing. Then I put away the food, wiped up the kitchen and finally brought another piece of wood in for the fire. There was nothing else I could do so I sat on the floor in front of Momma because I knew she was waiting for me.

She said a lot of things I didn't want to hear. Things about taking care of the little ones and the apartment and myself. It isn't fair for her to think about dying and leaving me alone to take care of everything. She sounded tired and I told her to rest but she kept talking like it was important for her to get everything said before she fell asleep. I've got to make her eat. I can't take care of all of us.

Momma is dead. Jane and Baby Anna woke me up crying. They said Momma was cold and when I tried to wake her I knew. I'm so frightened. I don't know what to do. I almost hate Momma for giving up and dying and leaving me alone.
Marie came up to remind me of Line. I don't think she is surprised about Momma. She is making me go to Line and she says we will decide what to do when we get back.

My new journal was my surprise birthday present. When I hold it in my lap and look at it I can feel Momma's love. I can see her and Marie saving all the bits of paper to make the pages.
Marie came to sit with me like she promised. I don't know what to do with Momma's body. We can't tell the protectors because if they know they will cut our food again. So many people have died that the protectors dug a grave-ditch for the bodies. I can't stand the thought of them taking Momma there and throwing her in.
Marie picked up my journal and held it. On the cover Momma wrote, "To my daughter Alexandria Dorian Thomas on her thirteenth birthday." I watched Marie trace the words with her fingers and I knew she was thinking of Momma. Marie told me then about how she and Momma made my journal. She said, "The night before your birthday your mother came down after all of you were asleep. We tore all the sheets into the same size and your Momma pushed the holes in the sides with a fork. She had to wait three weeks to get a cardboard box from the protectors and we used a side of it to make the covers but we couldn't figure out how to tie it together until your mother had the idea of unraveling part of her sweater. We cut the yarn in pieces and braided it to make the ties. We worked on it all night."
Then Marie said to me, "Your mother was a very beautiful person but she was not strong and she was not a survivor. She could have done things to get more food. But your mother wouldn't."

When I came home the little ones were crying and Ned's face was bloody. Carrie was curled up in Momma's chair and she wouldn't say anything or even look at me.

Momma's body is gone.

Poor Neddy isn't very strong but he tried to stop them. I don't think he's hurt. I cleaned off the blood and looked for cuts but I think he just got a bloody nose and bumped his head when the woman pushed him down.

I had to shake Carrie to make her look at me. She started crying and saying that it was her fault because she told the little girl across the alley that Momma was dead. It was the little girl's mother who came and took Momma's body. At least the woman will not tell the protectors about Momma because she knows I would tell them what she has done.

Carrie is still crying. But she is only ten and I think she will eventually forget. I've told her I'm not angry and I will keep telling her that it will be all right because I think that is what Momma would have done. But I don't know what I will say when she asks me why the people took Momma's body. I cannot think about it anymore.

It is getting colder. This morning there was frost on the windows on the inside. I made Anna and Jane get in bed with Ned and Carrie and told all of them to stay there and keep each other warm until I got back.

When I knocked on Marie's door she did not answer for a long time. When she opened the door just a little and told me to go on without her, I saw the gray uniform on the chair through the crack in the door.

The cement was very cold and my bare feet hurt before I was to the end of the first block. I will make shoes this afternoon for me and Ned and Carrie. It will snow soon and we can make a little money fetching wood bundles for people. I have enough cardboard to make the soles double-thick if I can remember how to cut the feet part the way Momma did last winter. We still have some wool cloth and I can use some yarn from Momma's sweater to sew them together. Anna and Jane will want shoes, too, to play outside. They will not understand that I don't have enough material to make shoes for all of us.

The protectors have cut the allotment again. Only one can of milk and one can of soup each day and only half a loaf of bread a week. Nextplease could not even glance at the people. He asked for names and did not take his eyes off the checklist.

Ned and Carrie have worked hard and earned a dollar. I took the money to Marie and asked her to get me some meat. She took my money and told me she will bring me what she can find. I know she will buy human meat with the money but I cannot do anything about that. We are hungry and we must have more food.

Marie brought back a little bundle wrapped in old yellow paper. She showed me how to use a little bit in the soup and cook it a long time to make sure it is done. Then she told me it is cold enough that if I put the meat by the kitchen window at night it will not spoil. During the day I must wrap it tightly so water cannot get in and put it in the back of the toilet where the water is always cold.

When we are finished with the meat I can dry the wrapping paper and use it for more pages for my journal. I think I will give half of it to Carrie, too, so she can draw a real picture that we can hang on the wall and keep. I hope she can remember how to draw Momma sitting in her chair.

I went down to find Marie after I put the kids to bed but when I knocked there was no answer. I turned to go back upstairs and the man was standing by his door watching me. He said he had a few extra cans of food and asked if I would like to have them for the children. I remembered what Marie said about him. But I remembered, too, that Momma said we should be kind to people like him and they would begin to be kind back. I followed him through the door. It was dark in his room but when I turned around I saw him shut the door and stand in front of it. I was suddenly very scared but I asked him where the cans were. He said I would have to pay for the food and I told him I didn't have any money. He said I didn't need money and I knew what he meant. I stood still while he took off my dress. He pushed me down on his bed, unzipped his pants and got on top of me.

I lay still and tried not to think about what he was doing. When he rolled off me I jumped up and grabbed my dress. I made myself stand still, put it on and ask him where the food was. He started laughing and I knew then that he didn't have any extra food and I wanted to hit him in the face and stop his laughing but I ran instead.

In our bathroom I washed myself again and again. After my bath I put another piece of wood on the fire and curled around Jane and Baby Anna and tried to get warm.

I have thought about it a lot. What the man did to me was ugly and it hurt but I know Marie gets food and money from the protector for it. I am going to ask her how I can do that, too. And how I can make the man pay me to let him touch me.

This morning when I went to get Marie to go to Line I told her about what the man did. I asked her about letting a protector touch me for food and she looked at me for a long time. Then she began crying and I got embarrassed and left. I don't know if she will help me get to know a protector or not.

Marie didn't come up to have supper with us and I was afraid she was still upset, so after I put the kids to bed I went down to talk to her. The man's door was open and I heard Marie call me from his room. She was lying on the floor covered with blood. The man was on the floor, too. There was blood and hair and skin and brains where his head should be. It made me sick. When I stopped throwing up I went upstairs and got Ned. We dragged Marie to her room and put her on the bed.

I've cleaned her up and her shoulder has finally stopped bleeding. She is very white and cold. I had Ned bring down another blanket but her skin still feels cold. While I was cleaning her she talked to me a little. She said she was very angry at the man because of what he did to me and she went to tell him to leave me alone. The man laughed at her and she slapped him. He came at her with the knife. She saw the hammer, grabbed it and hit him. Sometime while they were fighting he cut her with the knife. She said she kept hitting him until he fell down and didn't move anymore. She cried while she was telling me about it. She cried until she fell asleep.

I've sat with Marie all night. I don't know what to do to help her. I don't know what to do about the man across the hall. I have to go to Line and get our food.

I walked the two blocks to Line and tried to figure what to do. No one ever speaks to the protectors but I knew I had to ask them to give me Marie's food for her. When I was in front of Nextplease I asked him if I could please have the food for my friend Marie Christen. When he looked up at me I wanted to turn and run and I almost did but Grayeyes stepped over and laid his clipboard down beside the name book. When he spoke to me I looked into his eyes and I knew it would be all right because they were soft gray and not angry and there was understanding in his voice. He told me that I could have the food this time but the next time my friend was ill she must send a written message that I was to pick up her food. Nextplease marked off both my name and Marie's. When I picked up the bag of food Grayeyes spoke to me. He said, "Tell Marie I will be there soon."

Marie is still very white and cold and I cannot wake her up. I've made a fire and there is nothing to do but wait for Grayeyes.

It was snowing and the room was almost dark when he came. He asked me what had happened and I told him everything. About the man touching me and about Marie getting mad and the man cutting her and her killing him. While he listened we moved Marie's mattress closer to the fire and he had me light the candle so he could look at her shoulder. He held her wrist and told me to be quiet a minute, then, after a little time, he told me to go on.

When I finished talking he sat on the mattress by Marie and

stared at the candle. We didn't say anything or look at each other until Ned came down to ask about supper. He stopped talking when he saw the protector sitting by Marie, but Grayeyes smiled at him and told me to go upstairs and take care of the kids. When I had fed them and made them get into bed to keep warm, I told Carrie to read to them and took a cup of soup down to Grayeyes.

He took the soup and thanked me. I sat on the floor by him and watched him eat. A little later he put his jacket around me and I fell asleep leaning against his knee while he stroked my hair.

My life has changed very quickly. Marie is dead. She died two days after she killed the man. Grayeyes and I stayed with her all the time but she never woke up. A week ago the protectors took away both Marie's body and the body of the man across the hall. I went down and brought all of Marie's things to our apartment. Her clothes and shoes are only a little too big for me. Ned and I went through the man's apartment and found shirts and pants that I can make over for him and Carrie. There were also a pair of boots and a blanket. We will be warm now through the winter.

I made Ned help me drag Marie's and the man's mattresses upstairs. We laid them together on one side of the stove for Ned and Carrie. Jane's and Baby Anna's mattress is on the other side. They will be warm that way. Then we dragged the other mattress into the kitchen.

I will be colder sleeping alone in the kitchen away from the fire. But Grayeyes has come to me a few nights already and I will not always sleep alone. In the kitchen the little ones cannot see what I do. On those nights when Grayeyes comes he brings us things. He brought Carrie a tablet for drawing and he brought me a dictionary. He also brings extra food or a little money to buy extra food. We will survive through the winter.

ON THE NORTH POLE OF PLUTO

Kim Stanley Robinson

Sometimes I dreamed about Icehenge, and walked in awe across the old crater bed, among those tall white towers. Quite often in the dreams I had become a crew member of the *Persephone,* on that first expedition to Pluto in 2541. I landed with the rest of them on a plain of crater-pocked, shattered black basalt, down near the old mechanical probes. And I was there, in the bridge with Commodore Ehrung and the rest of her officers, when the call came in from Dr. Cereson, who was out in an LV locating the magnetic poles; voice high, cracked with excitement that sounded like fear, radio hiss sputtering in his pauses: "I'm landing at the geographical pole— You'd better send a party up here fast. . . . There's a . . . a *structure* up here. . . ."

Then I would dream I was in the LV that sped north to the pole, crowded in with Ehrung and the other officers, sharing in the tense silence. Underneath us the surface of Pluto flashed by, black and obscure, ringed by crater upon crater. I remember thinking in the dreams that the constant radio hiss was the sound of the planet. Then—just like in the films the *Persephone* brought back, you could say I dreamed myself into the films—we could see forward to the dark horizon. Low in the sky hung the little crescent of Charon, Pluto's moon, and below it—white dots. White . . . a cluster of white towers. "Let's go down," said Ehrung quietly. A circle of white beams, standing on their ends, pointing up at the thick blanket of stars. . . .

Then we were all outside, in suits, stumbling toward the structure. The sun was a bright dot just above the towers. Far away as it was, it still cast as much light as the full moon does on Terra. Shadows of the towers stretched over the ground we crossed; members of the group stepped into the shadow of a beam, disappeared, reappeared in the next slot of pale sunlight. The regolith we walked over was a black dusty gravel. Everyone left big footprints.

We walked between two of the beams—they dwarfed us—and were in the huge irregular circle that the beams made. It looked as if there were a hundred of them, each a different size. "Ice," said a voice on the intercom. "They look like ice." No one replied.

And here the dreams would always become confused. Everything happened out of order, or more or less at once; voices chattered in the earphones; my vision bumped and jiggled, just as the film from that first handheld camera had done. They found poor Seth Cereson, who had pressed himself against one of the largest beams, faceplate directly on the ice, in a shadow so that he was barely visible. He was in shock as they led him back to the LVs, and kept repeating in a small voice that there was something moving inside the beam. That frightened everyone a bit. Several people walked over and investigated a fallen beam, which had shattered into hundreds of pieces when it hit the ground. Others looked at the edges of the three triangular towers, which were nearly transparent. From a vantage point on top of one of them I looked down and saw the tiny silver figures scurrying from beam to beam, standing in the center of the circle looking about, clambering on top of the fallen one. . . .

Then there was a shout that cut through the other voices. "Look here! Look here!"

"Quietly, quietly," said Ehrung. "Who's speaking?"

"Over here." One of the figures waved his arms and pointed at the beam before him. Ehrung walked swiftly toward him, and the rest of us followed. We grouped behind her and stared up at the tower of ice. In the smooth, slightly translucent surface there were marks engraved:

. . . .

For a long time Ehrung stood and stared at them, and the crew behind her stared, too; and in the dream, I knew that they were two Sanskrit words, carved in the Narangi alphabet—*abhy-ud* and *aby-ut-sad*. And I knew what they meant:

> to move, to push farther out;
> to cause to set out towards.

Another time, caught in that half-sleep just before waking, when you know you want to get up but something keeps you from it, I dreamed I was on another expedition to Icehenge, a later one, determined to clear up, once and for all, the controversy surrounding its origins. And then I woke up. Usually it is one of the few moments of grace in our lives, to wake up apprehensive or depressed about something, and then realize that the something was part of a dream, and nothing to worry about. But not this time. The dream was true. The year was 2621, and we were on our way to Pluto.

There were seventy-nine people on board *Snowflake:* twenty-four crew, sixteen reporters, and thirty-nine scientists and technicians. The expedition was being sponsored by the Waystation Institute for Higher Learning, but essentially it was my doing. I groaned at the thought and rolled out of bed.

My refrigerator was empty, so after I splashed water on my face, I went out into the corridor. It had rough wood walls, set at just slightly irregular angles; the floor was a lumpy moss that did surprisingly well underfoot.

As I passed by Jones's chamber the door opened and Jones walked out. "Doya!" he said, looking down at me. "You're out! I've missed you in the lounge."

"Yes," I said. "I've been working some."

"I understand Dr. Brinston wants to talk to you," he said, brushing down his tangled auburn hair with his fingers. "You going to breakfast?"

I nodded and we started down the corridor together. "Why does Brinston want to talk to me?"

"He wants to organize a series of colloquia on Icehenge, one given by each of us."

"And he wants me to join it?" Brinston was the chief archeologist, and as such probably the most important person aboard, even though Dr. Lhotse of the Institute was the nominal leader. It was a fact Brinston was all too aware of. He was a gregarious Terran (if that isn't being redundant), a bit overbearing, and I didn't like him very much.

We turned a corner, onto the main passageway to the dining commons. Jones was grinning at me. "Apparently he believes that it would be essential to have your participation in the series, you know, given your historical importance and all."

"Umph." I wasn't amused.

In the white hallway just outside the commons there was a large blue bulletin screen in one of the walls. We stopped before it. There was a console under for typing messages onto the board. The new question, put up just three days before, was the big one, the one that had sent us out here: "Who put up Icehenge?" in bold orange letters.

But the answers, naturally, were jokes. In red script, near the center of the board, was "GOD." In yellow type, "Remnants of a Crystalized Ice Meteorite." In a corner, in long green letters: "Nederland." Under that someone had typed "No, Other Aliens." I laughed at that. There were several more solutions (I liked especially "Pluto Is a Message Planet from Another Galaxy"), most of which had been offered first in the ten years after the discovery, before Nederland published the results of his work on Mars.

Jones stepped to the console. "Here's my new one," he said. "Let's see, yellow Gothic should be right: 'Icehenge put there by prehistoric civilization' "—this was Jones's basic contention, that humans were of extraterrestrial origin, and had had a space technology in their earliest days—" 'Inscription put there by the miner starship.' "

"Jones," I said. The miner starship was Nederland's theory. "You're too frivolous for me, Jones."

"And you, Edmond Doya, are too serious for me."

"How many of those answers have you put on that screen?" I demanded.

"No more than half," he said, and seeing my shaking head and weary expression, he cackled. We left the screen and entered the dining commons.

Inside, Bachan Nimit and his micrometeor people were seated at a table together, eating with Dr. Brinston. I cringed when I saw him, and went to the kitchen.

Jones and I sat down at a table on the other side of the room and began to eat. Jones, system-famous heretic scholar of evolution and prehistory, had nothing but a pile of apples on his plate. He adhered to the dietary laws of his home, the asteroid Icarus, which decreed that nothing eaten should be the result of the death of any living system. Jones's particular affinity was for apples, and he finished them off rapidly.

I was nearly done with my omelet when Brinston approached our table. "Mr. Doya, it's good to see you out of your cabin!" he said loudly. "You shouldn't be such a hermit."

This comment confirmed my opinion of him. "I'm working," I said.

"Oh, I see." He smiled. "I hope that won't keep you from joining our little lecture series."

"Your what?"

"We're organizing a series of talks, and hope everyone will

give one." The micrometeor crew had turned to watch us.

"Everyone?"

"Well . . . everyone who represents a different aspect of the problem."

"What's the point?"

"What?"

"What's the point?" I repeated. "Everyone on board already knows what everyone else has written about Icehenge."

"But in a colloquium we could discuss these opinions."

"In a colloquium there would be nothing but a lot of contention to no purpose. We've wrangled for years without anyone changing his mind, and now we're going to Pluto to find out. Why stage a reiteration of what we've already said?"

Brinston was flushing red. "We hoped there would be new things to be said."

I shrugged. "Maybe so. Look, just go ahead and have your talks without me."

Brinston paused. "That wouldn't be so bad," he said reflectively, "if Nederland were here. But now the two principal theorists will be missing."

I felt my distaste for him turn to dislike. He knew of the relationship between Nederland and me. "Yes, well, Nederland's been there before." He had, too, to dedicate the plaque commemorating the expedition of asteroid miners he had discovered; at the time his explanation was so widely believed that the monument hadn't been examined closely, hadn't even been excavated. . . .

"Even so, you'd think he'd want to be along on the expedition that will either confirm or contradict his theory." His voice grew louder as he sensed my discomfort. "Tell me, Mr. Doya, what did Nederland say was his reason for not joining us?"

I stared at him for a long time. "Because, Dr. Brinston, he was afraid there would be too many colloquia." I stood up. "Now, excuse me while I return to my work." I went to the kitchen and got some supplies, and walked back to my cabin, feeling that I had made an enemy, but not caring much.

Yes, Hjalmar Nederland, the famous historian of Icehenge, was my great-grandfather. It was a fact I could always remember knowing, though my father never encouraged my pleasure in knowing it. (Father wasn't his grandchild; my mother was.)

I had read all of Nederland's books—the works on Icehenge, the four volumes of the autobiography, the earlier works on Terran cultures—by the time I was ten years old. At that time Father and I lived on Jupiter Thirteen. Father had gotten lucky and was crewing on a sunboat entered in the InandOut, a race that takes the boats into the top layer of Jupiter's atmosphere.

Usually he wasn't that lucky. Sunboat sailing was for the rich, and they didn't need crews often. So most of the time Father was a laborer. Street sweeper, carrier at construction sites, whatever was on the list at the laborer's guild. As I understood later, he was poor, and shiftless, and played the edges to get by.

He was a small man, my father, short and spare-framed; he dressed in worker's clothes, and had a droopy moustache, and grinned a lot. People were often surprised to see him with a kid —he didn't look important enough. But when he lived on Phobos he had been part of a foursome. The other man was a well-known sculptor, with a lot of pull in artistic circles. And my mom had had connections with the University of Mars. . . . Between them they managed to get that rarest of official sanctions, the permission to have a child. Then, when the foursome broke up, Father was the only one interested in taking care of me. Into his custody I went (I was six, and had never set foot on Mars) and we took off for Jupiter.

After that Father never discussed my mother, or the other half of the foursome, or my famous great-grandfather (when he could keep me from bringing up the topic) or even Mars. He was, among other things, a sensitive man—a poet who wrote poems for himself, and never paid a fee to put them in the general file. He loved landscapes and skyscapes, and after we moved out to Ganymede we spent a lot of time sightseeing, hiking in suits over Ganymede's stark hills, to watch Jupiter or one of the other moons rise, or to watch a sunrise, still the brightest dawn of them all. We were a comfortable pair. Ours was a quiet pastime, and the source of most of Father's poetry. Here is one of his earlier poems:

> In the Lazuli Canyon, boating.
> Sheet ice over shadowed stream,
> Crackling under our bow.
> Stream grows wide, bends out into sunlight:
> A million turns
> Following the old rift.
> Plumes of frost at every breath.
> Endless rise of the red canyon,
> Mountains and canyons, no end to them.
> Black webs in rust sandstone:
> Wind-carved boulders hang over us.
> There, on the wet red beach:
> Dull green tundra grass. Green.
> In the canyon my heart is pure—
> Why ever leave?
> The western sky deep violet,
> In it two stars, white and indigo:
> Venus, and the Earth.

Even though Father disliked Nederland (they had met, I gathered, several times) he still indulged my fascination with Icehenge. On my eleventh birthday he took me down to the local post office (at this time we were on bright Europa, and took long hikes together across its crystal plains). After a whispered conference with one of the attendants, we went into a holo room. He wouldn't tell me what we were going to see, and I was frightened, thinking it might be my mother.

The room came on, and we were in darkness. Stars overhead. Suddenly a very bright one flared, defining a horizon, and pale light flooded over what now appeared as a dark, rocky plain.

Then I saw it off in the distance: the monument. The sun (I recognized it now, the bright star that had risen) had only struck the tops of the liths, and they gleamed white. Below the sunlight they were square black cutouts blocking stars. The line quickly dropped (the holo was speeded up) and it stood revealed, tall and white. Because of the model of it that I owned at the time, it seemed immense.

"Oh, *Dad.*"

"Come on, let's go look at it."

"Bring it here, you mean."

He laughed. "Where's your imagination, kid?" He dialed it over—I went straight through a lith—and we were standing at its center. We circled about slowly, necks craned back to look up. We inspected the broken column and its scattered pieces, then looked closely at the brief inscription.

"It's a wonder they didn't all sign their names," said Father.

Then the whole scene disappeared and we were standing in the bare holo room. Father caught my forlorn expression, and laughed. "You'll see it again before you're through. Come on, let's go get some ice cream."

Soon after that, when I was just fourteen, he got a chance to go to Terra. Friends of his were buying and taking a small boat all the way back, and they needed one more crew member. Or perhaps they didn't *need* one, but they wanted him to come.

At that time we had just moved back to Ganymede, and I had a job at the atmosphere station. We'd lived there nearly a year, off and on, and I didn't want to move again. I had written a book (describing the post-Icehenge adventures of the Vasyutin Expedition), and with the money I was saving I planned to publish it. (For a fee anyone can put their work in the data banks and have it listed in the huge general catalog; whether anyone will ever read it is another matter. But I had hopes, at the time, that one of the book clubs would buy the right to list it in their own index.)

"See, Dad, you've lived on Terra and Mars, so you want to go back there so you can be outside and all. Me, I don't care about that stuff. I'd rather stay here."

Father stared at me carefully, suspicious of such a sentiment, as well he might be—for as I understood much later, my reluctance to go to Terra stemmed mainly from the fact that Hjalmar Nederland had said in his autobiography that he didn't like it.

"You've never been there," he said, "else you might not say that. And it's something you should see, take my word for it! The chance doesn't come that often."

"I know, Dad. But the chance has come for you, not me—"

"There's room for you."

"But only if you make it. Look, you'll be back out here sailing in a couple years—and I'll get down there some day. Meanwhile I want to stay here. I got a job and friends."

"Okay," he said, and looked away. "You're your own man, you do what you want." I felt bad then, but not nearly so much as I did later, when I remembered the scene and understood what I had done. Father was tired, he was going through a hard time, he needed his friends. He was about seventy then, he had nothing to show for his efforts, and he was tired. In the old days he'd have been near the end, and I suppose he felt that way—he hadn't yet gotten that second wind that comes when you realize that, far from being over, the story has just begun. But that second wind didn't come from me, or with my help. And yet that, it seems to me, are what sons are for. . . .

So he left for Terra, and I was on my own. About two years later I got a letter from him. He was in Micronesia, on an island in the Pacific Ocean somewhere . . . he'd met some Marquesan sailors. There were fleets of the old Polynesian sailing ships, called *wa'a kaulua,* crisscrossing the Pacific, carrying passengers and even freight. Father had decided to apprentice himself to one of the navigators from the Carolines—one of those who navigate as they did in the ancient times, without radio or sextant, or compass, or even maps.

And that's what he's been doing, from that day to this: thirty-five years. Thirty-five years of learning to gauge how fast the ship is moving by eye; memorizing the distances between islands; reading the stars and the weather; lying at the bottom of the ship, on the keel, during cloudy nights, and feeling the pattern of the swells to determine the ship's direction. . . . I think back to the hand-to-mouth times of our brief partnership, and I see that he has, perhaps, found what he wants to do. Occasionally I get a note from Fiji, Samoa, Oahu. Once I got one from Easter Island, with a picture of one of the statues included. The note said, "And this one's not a fake!"

That's the only clue I've gotten that he knows what I'm doing.

And so Icehenge, and Nederland's theory, the romantic story of the Vasyutin Expedition, remained part of my life—one of the myths that I believed in and lived by—as I grew up alone, moving from satellite to satellite, and then out to Saturn and the colonies surrounding it. I believed it until I was nearly thirty years old. Though it is a coincidence that may seem too appropriate to be true, coincidences are like that; the turning point in my history, the end of my innocence, came on New Year's Eve, 2599.

I was on Titan, working for the Titan Weather Company. Early in the evening I was on the job, helping to create a lightning storm that crackled and boomed above raucous Ed's Town. Just after the big blast at midnight (two huge balls of St. Elmo's fire colliding just above the dome), we were let off, and we hit town ready for a good time. The whole crew—sixteen of us, good friends all—went to Jacque's. Jacque was dressed up as the Old Year, and his pet chimpanzee was in diapers and ribbons, representing the New. I drank a lot of alcoholic drinks and once again observed how quickly one became incapable of tasting. Every New Year's Eve I drank alcohol, and every New Year's Day I wondered how humanity had managed to get by for so long with such an awful drug.

We soon got very drunk. My boss, Mark Starr, was rolling on the floor, wrestling the chimp. It looked like he was losing. An impromptu chorus was bellowing an old standard, "I Met Her in a Phobos Restaurant," and, inspired by mention of my native satellite, I started singing a complicated harmony part. Apparently I was the only one who perceived its beauties; there were shouts of protest, and the woman seated beside me objected by pushing me off the bench. She stood up and I retaliated by shoving her into the table behind us. People there were upset and began pounding on her. Feeling magnanimous, I grabbed her arm and pulled her away. The moment she was clear of them she punched me hard in the shoulder and began swinging with serious anger. I saw that I was outmatched and slipped through the throng at the bar, out the door and onto the narrow street.

I sat down at the curb and relaxed. I felt good. There were lots of people on the street, many of them quite drunk. One of them failed to notice me, and tripped over my legs. He looked around, taking stock of his situation, and slid himself over so that he was lying comfortably in the gutter, out of people's way.

He was a long-haired man. His torso was broad and round, but his limbs were thin, and under the tangle of hair his head seemed unnaturally small. After a moment he raised his head, opened a vial in his hand, and with awkward care waved the vial under his nose.

"You shouldn't use that stuff," I advised him.

"And why not?" His voice was scratchy.

"It'll give you high blood-pressure."

He looked up at me. "High blood-pressure's better than no blood-pressure at all."

"There is that."

With a series of slow movements he levered himself into a seated position on the curb next to me. Sitting, he looked like a spider. "You got to have blood pressure, that's my motto," he said.

"I see."

He looked around. "Man, on New Year's Eve everybody just goes *crazy.*"

"And all because Terra returned to its magic zero-point."

"Yeah. Just wait till Saturn's New Year comes around." Saturn's year was reckoned to have started when the first colony was established, and its eighth New Year was coming soon.

"Yeah, but tonight every town in the system will be like this. It's New Year's Eve everywhere. On Saturn's New Year nobody will be celebrating but us locals."

"Yeah, but it'll be crazy."

Then Mark and Ivinny and a few more weather people crashed out of Jacque's. "Come on, Ed, the chimp has got a fire extinguisher."

I stood up, much too quickly, and motioned to my companion.

He got up and we trailed the group, talking continuously. We had the opportunity to join several fights, for Ed's Town was filled with Caroline Holmes's shipworkers, and it was nearing dawn, but we only got caught in one, and it was an amiable free-for-all in a wide street. I got hit on the side of the head by an elbow and thought, "This goes too far." My new friend helped me away, we saw Mark and Ivinny down a side street, and were off again in pursuit. In this manner we passed a couple of hours.

At dawn we were on the east edge of town, sitting on the wide concrete strip just inside the dome. There were seven or eight of the weather crew left. My new friend arranged pieces of gravel in patterns on the concrete. On the horizon a white point appeared, and lengthened into a knife-edge line dividing the night: the rings. Saturn would soon be rising.

My companion had grown a little melancholy. "Sports," he scoffed in reply to a comment of mine. "Sports, it's always the same story. The wise old man or men against the young turk or turks, and the young turk, if he's worth his salt—which he is by definition—always seems to win it, every time. Even in chess. You heard of that guy Goodman. Guy studies chess religiously for a mere twenty-five years, comes out at age thirty-five and wins three hundred and sixty tournament games in a row, trounces five-hundred-and-fifteen-year-old Gunnar Knorrson twelve-four-two—Knorrson, who held the system championship for a hundred and sixty-some years! It's depressing."

"You play chess?"

"Yeah. And I'm five hundred and fifteen years old."

"Wow, that's old. You're not Knorrson?"

"No, just old."

"I'll say."

"Yes, I've seen six of these new-century eves—though I can't say I remember twenty ninety-nine very much. . . ."

"You must have seen a lot of changes."

"Oh yeah. Not as many, though, these last couple of centuries. It appears to me things don't change as fast as they used to—not as fast as in the nineteenth, twentieth, twenty-first. Inertia, I guess."

"Slower turnover in the population, you mean."

"Yeah. I suppose it's a commonly observed phenomenon."

"Is it?"

"I don't know. But damn it, why doesn't the wise old man beat the young turk? Why don't you just keep getting better? Where does your creativity go?"

"Same place as memory," I said.

"I guess. Well, what the hell. Winning ain't essential. I'm doing fine without it. I wouldn't have it over." He shook his head. "Wouldn't do like those Phoenixes. You heard of them? Folks banded together, 'way back when, in a secret organization, and now they're knocking themselves off on their five-hundredth birthdays?"

I nodded. "The Phoenix Club."

"Phoenixes. I wouldn't do that, not me. Never will understand those folks. Never understand those daredevils, either. Seems like the more you have to lose, the bigger thrill you get from risking your life for no reason. Those damn fools dueling with knives, trying to stand on Jupiter, having picnics on some iceberg in the rings—get themselves killed!"

"You really think people have more to lose by dying now than they did when they lived their three-score-and-ten?"

"Sure."

"I don't."

"Well, what the hell, you're just a kid. You don't know how strange it's going to get. As far as I can tell there are only a couple hundred people in the whole system older than me. And they're going fast. One of these days, if I'm like the rest of them, and I don't doubt that I am, my body is gonna toss off all this medical manipulation and *go*—" he snapped his fingers—"just like that. They still don't know why. And I tell you, closing in on it, I wouldn't mind having another six hundred years. I try talking my body into the idea all the time. And I'm *damn* glad I didn't go at seventy or a hundred. What kind of a life is that? I've been careful, and lived long enough to do so many things. . . ." He paused, and his eyes, aimed at the concrete we were sitting on, were focused for infinite distance.

"You done everything you wanted to?"

"'Course not, didn't you hear me?"

"Me neither."

He laughed. "I should hope not."

"I'd like to see the Vasyutin megalith."

He looked up at me. "The *what?*"

"The Vasyutin megalith, you know, that thing on Pluto."

"Yeah, I know, but *Vasyutin?*"

"He headed the expedition that put it there."

"He did not."

"What?" Now I was surprised.

"Where did you learn that?"

"Um, a historian named Nederland tracked the story down on Mars. . . ."

"Well, he was wrong."

I was taken aback. "I don't think so, I mean, he has it all well documented—"

"Idiot! He does not! What's he say, some asteroid miners put together a half-baked starship and take off—what's that got to do with Pluto?"

"They were the only ones out there, process of elimination—"

"Naaah. Listen, kid, I'm not going to sit here and argue with you about it. I'll tell you why Vasyutin didn't put up that thing—" He leaned toward me, leered. "Because I know who did."

He leaned back and stared at me calmly, and looking back at him I felt an uncanny certainty—something in his expression told me that he knew. He was telling the truth. "I *know,*" he repeated.

Just then Saturn broke over the horizon, and everyone started to cheer. All over Ed's Town voices and sirens and whistles and bells marked the dawn of the New Year with their ragged chorus. My companion stood and whooped several times, then lifted a hand to me and moved through the crowd, back toward the streets. After a moment's indecision I struggled after him. It took me a long time to reach him. I grabbed his sleeve and pulled at it, like a kid. He turned around.

"How do you know? *How?*"

He said nothing, looked thoughtful. Finally he grinned, a big toothy grin that stretched all across his thin face. He pursed his lips, bugged his eyes out, and tapped a forefinger against his mouth. Then he poked me in the chest with the other forefinger.

"You find that out," he said, and turned and left me standing there.

Later on I figured he helped put the monument up, or maybe he helped plant the hoax on Mars. That was why he was so sure. But at the time, I didn't have the slightest idea. I just knew that I believed him—and that my life had been changed. Changed for good.

My food had run out, and my memory was exhausted, so I decided to take the day off and hang around in the commons. Perhaps I would visit Jones in the afternoon. Several people aboard, I had heard, had been surprised or affronted to hear that I had invited Jones along; for Theophilus Jones was an outcast, he was one of those strange scientists who defied the basic tenets of his field. But I found the huge red-haired man to be one of the most intelligent and diverting people on the *Snowflake,* and more inclined than the others to talk about something other than Icehenge. Before I left for the commons I went to my library console to print up one of Jones's books. Should I read from *Prehistoric Technology?* I typed out the code for it.

In the kitchen I got a large bowl of ice cream, and went to a table to eat and read. The commons was empty—perhaps this was the sleeping time? I wasn't sure.

I opened my crisp new book, pages still stiff around the ring binding, and began to read:

> We must suspect alien presence in the unsolved problem of human origins, for science has significantly failed to discover the beginnings of human evolution, the point at which human beings and a terrestrial species might meet; and the recent finds in the Urals and in southern India, in which fossilized human skeletons one hundred million years old have been found, show that the scientific description of human evolution held up to this time was wrong. Alien interference, in the form of genetic

engineering, crossbreeding, or most likely, colonization, is almost a certainty.

So it is not impossible that a human civilization of high technology existed in prehistoric times—an earlier wave of history, now lost to us. That such a civilization would be lost to us is inevitable. Continents and seas have come and gone since it existed, and humanity itself must have come close to extinction more than once. If there had been a great and ageless city on the wide triangle of India, when it was a splinter of Gondwanaland inching north, what would we know of it now, crushed as it must have been in the collision between Asia and India, thrust deep beneath the Himalayas by the earth itself? Perhaps this is why Tibet is a place where humans have always possessed an ancient and intricate wisdom, and what we now know to be the oldest of written languages, Sanskrit. Perhaps some few of that ancient race survived the millennial thrust skyward; or perhaps there are caves the Tibetans have found, with deep fissures winding down through the mountain's basalt to chambers in that crushed city

My ice cream bowl was empty, so I got up and went to the kitchen to refill it, shaking my head over the passage in Jones's book. When I returned, Jones himself was in the room, deep in conversation with Arthur Grosjean. They were at the long blackboard, and Grosjean was picking up a writing stick. He had been the chief physicist on the *Persephone* in 2541, and had coauthored the only detailed description of the monument. He was an old man, nearly five hundred, short and frail. Now he was tying a piece of string around the stick, listening to Jones's excited voice. I sat down and watched them as I ate.

"First you draw a regular semicircle," said Grosjean. "That's the south half. Then the north half is flattened." He drew a horizontal diameter, and a semicircle below it. "We figured out the construction that will flatten the north half correctly. Divide the diameter into three parts. Use the two dividing points B and C for centers of the two smaller arcs, radius BD and CE." He drew and lettered busily. "At their meeting point, F, draw a perpendicular line through centerpoint A to south point G. Draw GBH—and GCI—then the arc HI, from center G. And *voilá!*"

"The construction," Jones said. He took the writing stick and began making little rectangles around the circle.

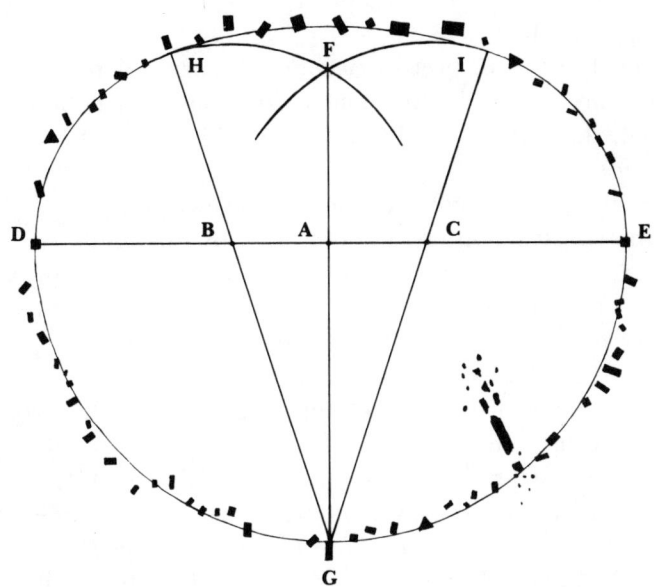

"All the sixty-six liths are within three meters of this construction," Grosjean said.

"And this is a prehistoric Celtic pattern, you say?" asked Jones.

"Yes, we discovered later that it was used in Britain in the second millennium B.C. But I don't see how that supports your theory, Mr. Jones. It would be just as easy for later builders of Icehenge to copy the Celts as it would be for the Celts to copy earlier builders of Icehenge—easier, I'd say."

Jones, facing the board, didn't reply.

Then Brinston and Dr. Nimit walked in. Jones looked over and saw them. "So what does Dr. Brinston think of this?" he said to

Grosjean. Brinston heard the question and looked over at them.

"Well, I'm afraid," Grosjean said uncomfortably, "that he believes our measurements of the monument were inaccurate."

"What?"

Brinston left Nimit and approached the blackboard. "Examination of the holograms made of Icehenge show that the on-site measurements—which were not made by Dr. Grosjean, by the way—were off badly."

"They'd have to be pretty inaccurate," Jones said, turning back to the board, "to make this construction bad speculation."

"Well, they were," said Brinston easily. "Especially on the north side."

"To tell you the truth," Grosjean informed Jones, "I still believe the construction was the one used by the builders."

"I'm not sure that's a good attitude," Brinston said, his voice smooth with condescension. "I think the fewer preconceived notions we have before we actually see it, the better."

"I have seen it," snapped Grosjean.

"Yes," said Brinston, voice still cheerful, "but the problem wasn't in your field."

Jones slammed down the writing stick and turned. "You're a fool, Brinston." There was a shocked silence. "Icehenge is not exclusively your problem because you are *the archeologist.*"

I stood up, jarred by the tableau: round Brinston, still trying to look unconcerned, angry redheaded Jones towering over him, frail grim Grosjean completing the triangular composition; and Nimit and I across the room, watching.

Jones's lip curled and Brinston stepped back, jaw tensed. "Come on, Arthur," said Jones. "Let's continue our conversation elsewhere." He stalked out of the room, and Grosjean followed.

It will become a circus, I thought, hearing it in Nederland's voice. Brinston approached us, his face still tense. He noticed Nimit and me staring, and looked embarrassed. "A touchy pair," he said.

"They're not touchy. You were harassing them, being a disruption."

"*I'm* a disruption!" he burst out. "You're the disruptive force on this ship, Doya, hiding in your cabin all the time as if you had nothing to do with us! Refusing to join our talks! Living on Waystation for twenty years like a bum has made you some sort of misanthropist."

"I'm working," I said.

"Working," he sneered. "Your work is done." He walked into the kitchen, leaving Nimit and me to stare silently at each other.

Waystation—where I lived for fifteen years, not twenty—is the freight train, the passenger express, the permanent high-speed rocket of the Outer Satellites. It uses the sun and the gas giants as buoys, gravity handles to swing around. It travels about the same distance as Saturn's orbit in a year—a fast rock. It began as an idea of Caroline Holmes, the shipping magnate who built most of the Jupiter colonies—and she profited from it most, as she did from all the rest of her ideas. Her company Jupiter Metals took a roughly cylindrical asteroid, twelve kilometers long and around five across. The inside was hollowed out, one end was honeycombed by the huge propulsion station, and off it went, careening around the sun, constantly shifting orbit to make its next rendezvous.

I remember when I first boarded it, on a shuttle from Titan. My name had finally come up on the hitch-hikers' list—the Outer Satellites Council provides free travel between the satellites (which otherwise would be too expensive for most individuals), and all you have to do is put your name on the list and wait for it to come to the top. I had waited four years.

Jumping on Waystation is like running in a relay race, and handing the baton to a runner five times faster than you—for getting a transfer craft up to Waystation's velocity would defeat the purpose of having Waystation at all. Our shuttle craft was moving at top speed, and we passengers were each in anti-G chambers (called the Jelly) within tiny transfer vessels. As Waystation flashed by, the transfer vessels were fired after it, at tremendous acceleration, and the transfer crews on Waystation then snagged them and reeled us in.

Even in the Jelly the sudden accelerations were a strain. At the moment we were snagged, the breath was knocked out of me and I blacked out for a second. While I was unconscious I had a brief vision, intense and clear. I could see only black, except for the middle distance, directly before me: there stood a block of ice, cut in the shape of a coffin. And frozen in this glittering bier was me, myself—eyes wide and staring back at me.

The vision passed, I came to, shook my head, blinked sparks and floating lights out of my eyes. Waystation people helped me out of the Jelly, and I joined the other passengers in a receiving room. Several of them looked distinctly ill.

A Waystation official greeted us, and without further ceremony we were escorted through the port and into the city itself. It was crowded at that time—dropoffs to Jupiter were just about to be made, and there were a lot of merchants in town moving goods. I found a job washing dishes first thing, then went out to the front end of Waystation, on the surface near the methane lake, and sat for a long time. I was on Waystation, the next step outward.

Some years after that I woke up one morning in the park, arms wrapped around a very young girl. The Sunlight had just come on and was still at half strength, giving its comforting illusion of morning. I stood up, went through a quick salute-to-the-sun exercise to alleviate the stiffness in my legs. The girl woke up—in the light she looked about fifteen or sixteen—and stretched. Her coat was wrinkled. She had joined me the previous night, waking me up to do so, because it was cold, and I had a blanket. It had felt good to sleep with someone, to spoon together for warmth, to feel human contact, even through coats.

She got up and brushed off her pants. She looked at me and smiled, and for the first time in weeks, I smiled myself.

"Hey," I said. "You want to go over to the Red Café and get some breakfast?"

"No," she said. "I have to go to work. Thanks for taking me

in." She turned and walked off through the park. I watched her until a stand of walnut trees blocked my sight of her.

I went and ate—said good morning to the cashier as she typed my money from me to them, but she just shrugged. I went out and strolled aimlessly up the curved streets, feeling low. Though in this real world you can smell and taste and touch things, it is still too often distressingly like the inside of a hologram, where nothing you say or do will have the slightest effect on what is happening around you . . . well, so be it. I don't like people that much, anyway.

For something to do I went down to the post office and checked my mail. And there, in my March 2608 issue of *Shards,* was *my own article.* I hadn't expected it to appear for months yet. I whooped once and disturbed people in the booths next to mine. I read quickly through the introduction, working hard to comprehend that the words were still mine:

Vasyutin and Icehenge:
A Reexamination by Edmond Doya

There are many reasons for supposing that Icehenge was constructed within the last two centuries, by an unknown group.

1) 2402, when the Ferrando-class spaceships were introduced, is the earliest year that ships capable of making the round trip from the outermost human colony to Pluto were available.

2) The Vasyutin theory, which is the only theory that pushes back this necessary time limit, provides an explanation that is possible, but apparently is not true. Though Mars Development Committee records show that an asteroid miner commanded by an Ivan Vasyutin did disappear, the sole evidence supporting the rest of his story is the journal of Emma Weil, discovered by Hjalmar Nederland in 2547. New evidence indicates that this journal is a hoax. The "grandson" who gave Nederland the number of the bank file that the journal was found in can no longer be located; nor can any trace of his existence now be found. Additionally, Jorge Balder, the famous historian of the Martian Revolution, made a thorough check of those very bank files while doing research in 2392; yet he made no mention of Weil's journal. It is certain that he would have found and reported it had it been there, and therefore we must assume that the journal did not then exist.

Thus the journal, and the Vasyutin explanation that depends on it, are apparently evidence manufactured by an agent who is presumably responsible for the construction of Icehenge as well.

And the article went on, recounting in meticulous detail my sources and methods . . . making further points that I could not prove for certain (like the total lack of evidence for the existence of the Mars Starship Association). . . . It was, I knew, a body blow to the Vasyutin explanation—it threw the whole issue into question again! And *Shards* was one of the major journals, it was read system-wide. Nederland himself would read the article, was reading it, perhaps, even as I did. It was a disturbing notion. The battle, I thought, was on.

Quitting time, graveyard shift at the restaurant. I went over to see Fist Mathews, one of the cooks. "Fist, can you lend me ten till payday?"

"Why do you want money, Edmond? The way you eat here you ain't hungry."

"No, I need to pay off the post office before they'll let me see my mail."

"What's a dishwasher like you doing with mail? Never mess with it myself. Keep your friends where you can see 'em, that's what I say."

"Yeah, I know. Listen, I'll pay you back payday, that's the day after tomorrow."

"You can't wait till then? Okay, what's your number . . ."

He went to the restaurant's register and made the exchange. "Okay, you got it. Remember payday."

"I will, thanks, Fist."

I threw a few more dishes on the washer belt—grabbed a piece of lobster tail the size of my finger, tossed it in my mouth, fuel for the fire, waste not, want not—until my replacement arrived, looking sleepy.

The streets of Waystation were as empty as they ever get. In the green square of the park, up above me on the other side of the cylinder, a group was playing cricket. I hurried past one of my sidewalk sleeping spots, stepping over prone figures. As I neared the post office I skipped. I hadn't been able to afford to see my mail for several days—it happened like that at the end of every month. Post office has mail-freaks over a barrel, and they know it.

When I got there it was crowded, and I had to hunt for a console. More and more people were going to general delivery, it seemed, especially on Waystation where almost everyone was transient.

I sat down before one of the grey screens and began typing, paying off the post office and identifying myself, calling up my correspondence from the depths of the computer. . . . I sat back to read.

Nothing! "Damn it!" I shouted, startling a young man in the booth next to me. Junk mail, nothing but junk. Why had no one written? "No one writes to Edmond," I muttered, in the singsong the phrase had taken on over the years. There was an issue of *Archeological Review*, and a notice that my subscription to *Marscience* had run out, for which I thanked God; and an inquiry from a local politician asking if this was my current mail number.

I blanked the screen and left. Keep your friends where you can see them. There were more people in the streets, on the peoplemovers; going to work, getting off work. I didn't know any of them. I didn't know anyone on Waystation, I thought, except the people at the restaurant, and I only knew them there. Yet it was 2612, I had lived on Waystation ten years!

I got on the peoplemover going to the front of the cylinder, and slumped down in a seat. At the front I got off and took the short subway through the wall of the asteroid to the surface. Once through, I got off and walked down to the big room fronting on Emerald Lake. We were somewhere outside Uranus, so the lake was there. The room, however, was nearly empty. I went to the ticket window, and they took more of Fist's ten. The suit attendant helping me looked sleepy, so I checked my helmet seam in the mirror. The black, aquatic creature—like a cross between a frog and a seal—stared back at me out of its facemask, and I smiled. In the reflection the humorless fish-grin appeared. The slug-broad head, webbed and finned handscoops, long finny feet, torso fins, and the cyclops-like facemask, transformed me (appropriately, I thought) into an alien monster. I walked slowly into the lock, lifting my knees high to swing my feet forward.

The outer lock door opened, I felt the tiny rush of air, and I was outside, on my own. It felt the same, but I breathed quicker for a time, as always. A ramp extended out into the lake, and I waddled to the end of it.

Around the lake, flat blue-grey plains rose up to the close horizon of an ancient, worn-down crater wall. It looked like the surface of any asteroid. Waystation's existence—the hollowed interior, the buildings and people, the complicated spaceport, the huge propulsion station on the other end—the rock's extraordinary speed itself—all could seem the work of an excited fancy, here by this lake of liquid methane, trapped in an old crater.

Below me the stars were reflected, green as—yes, emeralds—in the glassy surface of the methane. I could see the bottom, three or four meters below. A series of ripples washed by, making the green stars dance for a moment.

Out on the lake the wave machine was a black wall, hard to distinguish in the pale sunlight. Its sudden shift toward me (which looked like a mistake in vision made while blinking) marked the creation of another tall green swell. The swells could hardly be seen until they crossed the submerged crater wall near the center of the lake; then they rose up, pitched out and fell, breaking in both directions around the submerged crater, throwing sheets of methane like mercury drops into space, where they floated slowly down.

I dove in. Under the surface I was effectively weightless, and swimming took little effort. Over the sound of my breath was the steady *krkrkrkrkrkrkrkr* of waves breaking, and every ten or fifteen seconds I heard the emphatic *kaTHUNKuh* of the wave machine. Ahead of me the green of the methane became murky, because of the turbulence over the submerged crater. I stuck my head above the surface to see, and all sound except that of my breathing instantly ceased.

Few other swimmers were out. I swam around the break, out

beyond the crater, where the swells first hit the shelf and started to rise to their full height, which today was nearly ten meters. There were three other swimmers there, and I floated on my back and waited for them to take their turns. Rising and falling on those smooth swells, I felt quite inhuman; all that I saw, felt, and heard—even the sound of my own breath—was strange, alien, too sublime for human sensibility.

Then I was alone. A swell approached and I backstroked away from it, toward the point where it would first break, adjusting my speed so I would be just ahead of that point when the wave picked me up.

The wave reached me and I felt its strong lift. I turned luxuriously onto my stomach, skimmed down the steepening face until I felt that the swell was pitching out over me. From my thighs up I was clear of the methane, skating on my handfins—I turned them left and swerved across the wave, just ahead of the break, flying, flying. . . . I moved my feet to retard my speed a fraction, and the roof of the breaking wave moved ahead of me. It got dark. I was in the tube. My hands were below me, jammed into the methane to keep me from falling down the face. I was motionless yet flying, propelled through the blackness at immense speed by the liquid which rushed up past my left shoulder, arched over my head and fell out beyond my right shoulder. Before me there was a huge tunnel, and at the end of this swirling obsidian tube a small ellipse of velvet black, packed with stars.

The opening got smaller, indicating that the wave was past the submerged crater, and receding. I dropped to gain speed, turned back up and shot through the hole, over the swell and back onto the smooth glassy surface, under the night.

I swam slowly back to the point break, watching another swimmer spin silently across the next rushing wall. He rose too high and was thrown over with the lip of the wave. If he hit the crater-reef and broke the seal of his suit, he would freeze instantly—but he knew that, and would be careful to avoid being forced too deep.

I radioed the shore and had them pipe Gregorian chants into my headphones; and I swam, and rode waves, and hummed with the voices when I could catch my breath, and thought not at all. I swam till there was too much sweat in my suit, and not enough oxygen.

Back on the peoplemover, I felt good: free and self-sufficient, cosmopolitan, ready to work on the next part of the Icehenge problem. The next day I checked my mail again, just in case, and there was a note from Mark Starr, one of the variety that sent love and promised that a letter would arrive soon. PRINT, I typed, and out of the slot in the side of the console it appeared, blue ink on grey paper, just as always.

One day I went down to Waystation's News and Information Center to see if the Nederland press conference I had heard about was on tape. The lobby was nearly empty, and I went directly into a booth. The index I called up listed only Nederland's regularly scheduled lectures, and I had to search through the new entries to find the press conference I wanted. Finally I discovered it, hot out of space—it had arrived while I was searching. I typed the code to run it, and sat back in the center chair of the booth.

The room darkened. There was a click and I was in a large conference room, fully lit, filled with the holo images of Martians: reporters, students, some scientists I recognized. . . . Nederland was moving down an aisle next to me, toward a podium at the front. I moved through people and chairs to the aisle, and stood in front of Nederland. He walked through me. Smiling grimly at my ritual, and at my quick moment of involuntary fright at the unfelt collision, I muttered, "You'll see me yet," as I always did, and kicked about until I relocated my chair.

Nederland reached the podium and the irregular percussion of voices died. Underneath those manicured grey eyebrows there was a look of triumph, at the corners of the mouth, the tightening of a tiny smile. "You old son of a bitch," I said. "You've got something up your sleeve. . . ."

He cleared his throat, his usual sign that he was taking over. "I think my statement will answer most of the questions you have today, so why don't I start with that, and then we'll answer any questions you might have."

"Old fool," I said, but it was the only response. Nederland looked down at his notes, looked up—his eyes crossed mine—and extended a benedictory hand.

"The recent critics of the Vasyutin explanation claim that the Pluto monument is a modern hoax, and that in my work on the subject I have ignored the physical evidence. The absence of any disturbance in the regolith around the site, and our inability to find any signs of construction at all, are cited as facts which contradict, or do not fit, my explanation.

"I submit that it is the critics who are ignoring the physical evidence. If the Vasyutin Expedition did not build Icehenge, why did Vasyutin himself study the megalithic cultures of Terra for six years?"

"What?" I cried.

"—what are we to make of his stated intention to leave some sort of mark on the world? Can we label it coincidence that Vasyutin's ship disappeared just eight years before the date found on Icehenge? I think not. . . ."

He went on, outlining the arguments he had been espousing for the last sixty years. "Come on," I shouted. "Get down to it!" He droned on, ignoring the fact that his critics had shown the whole Vasyutin story to be part of the hoax. Then he flipped over a notecard, and an involuntary smile creased his face. I sat forward.

"My critics," he said in his let's-be-reasonable tone, "are simply attacking in a purely destructive way. Aside from the vague claim that the monument is a modern hoax—perpetrated by whom, they cannot say—there is no theory to replace mine; and nothing to explain away the evidence found in the archives on Mars—"

"Oh, my God."

"The general claim of people like Doya, Satawal and Jordan is that there is nothing at the site which will prove Icehenge's age. On the other hand, there is nothing there that shows the monument to be modern, either, which, given the sophistication of dating methods, there almost certainly would be, if it were indeed modern.

"In fact, there is now evidence conclusively proving that Icehenge cannot be modern." He stopped to let the statement sink in. "You are all aware that micrometeors, the dusty debris of space, are continually falling on all the bodies of the solar system; and that when they fall on those bodies without an atmosphere, they leave minuscule craters. Even the smallest of fragments leave their mark. The fall of these micrometeors is regular, and is a constant throughout the system. Professor Mund Stallworth, of our own University of Mars, has received a grant from the Holmes Foundation, and he has done extensive work in this field. He has established rates of fall for different gravities, and thus a micrometeor count can now be used as an accurate dating method. Professor Stallworth has made a detailed computer scan of the exposed faces of the liths, and of the surrounding grounds, which the builders swept clear; and the count is such that he puts the date of the erection of Icehenge at a thousand years before the present, plus or minus five hundred years. It is impossible to be more precise with the short time spans involved. This places the latest date of construction one hundred and fifty years before the date left on the Inscription Lith; but this may be explained by the fact that every blemish on the smooth surfaces of the liths can be clearly seen. In any case, it is impossible that so many micrometeors could have fallen in the short amount of time postulated by those who think that Icehenge is a hoax.

"Thus, my friends, there is nothing that factually disproves the Vasyutin theory—there are only the doubts and fanciful speculations of detractors. And there *is* something that factually disproves the notions that these detractors hold. I thank you for your attention."

Pandemonium broke loose among the previously attentive figures around me. Questions were shouted out, incomprehensible under the noise of cheers and applause. (The woman next to me was clapping and I wanted to restrain her, hit her, actually. . . .) As questions became audible order was reestablished, but apparently the news service people had considered the question-and-answer period unimportant. With another click the scene disappeared, and I was again in the dark, silent holo room. Lights came on. I sat.

Had Nederland proved his theory at last? Was the tall man I had met on Titan thirteen years before wrong after all? (And I as well?) "Son of a bitch," I said, no longer referring to the smiling man on the podium.

Woke up in the alley behind one of Waystation's main thoroughfares. I'd been sleeping on my side and my neck and hip were sore. Took off my coat and shook the dust off it. Pushed my fingers through my hair and made it all lie down flat, brushed my teeth with a fingernail, looked around for something to drink. Put my coat back on. Flapped my arms.

Around me prone figures were still slumbering. Waking up is the worst part of living on the streets of Waystation. They drop the temperature down to ten degrees during the nights, to encourage travelers to take rooms—helping out the hotel trade. A lot of people stay on the streets, anyway, since most of them are transients. They aren't bothered in any way aside from the cold, so they save their money for things more important than a room for the night. We all have the necessary shelter, inside this rock. . . .

Low on money again, but I needed something to eat. Onto the peoplemover.

Down at the spaceport I ate in the restaurant. Then I bought myself a bath, and sat in a corner of the public pool watching people wash, resting and thinking nothing.

When I was done I felt refreshed, and I walked around to the post office. Not much mail; but there at the end, to my great surprise, was a letter from a Professor Emanuel Rotenberg, head of the Fine Arts Lecture Series at the Waystation Institute for Higher Learning (which, like many of the institutions on Waystation, had been founded by Caroline Holmes): Professor Rotenberg, who had enjoyed my "series of interesting revisionist articles" on Icehenge, wondered if I would consider accepting a semester's employment, as lecturer and head of a seminar studying the Pluto megalithic monument— "My, my, *my,*" I said, and typed out instructions to print the letter, with my mouth hanging wide open.

I went out of my cabin for the first time in a while, to restock my supply of crackers and orange juice. The wood and moss hallways of the *Snowflake* were quite empty; it seemed that people were staying in their rooms, or in the tiny lounges that the rooms opened onto. Dr. Lhotse had brought Brinston by for a peace-making visit, and they had dropped in on Jones as well. Now we interacted, when necessary, with careful politeness; but mostly we were just settling in for the last wait. It would be a few more weeks until we reached Pluto. That wasn't long; everyone is patient, everyone is good at waiting in this world—in this life that goes so slowly.

Yesterday was my birthday—March 23rd, 2621. I was fifty years old. One tenth of my life done and gone—the endless childhood over. Those fifty years feel like eternity in my mind, and the thing is hardly begun. My God! . . . I thought of the ancient stranger I had met on Titan so long ago, and wondered: we humans, who live centuries and then die anyway, what have we become?

When I am as old as that stranger, my first half-century will be forgotten. Or it will recede into depths of memory beyond the reach of recollection—the same as forgotten—recollection being a power inadequate to our new time-scale. And how many other powers like it?

Autobiography is now the necessary extension of memory. Five centuries from now, bar accident, I will live; but the *I* writing this will be nothing in his mind but a bare fact. I write this, then, for that stranger, myself, so that he may know who he has been.

My father sent me a birthday poem that arrived just last night. He's given me one every birthday now for forty-four years; they're beginning to make quite a volume. Here it is:

Looking for the green flash
At sea, north of Hawaii.
Still day, no clouds:
On a dark blue plane,
Under a limpid blue hemisphere.
Our craft one mote in Terra's blue dance
Of wind water and light.
Sunset near.
To the west the ocean midnight blue
Broken by blued silver.
The sun light orange,
Slowing down,
Flattening as it touches horizon:
Earth is between us and sun by now,
Only light bending through atmosphere
Left to us: image of sun.
Half down, don't look, too bright.
Sky around sun white.
Mere sliver left, look now:
Bare paring turning back
From orange to yellow,
Yellow to yellow-green,
Then just as it disappears,
Bright green!

Walking back to my room with my food, saying his poem to myself in my mind, I realized that I miss him.

I met with the Institute seminar I was to teach about a month after I got the invitation from Professor Rotenberg. We decided to meet at the back table of a pub across the street from the Institute, and moved there forthwith.

It quickly became clear that they had read the literature on the subject. What more could I tell them?

"Who!" cried a man named Andrew. "Whodunit!"

"Wait a second, start at the beginning." That was Elaine, a good-looking hundredish woman on my left.

I told them my story as briefly as possible, feeling sheepish as I described the unscientific reason for my work, the appearance of the stranger on Titan.

"You must have been astonished," said Elaine.

"For a while. Soon the idea that the monument was put there by someone other than Vasyutin obsessed me . . . it made the whole problem unsolved again."

"Part of you welcomed it." That was April, an attentive woman sitting across from me.

"Yeah."

"But what about Vasyutin?"

"What about Nederland?" asked April. She had a rather sharp and scornful way of speaking.

"I wasn't sure. It didn't seem possible that Nederland could be wrong—there were all those volumes, the whole edifice of his story. And I had believed it for so long, everyone had. If he was wrong, what then about Vasyutin? Or Emma? Many times when I thought about it the certainty I had felt that night—that that stranger *knew* what had happened—faded right away. But the memory . . . refused to change. So the search was on."

"How did you start?"

"With a premise. Induction, same as Nederland. I started with the theory that Icehenge was a modern construct, made anonymous in a deliberate attempt to obscure its origins."

"A hoax." April.

"Well, yes, although it's not really the structure that's a hoax, I mean it's definitely there no matter who set it up—"

"The Vasyutin explanation." Elaine.

"Right. Suddenly I had to wonder whether Vasyutin—and Emma—whether any of them had existed at all."

"So you checked Nederland's early work." This from Sean, a very big, bearded man.

"I did. And both Vasyutin and Emma actually existed—Emma held some Martian long-distance running records for several years. And they both disappeared with their ships around twenty-two forty. But the only thing connecting them with Icehenge was Emma's journal. And as you have read, I couldn't find her grandson anywhere, or any sign he had ever lived. I got an engineer named Jordan interested in the case, and he determined that the starship Emma described would have been impossible to build with the resources available to those miners. And I worked with an archeologist named Satawal, who lives on Terra, and he figured out a list of equipment necessary to construct Icehenge, and the asteroid miners had very little of that equipment. The Vasyutin explanation began to look inadequate from every angle."

Hushed silence and attentive faces.

"So I started looking around for who might have done such a thing. I figured they were probably still alive. I figured they were rich. I figured there were more than one of them, certainly, although I suspected it was a single person's idea. I figured they had a big ship, and a lot of specialized equipment. From that I made more assumptions, but they concerned motivation and were less certain, though of great interest and aid to me—"

"But you could make assumptions forever! What did you do?" April again.

"Uh. Research. I sat in front of a screen and punched out codes, read the results, found new indexes, punched out more codes. I looked through shipping records, made quick investigations of various rich people. That sort of thing. It was boring work in some ways, but I enjoyed doing it. At first I thought of myself as working my way through a maze. Then that seemed the wrong image. In front of a library screen I could go anywhere. Because of the access-to-information laws I could look in every file and record that existed, except for the illegal secret ones—there are a lot of those—and if they had code call-ups—you know, were secreted somewhere in larger data-banks—then I could probably get into those, too. I bumped into file-freaks and learned new codes, and learning them took me into data banks that taught me even more. Trying to visualize it, I could see myself as a tiny component in a single communications network, a multibank computer complex that spanned the solar system—a dish-shaped, invisible, seemingly telepathic web, a wave pattern that added one more complication to the quark dance swirling in the sun's gravity well. So I was not in a maze, I was above it, and I could see all of it at once—and its walls formed a pattern, had a meaning, if I could learn how to read it. . . ."

I stopped and looked around. Blank faces, neutral, tolerant nods. "You know what I mean?" I asked.

No answers. "Sort of," said Elaine.

Wandering, wandering in the night of Waystation, the Sunlight out, and the other side of the cylinder a web of streetlights and colored neon points. The day after payday, and three hours before the seminar was to meet. I stopped at the News and Information Center, waited till I could get a booth. When I got one I sat down and aimlessly called up indexes. I wanted to be distracted. Eventually I selected Recreation News, which played continuously.

The room darkened and then revealed a platform in space. The scene moved to one side and I could see we were on the extension of a small satellite, in a low orbit around an asteroid.

The lilting voice of one of the sports commentators spoke. "The ancient game of golf has undergone yet another transformation out here on Hebe," he said. We moved farther out onto the platform, and two golfers appeared at the edge of it, in thin hoursuits. "Yes, Philip John and Arafura Aloesi have added a new dimension to their golfing on and around Hebe. Let's hear them describe it for themselves. Arafura?"

"Well, Connie, we tee off from up here, that's about it, in a nutshell. The pin is back down there near the horizon, see the light? It's two meters wide, we figured we deserved that much from up here. Mostly we play hole-in-one."

"What do you have to think about when you're hitting a shot from up here, Phil?"

"Well, Connie, we're in a Clarke orbit, so we don't have to worry about orbital velocity. It's a lot like every other drive, actually, except you're higher up than usual—"

"You have to watch out for hitting it too hard, gravity's not much around a small rock like this, if you drive with a one-wood you're liable to put the ball in orbit, or out in space even—"

"Yeah, Connie, I generally use a three-iron and shoot down at it, that works best. Sometimes we play where we have to put the ball through one orbit before it can hit ground, but it's hard enough as it is, and—"

"All right, let's see you guys put one down there."

They swung and the balls disappeared.

"Now how do you see where it's hit, guys?"

"Well, Connie, we got this radar screen following them down to the horizon—see, mine's right on track—then the green has a hundred-meter diameter, and if we land on that it shows on this screen here. Here, they're about to hit—"

Nothing appeared on the green screen beside them. Phil and Arafura looked crestfallen.

"Well, guys, any future plans for this new twist?"

Phil brightened. "Well, I was thinking if we were to set up just off Io, we could use the Red Spot as the hole and shoot for that. No problem with gravity there—"

"Yes, that'd be one hell of a fairway. And that's all from Hebe for now, this is Connie McDowell—"

My time ran out and the room was dark, then bright with roomlight. Eventually the attendant came in and roused me. Again my mouth was hanging open: the astonishment of inspiration. I jumped up laughing. "I got him!" I said. "Got the old fool," still laughing. "Got his ass nailed to the *floor!*" The attendant stared at me and shook his head.

Only a month later (I had written it in a week) this article appeared in *Shards:*

There is no good evidence concerning the age of Icehenge. Most dating methods developed by archeologists are applicable to substances and processes found only on Terra. In space the processes that are measured simply do not occur.

The ice of Icehenge, it has been determined, is about two and a half billion years old. But when that ice was cut into beams has proven more difficult to determine. A certain amount of the ice has sublimated spontaneously, but at seventy degrees Kelvin this process is extremely slow, and its effects at Icehenge are too small to measure.

The only dating method that has been applied to Icehenge is the micrometeor count method, developed by Professor Stallworth with the help of Hjalmar Nederland. This method is the equivalent of the terrestrial method of patination, and like patination, it relies on an intimate knowledge of local conditions, if it is to achieve any accuracy. Stallworth has assumed, and assumed only, that micrometeor fall is a constant both temporally and spatially. After making this assumption he has been fairly thorough, and has taken counts on artificial surfaces on Luna and in the asteroids, to establish a reliable short-term time chart. According to his calculations, micrometeors have fallen on Icehenge for a thousand years, plus or minus five hundred. This makes Icehenge at least a hundred and fifty years older than the 2248 dating, but is considered close enough by Nederland, who has used Stallworth's results to support his theory.

There are two problems with this dating. First, the entire method is based on an assumption that is not yet proved: that micrometeor fall is a constant. Second, and more important: the micrometeor fall on Icehenge could be part of the manufactured evidence, and there would be no way of telling. Micrometeors are, for the most part, carbon dust. A handful of it sprinkled from a few hundred meters over the monument would create exactly the same effect as a thousand years of natural micrometeor fall. It is, in addition, a precaution that would occur very quickly to a thoughtful hoaxer; for micrometeors would be the only force acting on the structure over a short period of time. Though a method for measuring this action did not exist at the time of the monument's construction (and still does not, in my opinion), the existence of micrometeor fall was known, and so the dating method could be both foreseen and dealt with, by an articial fall. Given the elaborate nature of the hoax, it is a possibility more likely than not.

At another seminar meeting, at the same table, after we'd all had a few drinks. We'd gotten to know each other pretty well.

"So give, Edmond," said April. "We want to know who put it there."

I waited, pretending to consider it. Then: "Caroline Holmes."

"No!"

"What?"

"No, noo . . ."

They became silent, watching my face. Sean said, "Why?"

I grinned. "Let me tell you about it. At first, it was because I kept running across her name. And not just because her company built most of the colonies outside Jupiter. She fulfilled all the criteria I had set: she had the money, ships and equipment to do it. She was interested in the monument when it was found. She financed the development of the micrometeor dating method by giving Stallworth a grant. And there was something about her personality—she wasn't overtly secretive, but it was curious how little I could find out about her, once I tried.

"She was the daughter of Johannes Tocquener and Jane Leaf. She was born sometime in the middle of the twenty-third century, I couldn't find the exact date. Jane Leaf was the chairperson of the Mars Development Committee for most of Carol's childhood, until she was killed in a docking accident on Phobos. The next year, on her Naming Day, Carol named herself Caroline Holmes, and took her share of the Leaf inheritance (which made her moderately wealthy) out to Ceres. She invested it in shipping, and was one of the first shipping magnates to buy the new Brindisi-class ships, that were large enough to go from Mars to Saturn and back. A lot of Mars corporations were in on the development of Jupiter's satellites, and many of them had much more experience than Holmes. But between twenty-two ninety-three, when she moved to Ceres, and twenty-four sixty, when the Outer Satellites Council was formed on Titan, she had won most of the economic battles, won the war certainly, and owned outright several of the biggest Jupiter colonies. I know most of you know this; does someone want to tell us how she managed to do that?"

"Good business sense," said Andrew, breaking his usual silence.

"She's completely ruthless," said April.

"Starting with so much money," Sean said. "As I understand it, she had a lot more than you made it sound like. And she was the first to start building the permanent colonies around Jupiter. Her company domed the Hyperion Crater on Ganymede, did you know that? That's where I was born. Almost all of the first colonies were hers."

"She had good business sense," insisted Andrew. "She could find minerals and ores that were in short supply on Terra, faster than any of her competitors. I worked in mining, I know. She was a legend. No one knew how she did it. She made the prospecting trips herself. The most celebrated case was the time they couldn't find any more manganese ore, anywhere. They thought it was all gone—the farther from the sun the less heavy metals, so there wasn't much hope held for finding it farther out. Holmes's Jupiter Metals supplied over a thousand tons of the ore in the twenty-three seventies. Nobody could believe it, it was like she was pulling the stuff out of her hat. That in itself made her rich."

"And after that," I said, "she could just leave it up to gravity."

"*What?*" A chorus.

"Acute students of finance will have observed that money, abstract concept that it is, actually behaves as if it had mass. Economic laws imitate physical laws. Everyone's collection of money is a planetary body, in other words, exerting influence on everyone else's. Thus the more money you have the stronger its gravity is, and the easier it is to attract more. People have recognized this law for years in the saying, 'The rich get richer and the poor get poorer.' " Laughter, and nods of understanding. "Now most of us own mere asteroids, meteorites even, of money. But some own stars of money, and some of those stars, like that of Caroline Holmes, reach their Chadresekhar Limit and turn into black holes. Nowadays, any money that comes close enough to Holmes is unavoidably sucked in. There is an event horizon, of course, where this captured money appears to slow down, like Apollo in Zeno's Paradox, ever closer by smaller degrees to Holmes's Jupiter Metals—but those 'subsidiary corporations,' in actuality, have flashed invisibly to the no-point of infinite mass which is Holmes's wealth. . . ."

They were staring at me again. "Edmond, you're crazy tonight," said Elaine, "but I have to go home."

"No, finish the story!"

"Later," I said. "Next time. Next time come with some information you've found about Caroline Holmes, and we'll see what you can find." Then we got up, and they left, and I was alone again, on the streets of Waystation. . . .

Next time we met, they were ready to go. Elaine began.

"She went to Terra only once, in her childhood, when Jane Leaf was still alive. In many ways it was a diplomatic visit. Apparently she didn't like it, and she stayed for just less than two years. She's never been back. But while she was there she visited

Athens, Luxor, Angkor Wat, Easter Island . . . and Stonehenge. She liked ruins—"

"Tenuous stuff," said April. Elaine looked annoyed.

"Yes, I know," she replied. "But if there's anything we've learned since lifetimes were extended so, it is that the concerns of youth endure, for a long time. Anyway, it was a fact that *I* thought was interesting."

"Aside from shipping and mining, what has she done with her money?" I asked.

"She started the Holmes Foundation," said April quickly, "which gives grants for scientific research of various kinds. In twenty-six sixteen the Foundation gave a grant to Dr. Mund Stallworth of the University of Mars, who used it to develop the dating method that places the construction of Icehenge around Vasyutin's time. He had had trouble getting the project funded up to that time."

"Is there anything to indicate that Holmes herself influenced the Foundation's decision?" asked Elaine.

"No," April said.

"Anything else?" I asked.

"Yes," said Sean, with a slight smile at me. "One of her companies built the dome over Hyperion Crater, as I said. That company also built Jupiter Thirteen, which was designed to be a colony for artists. Of course, very few artists went to live there, and eventually it became an enclave for rich exiles from Mars, and later, after all the really rich moved out to Saturn, it became just another city. There was a lot of attention given to these developments, especially in the artistic and intellectual media, most of it pointing out the stupidity of planning to remove artists from the society at large. So indirectly Holmes took a lot of criticism for that, and it could be that she took offense at it."

I nodded. "She was ultimately responsible for the Museum of the Outer Satellites, on Elliot, as well. You know how much critical condemnation that's received."

April said, "You know this isn't very good evidence."

"I know," I replied. "But they seemed to me interesting indications. I wanted to know why the hoaxer did it. Olaf Ohman, a nineteenth-century hoaxer, once said, 'I should like to do something that would bother the brains of the learned.' I thought perhaps Holmes might have had a similar feeling."

"But you're only guessing her reaction! The scorn of intellectuals may have just made her laugh."

"Who laughs at scorn?" said Elaine.

"Someone who has done as much as she has," said April. "To someone who's had such a major hand in the colonization of the Outer Satellites, that museum and that artist-place must look like very minor efforts! Why should she care what people say about them? She can look all over the space outside the asteroids and see her colonies, places she had built—and those are her cultural efforts."

"That's probably true," I admitted. "In all the research I've done on Holmes, I've never found a solid, central motive for building Icehenge. If she did it, then the reason remains a mystery. But I'm not really surprised. I think the reasons one might do such a thing are not the sort that can be discovered by examining the public records decades later." I sighed. "And there are these indications. . . . And something certainly was affecting her, because around twenty-five fifty she put a large satellite into a polar orbit around Saturn, and has lived in seclusion there ever since. No more projects of any kind."

"It would help," said Andrew suddenly, "if she had written an autobiography. But there isn't one to be found."

"That's true," I said. "That in itself struck me as odd. In this age of autobiography, who does not write one?"

"A hoaxer?" suggested Sean.

"Maybe she did write one," said April. "Maybe she just didn't catalog it."

"All right," I said. "You're right. But there are some more concrete things that point to her. She had an organization large enough to conceal the disappearance of a ship for a few years, something that would be difficult for a single ship owner, say, to do. So I examined all the records of her ships' movements, a major task, believe me. I found a Holmes Ferrando-class ship that spent nearly   in her shipyard on Titan, from twenty-five ten to twenty-t   teen. But it had been hit by a meteor—there were pictures—and there was no way of finding out if it had left the shipyard.

"So that was inconclusive as well, and I had the same doubts April is expressing. Then I got in touch with Holmes's father, Johannes Tocquener, who still lives on Mars. I asked him if he had ever written anything about Caroline, and if so, whether I could read it. He replied that portions of his autobiography discussed her youth, but that he had never published it. Upon my request he sent me the number of his file, and I read the autobiography avidly—and there was nothing of interest in it, except her age.

"You'll remember that no one knew her age precisely—it was a secret, Jane Leaf had concealed her pregnancy for reasons of her own, that sort of thing. Well. In this year twenty-six twenty she is three hundred and seventy-two years old. She was born July twentieth, twenty-two forty-eight. And it could have been coincidence, but somehow I was sure."

Later that evening, after we had taken a break for drinks, April said, "You sure do guess a lot."

I laughed. "I know. Call it inductive reasoning. My methods sometimes remind me of that Theophilus Jones—" They laughed. "But these days Jones has come to the conclusion that the monument was an alien message device sailing through space, that speared Pluto by coincidence and stuck there. Seriously! Now I think my theory is likelier than that, whatever my method."

"You need to go out there," said Andrew. "And make a rigorous investigation, with trained archeologists—"

"—which I'm not," I interjected.

"I know. You're a historian."

"A file-freak," said April.

"You need to find out how Holmes could have soft-landed such brittle ice without shattering all of it. You need to run as many different scientific tests as you can think of," Andrew continued.

"That's right," I said. "That's precisely what we need."

After the meeting had broken up, Andrew approached me.

"I found your stranger," he said quietly. "In the morgue. It was a murder, on Elliot, Uranus. The victim was named Paul Rebosky. He was five hundred and thirty-two—a ship design engineer. He was poisoned—apparently the murderer tried to make it look like a breakdown in his immune system, the usual thing, but a coroner on Elliot caught traces of the poison. Anyway, I got a picture of him."

He held it out—I looked at the dull colors of the Xerox. The dead. It was my stranger from Titan, the small pinched face looking worried at death. I remembered sitting near the edge of the dome, waiting for Saturn to rise.

"He worked for Holmes's Jupiter Metals from twenty-five oh-three to twenty-five thirty-nine," Andrew continued. "Is it him?"

I nodded.

"It could be a coincidence," he ventured.

"Maybe," I said. "Or she's getting serious."

"What are you going to do?"

I took the picture from him, put it in my folder of materials for the seminar. "Get serious myself."

Finally I decided to publish an article on the hoaxer; to try naming her without naming her. I sent this to *Shards,* and they published it in their very next issue:

We can list several necessary attributes of the agent who constructed Icehenge:
1) Access to a Ferrando-class spaceship, and the ability to remove it from the Outer Satellites Council monitoring system.
2) The cooperation of at least the ten persons necessary to operate a Ferrando.
3) Access to the 563-92-7246 data bank on Mars, where the Weil journal was found.

4) The means to convince somebody to impersonate the "grandson" of Weil.

5) The ability to remove ice-asteroids from the rings of Saturn without being detected.

6) The tools with which to cut these ice-asteroids into the liths of the structure, and the equipment needed to place the liths in position without leaving signs of construction (equipment which, as Jordan has shown, the Vasyutin Expedition, if it existed, could not have had).

7) The wealth necessary to accomplish all of the above.

8) A reason to perpetrate such a hoax.

Other attributes are not necessary, but are strongly indicated by the evidence:

1) A knowledge of the megalithic cultures of prehistoric Europe.

2) Some significant connection with the date 2248.

Two weeks later I received a letter:

18 September 2620

Edmond Doya
Box 510
Waystation

Dear Mr. Doya:

Please come visit me for a talk about matters of mutual interest. I will provide your transportation from Waystation to Saturn and back. If it is convenient to you, Captain Pada of the *Io* can leave Waystation immediately; and if you can stay for a week or ten days (which I urge you to do) she can return you to Waystation by the New Year.

Sincerely,

CAROLINE HOLMES
Saturn Artificial Satellite Four

Saturn was a striped basketball in the viewscreen of the *Io*. Five or six of its moons were visible as white crescents; Titan fuzzy at the edges because of its growing atmosphere. I watched it with the interest one has when seeing an old home.

Captain Pada, a quiet woman I had seldom seen on the voyage, pointed above the planet. "See that white point? That's her satellite. We'll meet it just below the Rings."

"Does it have a name?"

"No. Just Sas Four." Pada left the room.

I stayed and kept the screen locked on Saturn until the knife-edge of the Rings began to broaden, and the whole vista became too large for me, in my distraction, to focus on. I found the coordinates for Holmes's satellite and switched the screen to it.

We were closing on it, and it was big: a torus, spinning slowly, a wheel with spokes a kilometer long. A thin crescent on the sunward side was bright with reflected sunlight, and another half of the surface facing me was Saturn-lit, a dusky, burnished yellow. Locks, handrails and small bays studded the curving metal. There was a small, classically designed observatory, sticking out of the hub on the side opposite the dock; its telescope appeared to be trained on Saturn. The spokes connecting hub and wheel looked thin as wire. At regular intervals there were windows, some of them half-globes protruding into the vacuum. Many of the rooms behind the windows were lit, and I caught quick glimpses, as we circled it, of red and gold walls, rich brown furnishings, marble busts, a huge crystal chandelier. The entire thing brought to mind a nineteenth-century bathysphere, cast by some accident into the wrong time and medium. The largest of the windows was almost dark—the room behind it was filled with a pale blue light—and someone stood in it, close to the window. The rest of the rooms had been quite empty.

Captain Pada, over the intercom, called me to the transfer room. We were docking.

While crossing the ship I felt the bump of docking, and I stopped and tried to quell my excitement. Just an old woman, I thought, a rich old lady. The ancient epithets had little effect, however, and I was nervous as I floated into the transfer room.

The locks were already open. Captain Pada was there, and she shook my hand. "Nice having you aboard," she said, and waved me forward.

I passed through the docking sleeve and was in Holmes's satellite. A man dressed in red and gold was waiting. He smiled. "My name is Charles, Mr. Doya. Welcome to Sas Four. I'll show you your rooms and you can arrange your belongings. Caroline will receive you after that."

He took off with a neat leap and I hurried after him. We dropped down a hall with clear walls, in which terrestrial seashells were embedded (I thought again of the bathysphere), then took a long elevator ride. The room we entered was walled with reddish Persian rugs, and the ceiling and floors were a light wood. The floor was on several levels, with broad steps separating them.

"This is your room," said Charles. "That control panel over there will produce whatever furniture you need—wardrobe, bed, screens. The robots will obey you." He indicated a box on wheels.

"Thank you."

Charles left. I went to the control panel, which I found behind a tapestry, and pushed *Bed*. A circular section of floor slid away and a circular bed rose. I traversed the room to it, flopped down and waited for my things to arrive. And wondered what I would say to her. My stay there was going to be conducted entirely on her terms, I could tell; and that frightened me. I had a thought: I was about to meet Emma Weil.

I sat on the bed and waited—lying down to nap more than once—for what seemed like hours. There was no way of measuring the passage of time in the room; there were no buttons on the control panel labeled *Clock*. Presumably I could call somebody on the intercom, but I didn't know whom. Eventually I became hungry, and that, combined with growing irritation, drove me into the hallways. I tried to find my way back to the docking bay; my hope, though there was not much to support it, was that Charles would be there.

I got to the hallway with the clear walls and the hundreds of seashells. As I drifted down it I could see a wavery dark image moving down the hall with me, which I thought to be my reflection; but when I stopped for a moment to inspect a huge nautilus, the form continued to move. In surprise I caught up with it and pressed my face against the wall, but its thickness, and some ripples in it, reduced the image on the other side to a brown blob. The blob, however, had stopped across from me. It moved again, in the same direction, and I stayed across from it until the wall turned to wood. I stood there for a moment, and suddenly—back the direction I had come—a figure appeared in my hallway and approached me.

It was Holmes. She stopped when she saw me, and looked at me curiously for some time.

She was tall and had brown hair. Thick hair, tied back in a single knot and then let fall in a round stream down her back. She wore a long dress of simple design and plain brown material. She looked thin. Her face was handsome: lined, slightly tanned, with the finest of silky hairs just visible on her cheeks and upper lip. The line of her jaw, her cheekbones, nose and forehead, were all sharply defined, giving her an ascetic look. Her eyes were a rich brown.

Finally she moved up to me. "Hello," she said, in a well-modulated alto voice. "It's good to meet you. I've been reading your articles with interest."

"I'm glad," I said, and searched for more words, stupidly fumbling in a moment I had imagined many times. "Hello."

She said: "Why don't we go to one of the observation decks and have some food sent there."

"Fine." She had a long stride, one that revealed bare feet.

We went to a large dim room, walled and ceilinged in wood. The floor was clear; one of the windows I had seen while approaching. In the center of it Saturn shone like a lamp-globe. It was our only illumination. There were couches arranged in a small square near the middle of the room. Holmes sat on one, leaned forward and looked down at the planet. She appeared to have forgotten me; I sat down opposite her and looked down.

We were over one of the poles, looking at Saturn and its rings from a perspective none of its natural satellites ever had. The bands crossing Saturn (half of it was dark, though slightly illuminated by light reflected from the rings) were light greens and yellows, with streaks of orange. Seen from above they were full semicircles: bright cream in the equatorial bands, clearly defined streaks of yellow in the higher latitudes; a dusky green area at the Pole.

Outside the planet were the rings. The inner rings were a charcoal color, but quite visible. The outer rings were broad, pristine white bands, perfectly smooth and circular, as if drawn with a compass. The entire sight reminded me of a target, an archery target; the Pole the bull's-eye, the rings the outer circles; but it was impossible to imagine Saturn flat, because of its dark side, and the black bullet of its shadow, erasing part of the rings behind it.

This uncanny sight filled almost half of our floor-window. Around it a few bright stars gleamed, and seven of Saturn's moons were visible, all of them perfectly aligned half-moons. As we sat there silently and watched, the scene shifted perceptibly. Saturn's shadow on the rings was shortening, the moons were becoming crescent, the rings were tilting and becoming huge ellipses; all slowly, slowly, as in some inhuman, natural dance.

"Always the same but always different," I said.

"The landscape of the mind," she replied, after a long pause. I became aware of the profound silence in which we were speaking. "There are more beautiful places on Terra, but none that is so sublime."

"Perhaps that is because space itself has many attributes of sublimity—vastness, simplicity, mystery, that which causes terror—"

"It exists only in the mind, you must remember that. But space provides much that reminds the mind of itself, yes. . . ."

After a time I said: "Do you really think that if we did not exist, Saturn would not be sublime?"

I thought she wasn't going to answer. Then: "Who would know it?"

"So it is the knowing," I said.

She nodded.

Then she sat back and looked across at me. "Would you like to eat?"

"Yes."

"Alaskan king crab?"

"That would be fine."

She turned, and called out, "We'll have dinner in twenty minutes."

A small tray covered with crackers and blocks of cheese slid out of a new aperture in her couch. I blinked. A bottle of wine and two glasses were presented on individual glass trays. She poured wine and drank in silence. We leaned forward to look down at the planet. In the odd illumination—dusky yellow light, from below—her eye sockets were in shadow, and looked very deep. We leaned back to attend to the meal, which to my relief was brought in by Charles. Below us Saturn and its billion satellites still wheeled, a stately art-deco lamp. . . .

After the meal Charles took away our dishes and utensils. Holmes leaned forward on her side of the couch, and stared down at the planet with an intensity that discouraged interruption. Between watching Holmes and Saturn, I was kept busy enough.

Holmes remained in her contemplative position until the ringed ball was completely out of our floor-window and the room was quite dark. Then she stood up, said "Good night," in a companionable tone—as if this were a routine we had established through years of dining together—and walked out of the room. Filled with confusion, I sat in the dark room and looked down at the stars for quite some time; then I made my way without much difficulty back to my rooms.

When I awoke the next morning, I was sure I had slept for an uncommonly long time. I showered in water cold as I could stand, feeling disturbed by dreams I couldn't remember.

Apparently I was being left to my own devices again. After a long wait on my bed, during which I wondered if I should be as annoyed as I felt, I went to the control panel and called up every destination on the intercom. None of them replied. I couldn't even find out what time it was.

I left my room and ventured into the halls again, remembering the previous night; if I hadn't left my rooms, I wondered, would I ever have met Holmes?

Today she wasn't in the room we had dined in, or behind the seashell wall. I circled the satellite a couple of times, checking room after empty room, and became completely disoriented. Quite a few doors on every level were locked. The silence on board—actually it was a pervasive, soft, electric *whirr*—began to bother me.

I took an elevator up one of the spokes to the observatory and tried the door; to my surprise it opened. Inside there was a voice: I entered the weightless room. It was a tall cylindrical chamber, with a domed ceiling. The telescope was a long black thing, tricked out in brass. It extended from a vertical strip in the curving ceiling to the center of the chamber, where a crow's-nest with a leather and brass chair was welded to it.

Holmes was behind that chair, leaning over to look into the mask of the eyepiece. Every few moments she called out a string of figures. Charles, seated at a console in the wall of the chamber (still in his red and gold) tapped at a keyboard and occasionally quoted a set of numbers back to Holmes. I pulled myself down a railing set into the wall. Holmes looked up. She nodded, said "Mr. Doya," in greeting, and looked back into the eyepiece. I pushed off and floated to a platform just below her crow's nest. She continued working.

After a while she called to Charles, "Put it on the inside limit of the crêpe ring, please," and straightened up. She looked down at me.

"I've been reading your articles with fascination," she said. "I've been a student of the Icehenge controversy for a long time."

"Have you," I managed to say.

"Oh, yes, I followed it from the beginning. That last article of yours, the one in *Shards,* was tantalizing. But tell me. Who do you suspect was this marvelous hoaxer?"

I looked away from her, over at Charles, down at the end of the telescope. Adrenaline flushed through me, preparing me for flight, but not for conversation. . . .

"Do you really want to go into something so complex now?" I asked, and then, as she stared down at me, continued: "I really don't know who put it there. All that I have are hints, possibilities—conjectures."

"When you are inclined to it," she replied, with a slight smile, "I'd like to hear them. I've observed that I fit all of your hoaxer's attributes, and I want to know if I, too, am a suspect."

She stared at me for a long time, while I looked down at the telescope and tried to think. Finally I raised my eyes to meet hers.

"You are a suspect, Ms. Holmes."

She smiled. "Now that *is* exciting."

After another pause she appeared to sense how disconcerted I was, and she looked into the eyepiece again. She threw an occasional comment to me, and I replied when I could muster my attention.

"Have you lived on Waystation long?" she asked.

"Not long."

"Ah. My corporation had a good deal to do with the construction of it, you know. But where did you come from?"

I tried to pull myself together and make a coherent story of my past—a difficult task under the best of circumstances—but my distraction must have been very obvious. Eventually Holmes cut me off.

"Would you like to retire now, and continue this conversation later?"

I agreed that I would, and left hastily, remembering, as I returned to my room, her calm and enigmatic smile. What did she want of me? I called up my bed and collapsed on it, and lay pondering her purposes, more than a little fearful. Much later one of the robots brought me a meal, and I picked at it. Afterwards, though I thought I never would, I fell asleep.

"Tell me," demanded Holmes, "is it true that Hjalmar Nederland is your great-grandfather?" Her face loomed over me.

I didn't want to answer. "Yes."

"How odd," she said. Her hair was arranged on her head in a

complex knot (like my mother used to wear). She was wearing earrings, three or four to an ear, and her eyebrows had been plucked to thin black arches. She was looking out a window, at the sun.

"Odd?" I said, though I did not want to say anything.

"Yes," she said, annoyance in her voice. "*Odd.* All this marvelous work that you've done. If your theory is accepted, then Nederland's theory—his life's work—will be destroyed."

Her glare was fierce, and I had to struggle to reply. "But even if his theory was wrong," I said, "his work was still necessary. It is always that way in science. His work is still good work."

She followed me back, her face very close to mine. "Would Nederland agree?" she cried. She pointed a finger at me. "Or are you just lying to yourself, trying to hide what will really happen!"

"No!" I said, and weakly tried to strike back at her: "It's your fault, anyway!"

"So you say," she sneered. "But you know it's your fault. It's *your fault,*" she shouted, looming over me, her face inches from mine. *"You* are the one destroying him, him and Icehenge as well—"

A noise. I twisted around in my bed, looked down at my pillow, realized I was dreaming. My heart was hammering. I rubbed my eyes and looked up—

Holmes was standing over me, looking down at me with clinical interest (hair piled on top of her head)—

I jerked up into a sitting position and she disappeared. Nobody there.

I tossed the bedsheets aside and leaped out of bed. I hurried to the door; it was locked on the inside, though I couldn't remember locking it. The darkened room reeked of sweat; it was filled with shadows. . . . I ran to the control panel and switched on all the lights in the room. It blazed, white streaks everywhere on the polished wood. It was empty. I stood there for a long time, waiting for heartbeat and breathing to slow down. The image I had seen over me, I thought, could have been a hologram. I began circling the room, inspecting the wood for apertures.

... But the dream. Did she have a machine that created images within the mind, as a holograph created them without?

I didn't sleep again that night.

"Mr. Doya."

"What?"

"Mr. Doya." It was Holmes's voice, from the intercom.

"Yes?"

"The sun will rise over Saturn in thirty-five minutes, and I thought you might like to see it. It's quite spectacular."

"Thank you, I would."

"Fine. I'll be in the dome room, then. Charles will show you the way."

When I got there she was seated in the lotus position, staring out. The room was shoved out from the body of the satellite, so that the clear dome served as both floor and walls. Saturn, rather than directly below us, was off to one side, just clear of the surface of the satellite. Saturn was dark, but the north polar cap glowed green, as though lit from within. To the sides the rings, very thin now, shone brightly.

"Most of Saturn's mass is at its core," Holmes said, without turning her head. "The upper atmosphere is very thin, enough so that the sun shines through it, just before rising."

"Is that what that glow is," I said. The luminous green gained brilliance near the pole, and seemed even brighter contrasted with the dark side of the planet. Finally I could see the sun itself, a fiery green gem that flared to an intense white as it cleared Saturn. The green faded and became a crescent of reflected light: the sunward side of the planet. We could see more of the rings.

"Well," said Holmes. "Good morning."

"Hello." I sat. I stared at her closely. She ordered breakfast innocently enough, and we ate in silence. Afterwards she said:

"Tell me, am I your only suspect?"

I saw she intended to have it out. I said shortly, "I think you put it there."

"Genoa Ferrando fits the qualifications as well as I. So does Alice Waite. Why do you think it was me?"

I told her the tale of the long search, gave her all the pieces of the puzzle that she had left behind, put them together for her. It took quite a while.

At the end of it she smiled. "That isn't very much," she said, and left the room.

I took a long, deep breath and wondered what was going on. My head was spinning, my vision was a field of pointillistic dots: had my breakfast been drugged? Was I full of some sinister truth serum, thus to tell her everything I knew? Oh, I was becoming frightened, no doubt of it; yet I certainly did feel dizzy—I shrugged off the thought. Before me Saturn was a huge crescent of swirled cream and green. I watched for a long time as it and its delicate minions continued to turn, arcs and curves and ellipses of light, slow and inevitable and majestic, like the music Beethoven might have written had he ever seen the sea.

That night I couldn't sleep for dreaming.

The next morning I awoke sober and cold. I made my way up to the observatory.

She was there, working again with Charles. "Will you please try directing with some semblance of accuracy," she said to him waspishly as I opened the door.

She watched me enter, smiled politely. "Mr. Doya," she said. She put her head down to the eyepiece, then looked at me again. I was just below her. "Would you like to take a look?"

"Sure," I said.

"Want to see the rings first?"

"Sure."

She pushed buttons on a console beside her. The telescope and its vertical strip slid down, and there was a low, vibrating whir; though I could barely sense it, clearly the entire chamber was revolving. Holmes leaned forward and looked into the eyepiece, pushed buttons with her eye still to it.

"There." She pushed a final button and got up. I sat and looked in. The field was jammed with white boulders, irregular ice-asteroids.

"My." Even as close as we were in the satellite, with the naked eye the rings appeared to be a solid white sheet.

"Isn't it a nice view?"

"How big are they?"

"From a few kilometers diameter, down to icicles."

"It's amazing what a thin plane they stay in," I said.

"Oh, yes. It's a great example of gravity at work. I find it fascinating—a force the workings of which we can describe and predict with minute accuracy, without understanding in the slightest way. Here, the Cassini Division is a good display of the rigor of gravity's laws. All the ice debris is kept in a plane about twenty-six kilometers thick. Then about forty thousand kilometers from the planet, there's a ring four thousand k's wide, where nothing will stay in orbit." She pushed buttons and the field became a flurry of white, like a snowstorm, I imagined. When it cleared again there was the white rubble, still closely packed—and then, straight as a ruler, the boulders ceased and black starry space began. I was about to exclaim at this when one of the boulders, long and narrow like a beam, caught my eye. It occurred to me that she was showing me her quarry. . . .

"You know," I said casually, "some physicists on Mars have determined that the columns of Icehenge came from here."

"Yes," she replied. "A ring of ice boulders, made from ice taken from a ring of ice boulders. How nice."

I laughed, and continued to look into the eyepiece. "Some would say that fact tends to support the idea that a resident of the Saturn area built Icehenge."

"So they might, but it's just circumstantial evidence. Hasn't Nederland shown how easy it would have been for Vasyutin and his crew to pass by here?" Her voice was unconcerned. "Your whole case against me is circumstantial."

"True, but you can make a good case if there are enough circumstances."

"But you cannot *prove* your case, no matter how many circumstances." I pulled my head back to look at her, and she was smiling. "And if you can't prove it, you can't publish it, since it accuses me of a crime. I am fascinated by the monument, I have told you that, and it is amusing that you believe I built it; but both I and the monument have enough troubles without a connection being made between us. If you make one, I will assuredly see that you are destroyed."

I cleared my throat. "And if I find proof—"

"You will not find proof. There is none to be found. Be warned, Mr. Doya, I will not tolerate having my name associated with it."

"But—"

"There is no proof," she said, patiently but insistently. We hung in silence and I could feel myself blushing. Was this why I was here, and all that preceded it a preparation, lending force to her warning? The thought angered me, her self-assurance angered me, everything she had done angered me; and as an angry idea came to me I spoke it.

"Since you are so sure of this, perhaps you would, um, help me close my investigation?" She stared. "The Waystation Institute for Higher Learning wants to sponsor another expedition to Pluto, to investigate questions I and others have raised." I was making this up, and it was exciting. "Since you are so certain I will never find anything implicating you, perhaps you'd be interested in funding it, to lay all questions to rest? . . . and as a favor in return for my visit?" I nearly smiled at that.

She saw it and smiled in return. "You think I won't do it."

"I hope you will."

After a long pause she said, "I'll do it." And then, with a casual wave of her hand: "Now you must excuse me, I must return to my work."

After that conversation we seldom saw each other. I wasn't invited to dinner that evening, and after a long wait I had one of the little square robots bring a meal. For the next three days I was on my own; Holmes sent not a single message, and I didn't want to talk to her. I began to believe that supporting another expedition to Pluto disturbed her more than it had seemed. On the other hand, there was the old truism to consider, that every hoaxer wants to be discovered, eventually. . . .

One night I dreamed that Holmes and I were in a weightless, locked room: her hair waved around her nude shoulders like snakes, and she shrieked, *"Don't go on! Stop!"* I woke up immediately, sitting up with twisted bedsheets clutched in my hands, and after a while laughed uneasily; Holmes was prevented from violating my dreams, because it frightened me so badly that I would wake up.

The next day I was still thinking about a locked room. I wandered through the satellite, looking methodically for any sections that were closed off. There was one—an arc of the circle had a hallway to pass through, but above it was a section I couldn't enter. It took a lot of wandering around that area to make sure, and when I was, my curiosity grew.

That night my dreams were particularly violent; though Holmes never appeared in them, they were disturbing enough. My father was in several, always about to leave for Terra, always asking me to come with him. . . .

The next morning I decided to break into the closed arc. In a room down the hall from mine there was a console of the satellite's computer; I sat down before it, and went to work. It only took me half an hour of sifting through satellite layout diagrams to find the locking codes I wanted. I scribbled down a few numbers and left the console.

I checked to make sure Holmes and Charles were in the observatory—they were—then went to the hallway that allowed one to traverse the arc. I located a large elevator door that I had identified in the diagrams and began punching out the code commands I had written down. With the third one the elevator doors slid open. I walked in.

I was on, the interior control panel told me, the second of fourteen floors. I pushed fourteen. The doors closed and I felt the beginning of the elevator's rise.

The doors opened and I walked out into another passageway. The floors were black tile, the walls and ceilings darkest wood. I walked up and down hallways. Aside from the new walls and ceilings, nothing seemed to be different. Rooms I looked into were empty. I had walked for some time (always keeping in mind the location of my elevator), and was starting to feel disappointed, when I rounded yet another corner: there before me I saw a door that seemed to lead into the vacuum of black space; and in the center of that space was Icehenge.

It was small, and as I hurried toward it across a glass floor, I thought it was a holocube standing on a table. Then I saw that it was made instead of actual pieces of ice, standing in a big sphere of glass that rested on a white plastic cylinder.

The room itself was spherical, a tiny planetarium, with a clear floor bisecting the sphere. There were stars above and below, and the sun, just a few times brighter than Sirius, was just below the floor. It was Pluto's sky.

The ice liths of the model were nearly transparent, but aside from that it looked like a perfect representation. After a time I circled it slowly, and found an unmarked control console on the other side of the plastic stand.

There were small colored buttons in a row at the top. I pushed a yellow one, and a long narrow beam of yellow laser light appeared in the room. It just touched the top of one of the triangular liths, on the northwest side of the ring, and the top of the shortest lith, on the southeast side . . . Aligned like this, the slender cylinder covered the sun and turned it yellow.

The other buttons produced laser beams of different colors, marking the sight-lines established by certain pairs of liths, at a certain point in time—one moment in Pluto's long orbit—and not for observers on the surface of Pluto, since most of the sight-lines extended, in both directions, into space; established only if an elaborate model such as this were constructed. Violet was Sirius. Green was, I guessed, Pluto's moon Charon. A blue beam extended straight up out of the tallest lith, and defined Castor, Pluto's Pole Star. And red, stretching across the two remaining triangular liths, plunged into the sword-sheath of Orion: the galaxy Andromeda.

"Mr. Doya?" Holmes's voice on the intercom again.
"What." In my dream my father had been telling me a story.
"Captain Pada can leave for Waystation today, if you like."

"All right." I felt, all of a sudden, very angry.

"Would you join me for breakfast?"

" . . . All right. In an hour."

She wasn't in the dining room when I got there, so after a short wait I ate breakfast alone. I looked out at Saturn. When I was done with breakfast an image of Holmes, seated in a chair, popped into being across from me. I stared at her eyes.

"Excuse me for saying good-bye to you like this," she said. "I am indisposed. You are in a holo field yourself, so we can converse."

"Quite all right," I said.

"I hope you understand that my desire not to be associated with Icehenge is very serious."

"You shouldn't have built it, then," I said.

"I didn't."

"You did," I said, hoping my image's gaze met hers. "You built it and then built the false explanation that went with it." I was trying to control myself. "With all that money, Ms. Holmes, why did you build nothing but a hoax? Why construct just the story of a starship, when you have the means to make the story real? You could have done something great. As it is, you have done nothing but make a fool of an old man on Mars."

"Not if the Vasyutin explanation stands—"

"Someone will find out. The sooner it's done the less foolish he appears." I got up and walked toward the door.

"Mr. Doya!" I turned; her image was standing. "I had nothing to do with it."

"Then why is that model of it here in your home!"

She smiled, and for an instant I understood that she had meant me to find it. . . . "I told you," she said. "I am a student of it."

"If you analyzed the ice in that model," I said, "you would find it the same as the ice of the liths on Pluto."

She stared at me, calm and cold. "You may think what you like, Mr. Doya," she said. "But you will never know." She and her chair disappeared.

Charles opened the door. "The *Io* is ready," he said. "Your luggage is aboard."

I followed him to the docking bay, crossed into the *Io*. As I pulled myself to the bridge I felt the *clank* of our disengagement, and realized I was shaking.

The viewscreen in the lounge had an image of the satellite. Helplessly I hung before the great wheel and watched, still shaking. For a moment, seeing its windows and rails and the observatory, I thought again of an ancient bathysphere. As we moved away I could see the domed floor, a clear glassine bubble; and inside it the tiny figure of Holmes paced around the dome's perimeter, upside-down it seemed, watching us. Her purposes, I thought. No doubt she had accomplished them all. Then the satellite shrank, with great speed, to a white dot over the ringed eldritch ball. And we were on our way out again.

There was a holo-message transmitter on board the *Io*. After a month or so of waiting out the long reach back to Waystation, I went into the transmission room. I composed myself, and faced the empty row of chairs that indicated where the audience receiving the message would sit.

"Begin," I said. The red light in the center chair blinked on.

"Professor Nederland," I said. "This is Edmond Doya. Our previous interactions have all occurred in the periodicals, but now I want to communicate with you as directly as possible." I leaned against a table and kicked rhythmically at one of its legs. "The Waystation Institute for Higher Learning is mounting an expedition to Pluto, to make another investigation of Icehenge that will attempt to clear up the present mystery concerning its origins.

"I know you believe that there is no mystery concerning its origins. But—" I stopped, tried to recollect what I was going to say. All of the sentences I had thought of during the month jammed together, demanded to be spoken first. I stood up and paced back and forth, looking frequently to the red dot that represented my great-grandfather.

"But I think you must admit, having read my work, that there is at least the possibility of a hoax. Certainly the possibility. Yet in the present state of knowledge there is no way of telling who really built the monument; I truly believe that. . . ." I paused. "All of the serious researchers . . . and theorists of Icehenge, will be invited to join the expedition. As the senior and principal theorist your addition to the company would be valued."

Somehow that didn't sound right. I was being too stiff, too artificial: this was an invitation, I wanted to show how I felt. But it was too complex.

"I know that many people have construed my work to be an attack on you. I assure you, Professor Nederland, that isn't true! I admire the work you did, it was a good investigation, and if someone was deliberately misleading you . . . there was no way for you to know. And I don't agree that believing it a hoax destroys the monument's esthetic worth. Vasyutin or not, the monument is still there. Human beings still constructed it. Emma's story still exists, no matter who wrote it. . . ."

It was coming out wrong. I couldn't say it. I paced even more rapidly.

"Perhaps I am wrong, as you believe, and Vasyutin did build Icehenge. If so, then we should be able to document that on this expedition. I hope you agree to join us. I . . . bid you farewell. End transmission." The red light blinked off.

The following day, at about the same time, the reply arrived. I sat down in the chair with the red dot. The scene appeared and I blinked while my eyes accommodated the light.

He was sitting behind an anonymous university desk. He looked just as he did in the press conferences: short hair neatly combed, expensive suit (the latest Martian style) pressed and carefully adjusted. It was the official, pontificating image.

"Mr. Doya," he said, looking just to my right. I shifted.

"We haven't met before, even by means of this illusory medium, yet I'm aware that we're related—that I am your great-grandfather. How do you do. I hope we get to meet in the flesh someday, because I can tell we have common interests as well as common family." He smiled for a moment, and adjusted a sheet of paper on the desk. "Let me assure you, I understand that your arguments concern archeology and are not directed against my person." He moved the paper again and began tapping it with his forefinger. The corner of his mouth tightened, as if he were about to perform an unpleasant task.

"I disagree with many of the things you said in your invitation. There isn't any evidence in your work sufficient to convince me that the Vasyutin explanation is not true. So I don't believe that there is a need for your expedition. And I don't believe an on-site investigation made up of diverse theorists, each attempting to prove his own case, can become anything but a circus. For these reasons I decline your invitation, though I thank you for making it." He stopped, and appeared to consider what he had just said. He looked down at the paper again, then up, and this time he seemed to be looking directly into my eyes.

"When you say that Emma's story will still exist no matter who wrote it, you imply that it doesn't matter whether Emma's story is true or not. I say it does matter. I think in your heart you agree with that, and I ask you not to misrepresent the situation as if to disguise its meaning. If your theory is proven true, I know what that will mean as well as you do."

He looked down again, made desultory taps with his fingers. "I cannot wish you good luck. End transmission."

Blackout. I sat there and thought of many things—thought of the young Nederland trekking across the barren slopes of Olympus Mons, searching for answers; and suddenly I thought, it's been a hundred and fifty years since those things happened. He's changed, he's not the man who wrote the books you read when you were a child—not at all. I sat in the dark.

We were close, very close. Activity began on the *Snowflake*—like water thawing after a long winter, people began to move in the halls, to meander past each other, scuffing at moss, greeting shyly.... Jones and I went down to the crew's lounge and passed a couple of groups on the way; they were smoking and talking about Icehenge.

In the lounge we watched the viewscreen and drank. Occasionally we made comments to the crew there, to each other. We had reached the point where we could each talk about our thoughts concerning the monument without argument. We just listened to each other.

"So where is it?" said Jones to one of the crew. She pointed out Pluto, just ahead of Aries. It was about second magnitude. Jones pointed himself and said, "You're right! There's Icehenge, I see it right there on top!"

Later, when we were alone, I said, "I've been writing a lot of this down, Jones. A sort of journal." He nodded. "Sometimes it occurs to me that what I'm writing is the sequel to Emma Weil's journal, which I'm certain was written by Holmes. And my story tells of a voyage to Pluto, which is exactly what Emma said was going to happen—and this voyage is being paid for by Holmes —sometimes that old woman looks very much in control of things out here, Jones; sometimes I wonder how much of it she may have planned, what she has in store for us. . . ."

"Who knows?" said Jones. "There are so many influences on our lives that we don't control, you might as well not worry about another one that you may be making up. Whatever happens on Pluto, I'm looking forward to it. I'm anxious to get there. We are quite close, you know," pointing at the screen and staring at me seriously. "I wasn't joking when I said I could see those ice towers."

And then we were there. I was there, circling the ninth planet, and soon afterward, on its surface. My first impression was that the horizon was flat. It was, at any rate, less curved than any I had ever seen. "This is the biggest thing I ever stood on," I said aloud. "I'm on a planet. First planet I've ever stood on, and it's Pluto. . . . " Something in the thought was distressing, and though we were just a couple of kilometers from the monument, I waited till all the others trekked out and marveled at it, waited until most of them returned, and told me of it, and eyed me as if I were quite peculiar. Then I suited up, left the landing vehicle and walked north. The gravity wasn't very heavy.

Icehenge, Icehenge, Icehenge, Icehenge, Icehenge. I started running and almost immediately stumbled and fell to the ground; even that reminded me that the rocks were real, that I was really there.

Sitting there on Pluto's gravelly, dusty surface, and looking north, I could see the top three-quarters of the liths, rising just behind a low hill. The sun was off to my right, to the "east" (though every direction in reality soon became south)—it was a star just brighter than first magnitude, a few degrees above the horizon. On the eastern side the liths were long, gleaming white streaks—to the west they were barely visible black shadows. The southeastern triangular lith reflected a broad facet of white—other beam-ends were no more than white lines against the night.

I was shivering, as if I could feel through my suit a touch of Pluto's cold, only seventy degrees above the absolute zero of total stillness. I got up and established a rapid walk toward the monument.

There were four or five humans standing in and around the gigantic circle, and to my surprise I appreciated their presence, though I kept my intercom off. They were so small—one of them stood by the fallen lith, and even he appeared insignificantly short.

I passed between two liths and stood, looking down the curving row of columns; they seemed much more irregularly placed than they ever had in holograms—as if the act of transmitting and imaging had somehow given them more order. Here, in reality, their placement seemed random, the work of some alien intelligence.

I walked forward, head craned around to view the liths behind me. The awkward position left me feeling a bit faint.

From the center it appeared a rough circle—I couldn't perceive the flattened side on the north, for the different dimensions of each lith and the varying angles of placement created an irregular display of white and black parallelograms that were hard to get in spatial perspective. Most of the western liths shone with reflected sunlight, though many were darkened by the endless shadows of the eastern liths. The eastern liths themselves were black cutouts against the sky, except for a few that caught the reflected light from some more westerly lith, and gleamed dully. To the north the Six Great Liths stood like a huge curving wall; yet the jagged row of small liths near the fallen one seemed not much shorter, though the shortest ones were all there.

Four of the five people gathered near the south side of the ring. One of them waved at me and they took off for the landing vehicle. I assumed their air supplies were low. The remaining figure approached me—by his height and gait I had already identified him as Jones. He extended his arm and we shook gloved hands, clumsily. Through his faceplate I could see bright eyes and a wide grin. He drew me forward and hugged me, and then, without signaling for me to switch on my intercom, he turned and left.

I was alone at Icehenge. I sat down and let the feeling saturate me.

Over the next couple of weeks the teams established their pattern of investigation. Those working on the ice spent most of the time in the landing vehicle's labs. Dr. Hood and his team worked to determine what had been used to shape the liths. Bachan Nimit and his people from Ganymede were taking a new line of inquiry, and hoped to find out if as many micrometeors had fallen on the underside of some of the fragments of the Fallen Lith as had fallen on the upright beams.

But the most visible and, it seemed, the most energetic team was Brinston's excavation group. Brinston was showing himself to be extremely competent and well-organized, to no one's surprise. The day after we arrived he had his people out doing the preliminary line digs, and he spent long hours at the site, moving from trench to trench, consulting and giving instruction. In conversation he was confident, a dedicated archeologist certain that his methods would solve what was essentially an archeological problem. "The substructure of the monument will explain it," he said. At the same time he warned me against expecting any immediate information: "Digging is slow work—even with as simple a situation as this, one has to be very careful not to tear up the evidence one is looking for, which in this case is something as delicate as the marks of a previous excavation and fill, in regolith, no less. . . ." He would talk endlessly about the various aspects of his task, and I would leave him nearly as convinced as he that he would solve the mystery.

The teams established a common working period, and during this time the site swarmed with busy figures. Outside these times the landscape emptied.

I had no specific work to do; I was uncomfortably aware of that. The investigations I wanted made were being made, by professionals competent for the tasks. There was nothing left for me but to watch. So I quickly took to visiting the monument in the off hours. Those few who stayed into these times, or returned to visit, soon became still, contemplative figures, and we didn't bother each other.

At those times, as I wandered among the massive blocks in a vast silence, the abandoned equipment and trenches gave it the look of a work in progress, a work of giants left unfinished for unknown reasons . . . leaving behind the skeleton, the framework of something even larger. I sat at the center point of the ring for hours, and learned the various aspects it presented at different times of the Plutonian day. It was spring in the northern hemisphere—coldest, longest spring under the sun—and the sun stayed just over the horizon all the time. It took nearly a week for Pluto to spin around, for the sun to circle the horizon; and even at that slow speed I could see the movement of light and shadow, creating a different Icehenge at every moment, from every point of view.

My only regular companion during these meditations was Jones. It was natural enough that he should prefer these times, for only then did the monument fully regain its solitary power, its shadowed obscurity—but I thought, also, that he felt self-conscious doing his work in front of the others.

For work he was doing, laboriously and painstakingly. With a surveyor's transit, he was measuring the megalith. When I switched to the common band on my intercom, I could hear him muttering numbers to himself and humming snatches of music. He had arranged to have music piped in to him from the landing vehicle while he worked; usually, when I switched to that band, one of Brahms's symphonies was playing.

Occasionally he enlisted my aid, and I would aim a laser, or peer through a surveying instrument, while he paced across the central field and became a tiny figure against the beams on the other side. He measured and recorded hundreds of distances.

"Just what are you doing?" I once asked him, while we were engaged in this task. "You can't measure how far each lith is from every other lith, that's sixty-six times sixty-five—and why would you want to, anyway?"

"Numbers," he replied. "Whoever built this was very careful about numbers. I want to see if I can find the standard unit of measurement they used. You see, back in the twentieth century a man named Alexander Thom discovered that all of the stone megaliths in northern Europe used the same unit, which he called the megalithic yard. It was about seventy-four centimeters." He stopped what he was doing. "Now, no one but me has ever noticed that this megalithic yard from northern Europe is almost exactly the same length as the ancient Tibetan unit—"

"And the Egyptian unit used at the Pyramids, undoubtedly; but isn't that because they're the standard elbow-to-finger units?"

"Maybe, maybe. Anyway, since the general layout here, flattened-ring construction (they did that to avoid *pi*, did you know that?), is one of the common patterns for British henges, I thought I'd check to see."

I laughed. "You could find out in minutes on the computer."

He looked down at me. "Yeah?"

"Jones, I'm glad you're here with us."

He grinned. "You like having someone here crazier than you. But just wait. The numerology of Icehenge was always a rich field, even before these new measurements I'm taking. Did you know that if you begin at the Fallen Lith and count counterclockwise by prime numbers, the mass of each lith increases by one-point-two-three times? Or that the heights of each foursome of consecutive liths add up to either ninety-five point four, one hundred and one, or one-hundred-nineteen-point-five meters? Or that each length divided by width ends with a prime number—"

"Who says all this?"

"*I* do. You must not have read my book, *Mathematics and Metaphysics at Icehenge.*"

"I missed that one."

"One of my best. See how much you don't know?"

In this manner several weeks quickly passed. Brinston's face took on a slightly anxious expression, though he was finding out some interesting things. It appeared that for every lith a large cylindrical posthole had been dug—the ice beam had been positioned on the floor of the hole, which was invariably bedrock, and the hole was then filled. The only other fact they had discovered was that there were no individual postholes for the Six Great Liths. Perhaps because they were so near each other, a single big hole, still cylindrical, had been dug for all of them. Brinston's team had marked out the circumference of this cylinder, and it encompassed nine liths; but they hadn't found the bottom of it.

The day Brinston presented this information, Jones and I walked out to the site. Jones was excited, but he wouldn't tell me why.

We walked through the circle of towers and on to the pole, to watch the henge from there. We sat down directly on the pole, just beside the steel marker that Nederland had placed there to honor Vasyutin. The sun was on the other side of the monument, and the liths were more obscure than ever, faint reverse shadows, a dim lightness against the pervading black. The rock I sat on felt cold.

"Now we're spinning like a top," said Jones. "Feel it?" I laughed easily, yet as we sat there, silent, I could suddenly visualize Pluto as a tiny ball twirling, a handful of ice toothpicks stuck in its top, two antlike creatures seated on the axis of rotation.

I moved and the sun disappeared behind a lith. I felt the ancient fear—eclipse, sun-death. After a long time Jones took a small penlight from his suit, pointed it at the ring, turned it on. On Lith Number Three, the tallest of them all, a white spot appeared, brighter than any star. Jones moved the spot in a small circle on the lith.

"That one," he said, breaking an hour's silence. "There's something special about lith three."

"Aside from it being the tallest?"

"Yes." He jumped up and took off rapidly toward it. "Come on."

As we approached, he said: "I told you I would find something in those measurements. Though it wasn't exactly what I had expected."

We stopped before it, just outside the Six Great Liths. Number Three was massive, endlessly tall, big as a Martian skyscraper. On this side it was in total darkness, or rather, was illuminated only by starlight, which was barely adequate for our vision; the circle of shadows reared up into eerie obscurity. We stared up into it.

"If you take the centerpoint of the lith," Jones said, "at ground level and measure from there, then every center of every lith in the henge is an exact multiple of the megalithic yard away."

"You're kidding."

"No, seriously. It doesn't work for any other lith, either."

I looked up at his faceplate, but it was too dark—feet away, I could barely see him. "You used the computers."

"Yes."

"Jones, you amaze me."

"What's more, Number Three is right near the center of that big excavation Brinston and his folks found. That's interesting. For a long time I thought it was the triangular liths that our attention was being drawn to. Now I'm pretty sure it's this one —it's the center of the henge."

"But why?"

"I don't know."

"You don't know!"

"No! Perhaps to satisfy an alien geometry, perhaps to provide a key to a code—it could be anything. My brilliant investigation has gone only so far."

"Ho, ho." We circled it slowly, looking for some remarkable sign, some new attribute. There were none evident. A rectangular slab of ice—

A thought, slipping at the edges of consciousness. I stopped and tried to retrace my thinking. Stars, nothing . . . I shifted my head through the positions it had been in when I had the thought —tried all the other remembering tricks I knew. I looked up to the top of the lith and stepped back; and as I did so a bright star appeared, defining the top of the lith. Was it Castor? I found Pollux, checked the lineup—it was. The Pole Star.

I remembered. "Inside it," I said, and heard Jones's surprised breath. "That's it! There's something inside it."

Jones faced me. "Do you really think so?"

"I'm certain of it!"

"How?"

"Holmes told me. Or rather, Holmes gave it away." I told him of the model with the laser sight-lines, in the spherical planetarium: "And there was one beam of blue-white light pointing straight out of one of the tallest liths, very likely this one . . . it was the only laser beam coming directly out of a lith."

"That could be what it means, I suppose, but how do we find out?"

"Listen," I said. I pressed my faceplate against the surface of the lith and rapped hard on the ice. A certain vibration . . . I hurried to the adjacent lith and did the same. Vibrations again, but I couldn't tell if they were different.

"Hmmm," I said.

"I hope you don't melt holes in it—"

"No, no." The certainty of my guess, which had felt so much like an act of memory, didn't fade. I switched my intercom to a landing vehicle band. "Could you get me Dr. Lhotse, please?" The officer on duty called him up.

"Dr. Lhotse? This is Doya. Listen, could you run an easy test to find out if one of the liths had any hollow spaces in it?"

"Or spaces occupied by something other than ice?" Jones was on the band as well.

Lhotse considered it for a moment—it sounded as if he had

been asleep—and then supposed that some mass tests, or sonar and X-ray and such, could determine it.

"That's excellent," I said. "Could you bring out the necessary gear and people? . . . Yes, now; Jones and I have found the key lith and we suspect there is a hollow in it." Jones laughed aloud. I could imagine Lhotse's thoughts—the two strange ones had finally gone round the bend. . . .

"Is this serious?" Lhotse asked. Jones laughed.

"Oh, yes," I said. "Quite serious."

Lhotse agreed to do it and hung up. Jones said, "You'd better be right, or we may have to walk home."

"There'll be something," I said, feeling an apprehension that verged, curiously enough, on exhilaration.

There was a hollow column in the center of the lith, running from top to bottom.

"I'll be damned," said Lhotse. Jones and the sonar people were whooping. Searchlights flashed off the ice as from the surface of a mirror. Circles and ellipses of white bobbed around the ground and caught dancing figures, flashed in my eyes. The surrounding scene was blacker, more obscure. I could feel my heartbeat squashing my stomach.

"There must be an entrance at the top!"

There was an extension ladder that could be roped to the liths, on the other side of the site. Lhotse ordered the people he had brought with him to set it up, and he called back to the LV. "You'd better get out here," he told Brinston and Hood. "Jones and Doya found a hollow lith."

While they were moving the ladder across the dark old crater bed, Jones told Lhotse the story of our search. I could see Lhotse shaking his head. Then the ladder was moored against the lith and secured. Huge arc lamps, their beams invisible in the vacuum, made Lith Number Three a blazing white tower, and it cast a faint illumination over the rest of the henge, bringing the beams into ghostly presence. Lhotse climbed the ladder and set the next section in place. It just reached the top. I followed him up, and Jones clambered at my heels.

Lhotse kneeled on the top, roped himself to the ladder securely. I looked down, and the painfully bright arc lamps looked far below. Lhotse's quiet voice in my ear: "There are cracks." He looked up at me as my head rose over the edge, and I could see that his face was flushed red and dripping with sweat. I myself felt chills, as if we were in a wind.

"There's a block of ice here, topping the shaft. It's flush with the surface, I don't know how we'll get it out." He ordered another ladder set up. There were a lot of people talking on the common bands, though I couldn't see many of them. I tied myself to the ladder and climbed onto the top of the lith. Jones followed me up. It was a big flat rectangle, but I worried that it might be slippery.

Eventually we had to sink a heated rod into the block and set up a pulley above it. When those on the ground pulled, the trap door—a square block about six meters by six—rose up easily. The blocks of ice were too cold to stick to each other. Jones and Lhotse and I, standing on the ladders, stuck our heads over the black hole and looked down. The shaft was cylindrical. With a powerful light we could just distinguish an end or turning in the shaft, far below.

"Bring up some more rope," ordered Lhotse. "Something we can use for belay slings, and some of those expanding trench rods. If we used crampons we'd kick the lith down before we cut a step in this stuff." The ropes were brought up and we were tied into torso slings and given lamps. Lhotse climbed in and said, "Let me down slowly." I followed him in, breathing rapidly. Jones hung above me like a spider.

The walls of the shaft were slick-looking under our bright lights. We inspected the ice as we pushed off and descended, pushed off and descended.

Lhotse looked up. "You probably should wait till I get to the bottom." The people at the top of the ladder heard him and Jones and I slowed. Lhotse dropped away swiftly.

The descent lasted a long time. Our lamps made the ice around us gleam, but above and below us it was black. The ice changed to dark, smooth rock. We were underground.

Finally we hit a gravelly floor. Lhotse was waiting, crouched in the end of a tunnel pointing northward that descended at a slight slope. Ahead lay pitch blackness.

"Send another person down to this point for a radio relay," said Lhotse, and then, holding his lamp ahead of him, he hurried down the tunnel. Jones and I stayed close behind him. We walked for a very long time, down the bottom of the cylindrical tunnel. Except for the fact that the walls were rock—solid basalt, the tunnel had been bored through it—it might have been a sewer pipe. I was shivering uncontrollably, colder than ever. Jones was stumbling over me; he kept ducking his head at imaginary low points.

Lhotse stopped. Looking past him I could see a blue glow. I rounded him and ran.

Suddenly the tunnel opened up and we were in a chamber, a blue chamber. A cobalt-blue chamber! It was an ovoid, like the inside of a chicken's egg, about ten meters high and seven across. As Lhotse's lamp swung unnoticed in his hand, streaks and points of red light gleamed from within the surface of the blue walls. It was like a blue glass, or a ceramic glaze. I reached over and ran my hand over it, and it was a glassy but lumpy surface. The points and lines of dark red came from chips under the surface. . . . Lhotse raised his lamp to head-level and rotated slowly, looking up at the ceiling of the chamber. His voice barely stimulated the intercom's carbon: "What is this? . . ."

I shook my head, sat down and leaned back against the blue wall. "Who put this here?" Lhotse said.

"Not Vasyutin," I said. "There's no way they could have put this under here."

"Nor Holmes neither," suggested Jones. Lhotse waved his lamp and red points sparked. "Let's discuss it later," he said.

We stood, and sat, in silence, and watched the blue walls gleam with ruby light. The constantly shifting patterns created the illusion of extended space; the room seemed to grow ever larger as we watched. . . . I felt fear, fear of Holmes, fear that I had been in her power: who was she, to have created this? Could she have?

Questions, doubts, thought receded, and the three of us remained mesmerized by light. After a time white flashes from the tunnel, and voices on the intercom, snapped us awake.

Our air was low. Several others crowded into the chamber, and we moved out so they could see and marvel freely.

Jones, through his faceplate, looked stunned. His mouth was open. As we walked slowly back up the sloping tunnel, he was shaking his head, and I could hear his deep voice muttering: ". . . strange blue glass under Icehenge . . . star chamber, red light . . . a space . . . underground."

Then they hauled us up the long narrow shaft of the hollow lith. I stood on the rim at the top, and looked up, up to the great blanket of stars.

It gave the scientists a lot more to work on.

They soon reported that the chamber was directly under the pole—that is, the pole passed directly through the chamber. The walls were covered by a ceramic glaze, fired onto the bedrock.

Dr. Hood and his team soon discovered traces of the drill bits used to bore out the tunnel in the bedrock—small smears of metal, of an alloy just like that used for the bits of a boring machine designed to cut tunnels through asteroids. The machine had been first produced in 2514 . . . by Holmes.

And Brinston was ecstatic. "Ceramic!" he cried. "Ceramic! When they fired that glass up to melting temperature, they put a date on it clear as those marks on the Inscription Lith—with no chance of lying, either."

It turned out that thermoluminescence measurement was a method that had been used to date terrestrial pottery for centuries. Samples of the ceramic are heated to firing temperatures, and the amount of light released by them is a measure of the total dose of radiation to which the ceramic has been exposed since the last previous heating. The technique can determine age—even over short periods of time—with an accuracy of plus-or-minus ten percent.

After a week Brinston triumphantly released the results of the tests. The Blue Chamber was one hundred years old. "We got her!" Brinston cried. "It was Holmes! Doya, you were right. I don't know how she landed that ice, but I know she did it!"

The reporters had a field day. Icehenge was once again a nine-day wonder. This time the scoop was that it was a modern hoax. Speculation was endless, and Holmes was named directly by more people than she could sue—or destroy. They called this the Holmes explanation—or Doya's theory.

I sat around the site.

One day I heard that Nederland had been interviewed on the holonews. Several hours later I went down to the holo room and ran the scene through.

It wasn't at the usual University of Mars press-conference room. As the scene appeared, Nederland was leaving a building, and a group of reporters circled him.

"Professor Nederland, what do you think of the new developments on Pluto?"

"They're very interesting." He looked resigned to the questioning.

"Do you still support the Vasyutin theory?"

His jaw muscles tightened. "I do." The wind ruffled his hair.

"What about— But what about— What about the fact that a twenty-sixth-century drill bit was used to bury the Blue Egg?"

"I think there may be some other explanation for those deposits . . . for instance—"

"What about the thermoluminescence dating?"

"The ceramic measured is too deep for the method to work," he snapped.

"What about the alleged inauthenticity of the Weil journal?"

"I don't believe that," he said. "Emma's journal is genuine—"

"What's your proof? What's your proof?"

Nederland looked down at his feet, shook his head. He looked up, and there were deep lines around his mouth. "I must go home now," he said, and then repeated it in such a low voice the microphones barely caught it: "I must go home now. . . ." Then, in his full voice, "I'll answer all these questions later." He turned and made his way through them, head down, and twisted to avoid a reporter's grasp; and as he did so I saw his lowered face, and it looked haggard, exhausted, and I slammed the holo off and made my way blindly to the door, struck it with my hand, "Damn it," I said, "damn it, why aren't you dead!"

The day before we were to leave, a bulletin came in from Waystation. A group there at the Institute—led by my student April—had presented a new solution. They agreed that it was a modern construct, but contended that it was put up by Commodore Ehrung and her crew, right after they arrived on Pluto, and just before they "discovered" it. The group had a whole case worked up, showing how both Vasyutin *and* Holmes were red herrings, planted by Ehrung's people. . . .
"That's absurd!" I cried, and laughed harshly. "There's a dozen reasons why that can't be true, including everything that Brinston just found!" Nevertheless I was furious, and though I laughed again to hide it as I left the room, the people there stared at me as if I had kicked the teletype machine.

Later I walked out to the site. The henge was gleaming again, in the relative clarity of Pluto's day. It looked unchanged by all our new discoveries; as obscure as ever.
Jones was out there. He had taken to spending almost all of his time at the site; I had even chanced upon him lying between two pieces of the Fallen Lith, fast asleep. For days he hadn't spoken to anyone, not even—or especially not—to me. Brahms coursed through his intercom all the time.
This night, our last night on Pluto, he was sitting at the center point of the henge. I walked up to him, sat down beside him. The sight of the Six Great Liths left me numb.
We sat in silence for a long time. Eventually I switched to the common band. "Did you hear about the new theory from Waystation?"
He nodded. Put his arm around my shoulder.

"Jones," I said in a conversational tone, though my voice was quavering (I didn't know why), "Jones, what do you think happened here?"

He chuckled. "Still at it, are you? . . . I'm like the rest of us, I suppose. I think much as I thought before. I think . . . that more has occurred at this place than we can understand."

"And you're content with that?"

"Yes."

I was shivering, crying a little. "I just don't know why I did all this!"

After a while: "It's done." We sat. "Come on, Edmond, let's go back. You're tired." He stood up, put a hand to my shoulder. "Let's go back."

When we got to the low hill between the site and the landing vehicle, we turned and looked at it. Tall white towers against the night. . . .

"What will you do," asked Jones.

I shook my head, blinked away tears. "I don't know. I've never thought of it. Maybe—I'll go back to Terra. See my father. I don't know!"

Jones's bass chuckle, rumbling in the vacuum's silence. "That's probably as it should be." He put his arm around my shoulders, steered me around. We began walking toward the landing vehicle, going back to the others, going back. Jones shook his head, spoke in a sort of singsong: "We dream, we wake on a cold hillside, we pursue the dream again. In the beginning was the dream, and the work of disenchantment never ends."